"Go find my son," Mrs. Becenti said. "Talk to him."

Lillian frowned. She'd always found Johnny Becenti arrogant, uninterested in any viewpoint but his own. In fact, she'd come to feel it was her duty to annoy him whenever possible. "I don't understand," she said.

"He won't come back to the reservation," the old woman said. "He stayed away all winter. He has been alone too long."

"Perhaps you should go to the Peacemaker," Lillian suggested.

"He won't listen to the Peacemaker. *You* talk to him."

"Mrs. Becenti, Johnny wouldn't listen to me. I'm the *last* person who should talk to him. We've *never* gotten along."

"That's why he'll listen," Mrs. Becenti said with an assurance born of long consideration. "When he sees I have sent *you*—" clearly, Lillian was the most insufferable incentive Johnny's mother could devise "—he'll know how bad he's become!"

Dear Reader,

May is a time of roses, romance...and Silhouette Special Edition! Spring is in full bloom, and love is in the air for all to enjoy. And our lineup for this month reflects the wonder of spring. Our THAT SPECIAL WOMAN! title, *Husband by the Hour*, is a delightful spin-off of Susan Mallery's HOMETOWN HEARTBREAKERS series. It's the story of a lady cop finding her family... as well as discovering true love! And Joan Elliott Pickart continues her FAMILY MEN series this month with the frolicking *Texas Dawn*—the tale of a spirited career girl and a traditional Texas cowboy.

Not to be missed is Tracy Sinclair's warm and tender *Please Take Care of Willie*. This book is the conclusion to Tracy's CUPID'S LITTLE HELPERS series about matchmaking kids. And speaking of kids... *The Lady and the Sheriff* is Sharon De Vita's latest heartwarming installment of her SILVER CREEK COUNTY miniseries. This story features Louie, the kid who won readers' hearts!

May is also the month that celebrates Mother's Day. Cheryl Reavis has written a story that is sure to delight readers. Her FAMILY BLESSINGS series continues with *Mother To Be*. This story is about what happens when an irresistible force meets an immovable object...and deep, abiding love results.

Finally, we round off the month by welcoming historical author Barbara Benedict to Silhouette Special Edition. She makes her contemporary debut with the lighthearted *Rings, Roses...and Romance*.

I hope you have a wonderful month of May!

Sincerely,

Tara Gavin,
Senior Editor

Please address questions and book requests to:
Silhouette Reader Service
U.S.: 3010 Walden Ave., P.O. Box 1325, Buffalo, NY 14269
Canadian: P.O. Box 609, Fort Erie, Ont. L2A 5X3

CHERYL REAVIS

MOTHER TO BE

Silhouette®

SPECIAL EDITION®

Published by Silhouette Books

America's Publisher of Contemporary Romance

To "Grampy," with love, from "Grammy."

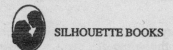

SILHOUETTE BOOKS

ISBN 0-373-24102-X

MOTHER TO BE

Copyright © 1997 by Cheryl Reavis

Books by Cheryl Reavis

Silhouette Special Edition

A Crime of the Heart #487
Patrick Gallagher's Widow #627
*One of Our Own #901
*Meggie's Baby #1039
*Mother To Be #1102

*Family Blessings

CHERYL REAVIS,

award-winning short-story author and romance novelist who also writes under the name of Cinda Richards, describes herself as a "late bloomer" who played in her first piano recital at the tender age of thirty. "We had to line up by height—I was the third smallest kid," she says. "After that, there was no stopping me. I immediately gave myself permission to attempt my *other* heart's desire—to write." Her Silhouette Special Edition novel, *A Crime of the Heart,* reached millions of readers in *Good Housekeeping* magazine. Both *A Crime of the Heart* and *Patrick Gallagher's Widow* won the Romance Writers of America's coveted RITA Award for Best Contemporary Series Romance the year they were published. *One of Our Own* received the Career Achievement Award for Best Innovative Series Romance from *Romantic Times* magazine. A former public health nurse, Cheryl makes her home in North Carolina with her husband.

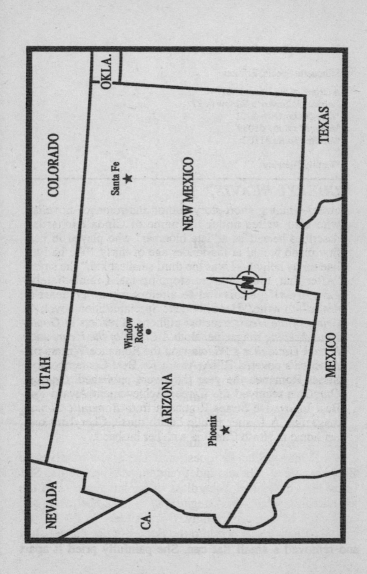

Chapter One

"This is a sad thing," the old woman said, her voice brittle with tears that had not yet been shed.

Lillian Singer made no reply, recognizing the remark as a formal prelude to the reason why Katie Becenti had come to Santa Fe to see her. It was important to the old woman that Lillian understand that the trouble was serious, even before she heard the details. Not that Lillian hadn't already guessed as much. It was unlikely that Katie Becenti ever left the Navajo reservation, and the fact that Lillian's own mother had escorted her here could only mean that both women considered the situation to be dire.

But Lillian asked no questions. She'd had relatives to teach her—her mother and grandmother, her aunts. She knew how to behave, regardless of her many years in the white man's world. And, regardless of her impatience, she conducted herself accordingly. She waited.

Katie Becenti reached into the pocket of her flannel shirt and removed a small flat can. She painfully pried it apart

with her arthritic fingers and took out the contents—one
tightly folded twenty-dollar bill. Then she set the can aside
and took the bill and carefully spread it out on the corner
of Lillian's desk, trying and failing to press out the creases
that had become permanent from having been in the can
for so long. The money—a mere pittance compared to Lillian's usual attorney's fee—smelled faintly of mint snuff.

"I can pay you," Katie said, pushing the money forward.
"You go find him. You go talk to him."

"Who?" Lillian asked, ignoring her good upbringing after all. She glanced at her mother, but Dolly Singer's expression was as impassive as the Becenti woman's and told
her absolutely nothing.

"My son, the policeman," Katie said.

Lillian frowned and leaned back in her chair. She had
expected a problem with some relative, but not *this* relative.
Johnny Becenti was a captain in the Navajo Tribal Police
force, and he was good enough at his job to have caused
her more legal aggravation over the years than she cared
to admit. She had always found him grimly intense, self-
assured to the point of arrogance and completely uninterested in any point of view other than his own. They had
had words more than once because of her criticism of tribal
police procedure, and she had come to feel that it was her
duty to annoy him whenever possible. Actually, she rather
liked to annoy him, simply because he was so determined
not to be annoyed. But in spite of their long adversarial
relationship, it was hard for her to imagine him doing anything that would drive his mother to take up a snuff can
that must contain her entire cash flow and come to Santa
Fe.

"I'm sorry. I don't understand," Lillian said, and the old
woman sighed, an eloquent comment on this daughter of
Dolly Singer's, who had obviously become too white to
fathom her own people.

"Please," Lillian said, stopping short of giving a sigh of
her own. "Just tell me what this is about."

"He won't come back," the old woman said. "He stayed up there at the homestead with the animals all winter. First, the snow piled up so high he couldn't get out. Now the snow is gone, but he stays there. I said he has been alone too long. I said it's because of her—the one who died. His sorrow was too strong and it let her *chindi* find him up there. Now he's not the same. He doesn't believe me. I am his mother and he tells me no. But he's changed. He's...no good now."

"You've talked to him?" Lillian asked, ignoring the theory that he'd been harmed by his dead wife's ghost.

"Yes. All his relatives have talked to him. He says to leave him alone."

"Mrs. Becenti, I think this is a family matter. It's not a legal problem. You should go to the Peacemaker Court. All of you should sit down together and talk about this."

"He won't come to hear what the Peacemaker will say. I have thought about this a long time and I know what is the best thing. You go up there to the homestead and you talk to him. You tell him he needs a ceremony to get back his harmony. I can pay you to do this." She pushed the twenty-dollar bill closer.

"Even if I did go, Mrs. Becenti, Johnny wouldn't listen to me. I am the last person who should talk to him. We've never gotten along. Not professionally and not personally."

"That's why he'll listen," Katie Becenti said with an assurance born of much consideration. "When he sees I have sent *you,* he'll know how bad he's become. He'll know that he's forgotten how to behave."

Lillian frowned again, not at all certain she wanted to be the most insufferable incentive his mother could devise. "Maybe he just needs more time. It hasn't been that long since—"

She nearly said, *since Mae died.* It would have been a terrible breach of her Navajo upbringing to actually speak the name of Johnny Becenti's dead wife, and it only served to point out how tired she was. Her head hurt. She had been in court all day. She still had hours of work to do. And she had a dinner date she could *not* be late for.

"Mrs. Becenti, I'm a lawyer. I talk for people when they have to go to court. I don't do this kind of thing."

"My son would listen to you. You can help him. He would believe what you say. I am his mother. I know this."

"I'm sorry, I can't. There must be somebody else who can go talk to him for you."

"He says he can't be a policeman anymore," the old woman said.

"Oh, I don't think he meant that."

"I remember," Katie said. "In my mind I can see his face the day he heard there was a place for him at the police school. He studied all those books to know the things the policeman knows—late in the night when he was too tired from working the homestead—when he should have been sleeping. But he didn't rest until he learned how to do the policeman's work. It made him happy. It made him a man. I have no grandchildren. I have only my son. And what is he if he is not a policeman anymore? What is he?"

What indeed? Lillian thought, but she said nothing.

Katie looked at Dolly Singer, and as inept as Lillian might have become at the subtle art of Navajo nonverbal communication, she sensed immediately what Katie Becenti didn't say.

Your daughter doesn't understand this.

The three of them sat in silence. Lillian was perfectly aware that she was facing two very formidable representatives of the Navajo matriarchy. But she simply didn't have the time to do what Katie Becenti asked, even if she wanted to—which she didn't. Johnny Becenti was a proud man. The idea of accosting him at some lonely reservation homestead and lecturing him about his behavior did *not* appeal to her. Nothing about this situation appealed to her. As aloof and emotionally restrained as Johnny Becenti had always seemed, Lillian believed that he had loved his wife.

Who was she to tell him he'd mourned long enough, even at the behest of his mother?

It was disturbing, though, that he supposedly intended to give up his career. Johnny Becenti *was* the Navajo Tribal Police. She would have been hard put to tell where the man began and the agency ended. It was also disturbing that she couldn't quite disregard one small truth. In spite of their professional differences, Johnny Becenti was one of the few men Lillian had ever met whose good opinion she would have liked to have. And, it was perhaps because she knew she *didn't* have it, that she went out of her way to provoke him. She knew only too well that she had done the unforgivable in his eyes. She had left the reservation and gone to live in the "white" world. She had refused to shoulder a personal responsibility for the welfare of the People, as he had done. Oh, she occasionally still participated in tribal matters on some level—usually at her mother's request—but Lillian had no doubt that Johnny believed she had willfully abandoned her own people. And he, *he* was the kind of man who had always been her worst fear—the decent and dedicated kind—who, if she had ever let her guard down, could have kept her from leaving the reservation life she had been so desperate to escape.

But there was nothing left to be said about this current matter, and all three women knew it. There was no point in prolonging the discussion. Katie Becenti painfully attempted to rise, finally taking Dolly's arm to get out of the chair. Lillian stood as well, but she didn't follow. The look Dolly cast over her shoulder as she helped Katie toward the door was enough to stop her. When Lillian was growing up, Dolly Singer had never had to raise her voice to make her point. She still didn't.

"Mother—" Lillian began, but Dolly shook her head.

"You do what you think is right," she said.

"I...hope to get home soon," Lillian said, in spite of the fact that what she "hoped" and what she actually did in that regard rarely equated.

"Yes," her mother answered, leading Katie Becenti out into the hallway. "Walk in beauty, daughter," she added in Navajo.

Lillian stood with her arms folded. She still had the ton of work to do, and she still had the headache. No, actually the headache was worse. One would think that she would have gotten used to inspiring her mother's disappointment by now. She'd embarked on that path at a very early age. When she wouldn't learn how to weave. When she barely learned to cook and herd the sheep. When she refused to marry. But she was neither weaver nor cook nor shepherd nor wife, and she'd known that about herself for as long as she could remember. She was a solver of problems. Not the mathematical kind. The human kind. The kind people ran headlong into just trying to live their lives. It didn't matter to her if their trouble was self-inflicted or not. It only mattered that she find a way to maneuver the law and the circumstances to fix it. Or at least make it better. Or at least help the person endure.

She smiled slightly at the downward spiral of her lofty ideals. "Realism born of experience," she said aloud.

Her smile faded. Her mother was disappointed. Katie Becenti was disappointed. And Johnny Becenti—who knew what he was?

"I can't do everything," she said, still talking to herself. She rubbed the place on her forehead that hurt the worst. How many times had she come to Window Rock to represent one of the People just because her mother had asked? Plenty of times. Plenty.

Yes, Lillian, but what have you done lately?

She gave a sharp exhalation of breath and smothered the urge to swear because the twenty-dollar bill and the snuff can still lay forlornly on her desk. She picked them both up and put them inside a manila envelope. She wouldn't chase after Katie and her mother to return it. It would only give them false hope that she'd changed her mind. She would mail it to Window Rock—Dolly would see that it was returned to Johnny's mother.

She looked around at hearing a soft knock. Her brother Lucas stood waiting in the open doorway. Her brother, who, like Johnny Becenti, was also a Navajo Tribal Policeman in Window Rock.

"What are you—the second wave?" she asked without prelude.

"I'm fine, thanks," he said, ignoring the remark. "Good of you to ask. My wife is fine, too. So are all the children. Or at least I think so. I haven't seen or heard from the Flagstaff nephew-by-marriage lately. Patrick is keeping to himself, for some reason. So how are you, Lillian? I have to ask, because I haven't seen or heard from you lately, either."

"Lucas, I am not in the mood for this. And I'm busy."

"So our mother tells me. But," he said with a shrug, "I'm here begging a favor anyway, so you might as well hear it."

"I am not going to talk to Johnny Becenti."

"I wish you would."

"Why? You don't even like Becenti."

"I respect him."

"Then *you* go talk to him."

"I can't."

"Why?" she said again.

"Because I can't."

Lillian raised both eyebrows. She was in no mood for some inverted male logic regarding appropriate manly behavior, either.

"He's my superior officer," Lucas said with a patience that annoyed her even more. "It's not my place to challenge him."

"Oh, yes, like you've never done *that* before."

"Whatever disagreements we've had were always part of the job. This is personal—private."

"Lucas—" she began, but she didn't go on. She couldn't

argue with the privacy issue, not when it was the same reason she herself had for not becoming involved. She finished putting the snuff can into the envelope.

"So has he officially left the tribal police?"

"No, not yet. He's on extended leave. But his mother is worried—you saw how worried she is. I think she's got good reason. I...owe him, Lillian, and I'm asking you to make some attempt to help repay my debt."

She didn't say anything.

"When have I ever asked you for a favor?" he said quietly.

"When? How about when your wife, Sloan, needed somebody to navigate her through the Navajo legal system? She wasn't even your wife then—for all I knew she was just another bored, rich white woman you had the hots for—like that other one, the anthropologist. But I came anyway, didn't I? I did the best I could for her. And then there was your youngest nephew-by-marriage, Will. You do remember when he got arrested for bootlegging whiskey on the rez?"

"That wasn't exactly his fault. He was trying to get Eddie Nez to teach him to be a medicine man. And he was going through that thing of not knowing if he wanted to be Navajo or white."

"Yes, well, I still had to drive all the way to Window Rock to get him out of jail. And what about your niece-by-marriage, Meggie?"

"Meggie's never been arrested in her life—well, except for the time when she and Jack inadvertently stole a horse. But she was only nine, and we managed to get that straightened out without you. I think you can cut her some slack on that one. You know Meggie won't even tear the tags off pillows."

"Don't be cute, Lucas. I'm talking about her husband—about Jack and *his* little run-in with those people from California—"

"They were trying to take away Meggie's baby, Lillian."

"That's not the point. The point is *I* did what you needed, each and every time—"

"Okay!" he said, holding up his hand to stop her from cataloging any more good deeds.

"Johnny Becenti wouldn't listen to me," she insisted. "And I can't for the life of me understand why you and our mother and *his* mother think he would."

"Because he's always valued your opinion," Lucas said.

"I'm not sure you and I are talking about the same Johnny Becenti," she said, but her exasperation abated somewhat. It was true that her brother owed the man. There had been a time in Lucas's life—before he married Sloan Baron—when he'd been foolish enough to become involved with another white woman whose only intent had been to annoy her wealthy parents with yet another unsuitable sexual liaison and to have a titillating topic of conversation at her pretentious academic cocktail parties. But Lucas had truly loved her, and she had been oblivious to that fact. So much so, that when she'd found herself pregnant with Lucas's child, she'd simply disappeared. No explanation. No words of farewell. No announcement or negotiation of her plans regarding their unborn baby.

Lucas had been devastated, and he'd abruptly become the "worthless Indian" she must have thought he was to have treated him so. It was the uncompromising Johnny Becenti who had intervened, who had refused to let Lucas throw away his life and his career on alcohol and feeling sorry for himself. It was Johnny Becenti who had forced Lucas to find his harmony again. If Becenti hadn't done it, there was no telling where Lucas would be now. Certainly not a respected tribal policeman. Certainly not the now sober husband of Sloan Baron and the much-loved second father to Sloan's orphaned niece and nephews. It didn't escape Lillian that Lucas might be dead now if not for Johnny Becenti, or that it might be *their* mother, Dolly, offering her snuff-can money to someone to try to talk some sense into him.

"Think about it, will you?" Lucas said.

"I don't have to think about it. I'm not going to do it."

Lucas looked at her gravely for a moment, then gave a quiet sigh. "There's nothing more to say, then, is there?"

"Nothing," she agreed.

"So how are you?" he asked, harking back to his earlier question.

"I'm fine. I'm busy," she said pointedly.

"You and the big state legislator—you're still to-gether?"

"Yes, Lucas," Lillian said pointedly. "He's going to take me to dinner tonight if I can ever get out of here."

"Dinner. But he's not going to marry you."

"That, my dear brother, is none of your business."

"When a man loves a woman, Lillian, he wants to marry her."

"Did it ever occur to you that *I* might be the one who doesn't want to get married?"

"No," he said, teasing now. "Never."

"Oh, get out of here, will you?" she said, shooing him away. "Go home, say hello to Sloan and the family for me."

"They'd rather you said hello in person."

"Window Rock gets on my nerves."

"So you've said," Lucas said. "Lillian, can't you do this one—"

"No!" she said. "I can't." She looked at him and then at her watch. When she looked back at him, he was waiting, giving her one last chance to change her mind.

"I can't," she repeated.

He hesitated for a moment longer, then abruptly reached into his shirt pocket and put a folded piece of paper on her desk.

"What is this?"

"A map to Becenti's homestead."

"Lucas, I told you—"

"I know, I know. This is just in case you decide to make an old woman *and* your brother rest a little easier."

The two of you *might rest easier if I went,* Lillian thought, but she wasn't at all sure Johnny Becenti would. She had, after all, been approached for this job because of her highly developed ability to vex the man senseless.

"Goodbye, Lucas," she said pointedly.

He gave a tolerant and forgiving smile before he stepped out of the office and walked down the carpeted hall, his footsteps muffled and soon inaudible.

"Damn it!" she said in exasperation. She didn't want to be tolerated or forgiven. Intellectually, she knew she had no reason to feel guilty. Intellectually—but not emotionally. And her family had no right to make her feel this way. She was a lawyer, not a psychiatrist. Johnny Becenti's problem was not a legal one.

She looked at her watch again. She needed to shower and change her clothes. She needed to put some real effort into this evening. Stuart Dennison, "the big state legislator," as Lucas had so inelegantly described him, would be waiting. Their relationship had been on such an even keel lately, and she wanted to keep it that way. Stuart had suddenly recovered all the cheerfulness and good humor that had first drawn her to him, and regardless of his uncharacteristic insistence that they find the time to have dinner together tonight *without fail,* she was truly looking forward to seeing him. She had known him since she was a young law student, and except for the last several months, they had been lovers for nearly as long. She respected him, perhaps loved him. She certainly needed him. He complemented her in every way, his sanguine nature perfectly offsetting her cynical intensity. His quick grasp of a legal situation had helped her more than once to win a case. And she liked to think that she had helped him, as well. Her unwillingness to suffer fools gladly and her uncanny ability to know what people meant regardless of what they said, had made it possible for him to weed out more than one political hanger-on, some of whose ulterior motives would have proved disastrous to Stuart's career. He made her laugh—or he used to—and he would again. Their relationship was definitely taking a turn for the better. She knew that without a doubt.

She sat down behind her desk and stared at the stacks of papers she needed to process, and the envelope with the snuff can she should have given to Lucas. She didn't have time to go home and change for dinner. And she didn't have time to start any of her legal tasks. Her mind went abruptly to Johnny Becenti. What in the world was going on with him? She hadn't seen him since just before his wife died. Surprisingly, the two of them had managed to work together then without getting into any major lawyer-policeman squabbles. In fact, they'd gotten along quite well trying to get Jack Begaye—who had defiantly married Lucas's Meggie—out of a great deal of legal trouble. Becenti hadn't broken any rules for Jack as far as Lillian knew, but he still had done everything he could to help Meggie's wild young husband fight the false accusations that could have destroyed their happiness and their marriage. And it was just that kind of thing that always puzzled Lillian so. Becenti was rigid and "by-the-book"—and yet he wasn't. He could have washed his hands of both Lucas and Jack on more than one occasion—no one would have blamed him—but he didn't. He'd thought them both worth salvaging, and he'd been right. And, if she admitted the truth, she "owed" Johnny Becenti as much as Lucas did.

She abruptly got up and walked around the desk to the window. The sun was almost gone, leaving a pale orange horizon in its wake. Spring was coming, but it was still cold. She looked out across the street. Cars. People. But no reservation trucks or Johnny Becenti relatives. No relatives of *hers,* either, for that matter. She was off the hook, but she certainly didn't feel like it.

She abruptly made up her mind. She would leave for the

restaurant now, even if she would be somewhat early. She got her purse out of her desk drawer and hunted through the jumbled contents for the silver-and-turquoise compact Stuart had given her early in their relationship—before he'd understood that Lillian Singer had already made her decision as to which world she would belong. She didn't wear Southwestern Navajo-type jewelry, or buttons, or bolos, or anything else. She wore gold and not much of that. Gold studs in her ears. A delicate gold chain around her neck. The compact Stuart had given her was the only silver-and-turquoise item she owned.

She brushed her hair, powdered her nose, painted her mouth. Better, she thought, looking into the compact mirror. But not as good as if she'd had the time to go home. Even so, she was looking forward to this evening. Candlelight. Breast of chicken in champagne. New Zealand raspberries. Stuart. Precisely what she needed after a day like today. She smiled at her reflection before she snapped the compact closed. She would work later, or early in the morning. But, for now, headache or not, guilt or not, she was going to relax and enjoy.

The restaurant was crowded when she arrived, somewhat surprising to her because the opera season hadn't yet begun. She stood waiting in the dark entry while the maître d' located Stuart's reservation at the lighted podium. She could smell the aroma of baking bread, hear the murmur of conversation in the dining area and the classical guitar music that played softly in the background. She noted immediately that she was surrounded by elegantly dressed women and that there was not a navy blue power suit like hers among them.

"This way, please," the maître d' said, sending her off with a tuxedoed hostess. Lillian followed, threading her way carefully in the dim light. All the tables were set with gleaming silver and glassware. The candles were lit, the napkins intricately folded.

She saw Stuart before he saw her. His table was well

away from the flow of traffic, a choice location beside floor-to-ceiling windows that looked out on the formal garden. He was not alone. She didn't recognize the blond-haired woman seated at the table with him—a young woman wearing a "little black dress" and pearls appropriate for the posh surroundings.

A colleague? Lillian wondered. *Relative? Friend of the family?*

The woman leaned forward to say something to Stuart, and he moved closer to hear. Lillian watched them, their whispered words, their bodies not touching but clearly wanting to. He was smiling, oblivious to anything but the woman in the black dress.

Lillian faltered.

None of the above.

A phrase immediately came to mind, one she'd actually seen in a newspaper advertisement for this particular restaurant.

Intimate dining.

Intimate.

Stuart saw her then and stood. He was smiling for her now. So happy to see her. Explaining to the woman in the black dress that Lillian Singer had indeed arrived.

She had no choice but to walk forward. Indeed, there was no reason why she shouldn't. She was here by invitation—by very insistent invitation, actually—and he was smiling still, his boyish handsomeness all too apparent.

"Working late again, I see," he said in spite of the fact that she had arrived early.

Early. And dressed wrong.

She let him pull out her chair, and she sat down heavily, as if her legs wouldn't hold her anymore. She took a quiet breath before she acknowledged the woman, but she felt anything but serene. She wanted to believe that she had jumped to some erroneous conclusion based solely on a split-second observation. Intellectually she knew that she had no reason to feel such anxiety or such a sense of intruding into a situation where she didn't belong. But it was that same inexplicable thing that had made her a good lawyer—a Navajo thing, perhaps—the ability to *know* what people were about, regardless of what they said or did. And Stuart's smile didn't fool her. He was *about* something. She could only sit here and awkwardly wait for the revelation.

She abruptly smiled at the woman. "Lillian Singer," she said, before Stuart could introduce her.

The woman returned the smile shyly, disarmingly really. Like a little girl. She just missed being beautiful, something only another woman would notice under the artful makeup. "J. B. Greenleigh," she said, her voice whispery soft. Unnaturally soft. Learned, like the makeup. "I've heard so much about you. From Stuart," she added.

"Oh, yes?" Lillian answered, glancing at Stuart. He was watching J.B. as if she were some doted-upon child who had just carried off her parents'-night recitation perfectly.

"I'm really glad you could make it, Lillian," he said, finally glancing in her direction.

Oh, really? Why? Lillian almost said, her penchant for outspokenness driving her hard. She needed to understand the significance of this unexpected threesome, and, in spite of her early Navajo training, she had never been one to patiently wait for events to unfold.

"Is anyone else coming?" she asked instead, her sarcasm subtle but not lost on Stuart. He looked at her sharply and then at J.B. Then, as if by some prearranged signal, J.B. suddenly slid back her chair.

"I must go powder my nose," she said. "I'll be right back." She smiled at them both and left.

"I'm sorry, Lillian," Stuart said immediately.

"Sorry?"

"I hadn't planned—well, J.B. wasn't going to be here. You're *early.*"

She looked at him, not knowing what he expected her to say about that. She forced herself to wait. The silence lengthened unbearably.

"Stuart, just get to the bottom line here, okay?" she said when he didn't go on.

He gave a slight smile. "The bottom line."

"Please," she said.

He took a deep breath. "Lillian, you know how important you've always been to me. The success I've had—I owe a great deal of it to your—"

"The bottom line, Stuart," she said again.

"All right. There's no use dragging it out, I guess. J.B. and I are...getting married."

Lillian heard him perfectly. She'd expected the worst, but even so, it took a moment before she could respond. "I...see," she finally managed. He looked miserable, as unhappy as she felt, but she showed him no mercy. "Isn't this rather sudden?"

"No—not really," he said in spite of the fact that his engagement *had* to be sudden or it had to have happened while he and Lillian were still lovers.

"How is it she's heard all about me and I seem to have missed any mention of her?"

"Lillian—"

"Isn't she a little *young*, Stuart?"

"I love her," he said quietly, his eyes begging her to understand.

But it was her brother's voice she heard.

When a man loves a woman, Lillian, he wants to marry her.

"Ah, yes," she said sarcastically. "Love. Well, then. That's that, isn't it?"

"We were hoping you'd come to the wedding."

She gave a short laugh. "Oh, please, Stuart, let's not torture *both* your women with your naive notion of civilized behavior. She's young enough to think she has to go along with it. I'm old enough—uncivilized enough—to tell you to go to hell."

She stood, dropping her purse off her lap. He retrieved

it for her, but he held on to it when she would have grabbed it out of his hand.

"Lillian, you know I care about you. I'll *always* care about you—"

"Don't," she said. "I don't want to call you a liar in front of all these people." She took her purse out of his hand, and she stared into his eyes for a moment.

But there was nothing left to say, not without yelling or crying or upending a perfectly set table. She abruptly turned and walked away.

Chapter Two

I'm fine with this, she kept thinking. No problem. Stuart had been all but out of her life even before he'd made his sudden wedding announcement. She had gotten used to his not calling, not asking her opinion, not being around. In fact, she had been so busy herself that there were times when she'd hardly noticed. But how much easier it would have been now if, in the last few weeks, he hadn't made her think he was coming back again.

Why did he do that?

Her mind belabored the question all that sleepless night and all the next day, and eventually it gave her an answer—whether she really wanted one or not. It had been her experience both personally and professionally that guilty men either found fault or made jealous accusations to justify their infidelity or to give themselves an excuse to get out. Clearly, Stuart hadn't felt the least bit guilty—he would have had to have some sense of commitment to their relationship for that. But Lillian Singer had simply been his longtime *in*significant other. He owed her no consideration, no explanations beforehand. He had "cared" about her enough to let her bask a little in the light of his newfound happiness, but not enough to tell her the reason for it.

I'm fine with this.

She must be fine. She was able to take care of her court cases with competence if not with her usual ease. She even managed to go for hours at a time without thinking of Stuart or his new bride-to-be. She went to work; she came home. She ate. She slept. And in spite of all she could do, she kept finding reasons to look at herself in the mirror.

Not young, she thought every time she did it. J.B. Greenleigh was young. Lillian had been brought up to revere old age and its wisdom, and until now, she hadn't minded any of her birthdays. She was reasonably attractive, educated, successful, healthy, *thin.*

But she was not young. And the more she looked at her reflection, the more she was certain that J.B. Greenleigh's appeal wasn't just that she was white and therefore more suitable to be a politician's wife. It was that J.B. Greenleigh wasn't knee-deep in her forties.

Face it, she thought. *You, my dear, have been dumped— big time.*

And there was nothing she could do about it. She couldn't be younger, even if she wanted to be, and she certainly couldn't be any less Navajo. She'd had years of practice living off the reservation, and she'd already gone as far as she could with that.

On Friday she lost the court case she'd been working so hard on—an outcome she hadn't expected despite all her courtroom experience. She had relentlessly and logically shown without a doubt that the prosecution had not proved its case. Unfortunately, all her stellar arguments had apparently gone right over the jury's head. In fact, she had been so surprised by the verdict that her considerably-less-than-gracious remark about it had cost her a two-hundred-dollar sanction.

She returned to her office that afternoon, poorer if not

wiser, to find a terse message from Stuart among the pile of yellow While You Were Out slips on her desk. She was to call him ASAP. Not a request, an order. And, he explained further, if she happened not to be able to reach him, he would come by her place later.

With or without J.B.? she wondered. She closed her eyes at the possibility of a "with J.B." scenario, and for the first time since that disastrous so-called dinner, she was ready to admit that perhaps she wasn't *fine* after all. She certainly didn't feel fine. She felt overwhelmed, exasperated and embarrassed—*hurt*, damn it! She wanted to cry, throw back her head and bawl until she felt better. And the last thing she needed from Stuart was some kind of token Let's-go-check-on-poor-poor-Lillian visit.

"I can't deal with any of this," she said aloud, tossing the message aside. Her secretary was just passing her open door.

"Did you say something, Lillian?"

"I've decided to run away, Gracie," she answered, leaning forward and resting her head in her hands for a moment.

The inconceivable notion that L. Singer, Esquire, would do such a rash and uncharacteristic thing made the woman smile. "Can I go, too?" she asked anyway, because it had been that kind of week.

"Next time, Gracie," Lillian answered. She slid back her chair to look for her purse. "You haven't seen me this afternoon, okay?"

"Except if Stuart calls, right?"

"You haven't seen me," Lillian repeated.

"What if the family calls? Will you be at home?"

"You *haven't seen me,*" she said, putting her purse strap over her shoulder.

"Aha!" Gracie said, holding up one finger. "I believe I've got it now. I haven't *seen* you. Have a nice weekend, Lillian—wherever it is."

There wasn't much chance of that, but Lillian didn't say so. Where exactly would she go if she did happen to decide that running away would be the most satisfying rebuttal to all her recent aggravation? In her current frame of mind, she was certain that she didn't want to go to some quiet, restful place where she had nothing to do but think. She didn't want to think—therefore she didn't want to hide out at home. Neither did she want to go to Window Rock to see the family. She needed a puzzle to unravel, a problem to solve.

She needed—

She abruptly began to move the papers around on her desk, and she found the map almost immediately. She unfolded it and looked at Lucas's meticulous drawing. She thought that she could find the Becenti place. The question was whether or not she felt up to the challenge of this particular brand of problem solving. She would be unwelcome, of course. And her wise counsel would likely go unheeded. There was no reason for her to even attempt it—except that she didn't like her current loser status, and she needed to try to accomplish the impossible to assuage her wounded ego. She'd taken two major hits in a week—but did she want to stand in plain view for another one?

She gave a quiet sigh. She could drive to Window Rock, or beyond toward the Becenti homestead, if she wanted, and she could bail out at any time. She hadn't accepted Katie Becenti's quest, even if she did still have the twenty-dollar bill and the snuff can. She wouldn't have to explain herself to anyone if, once she got there, she decided not to talk to Johnny Becenti after all. A long, quiet drive was certainly preferable to going home and having to worry about whether or not Stuart and his bride-to-be were going to sneak up on her.

She shoved the map into her purse and stepped into the hallway.

"Lillian!" Gracie called from the receptionist's desk. "Stuart's on the phone again!"

"You haven't seen me!" Lillian said over her shoulder, walking swiftly toward the private back entrance to the parking lot. She let the door quietly close on whatever Gracie replied.

Lillian lived several miles outside of town, and she drove too fast to get home. The red-roofed old stucco ranch house she'd bought years ago had always been a sanctuary for her—until today. She didn't want to take a chance on having Stuart turn up while she was still there, and she changed quickly into a pair of old jeans and a sweatshirt, boots and a leather jacket. She stuffed a change of clothes, a bar of soap, her toothbrush and toothpaste into a backpack, emptying a bowl of fruit and English walnuts and the nutcracker into it on her way out the back door.

To be clean and not to starve, she thought. *And to run.* How her life's goals had changed of late.

She managed to get away from the house unchallenged, and she took the interstate to Albuquerque and then on to Gallup. The day was bright and windy, the strong wind gusts buffeting her small car from time to time as she drove. She played the radio loud—country music—something she never listened to and therefore was guaranteed not to bring any disturbing memories to the forefront.

She did *not* want to think.

She made good time, getting into Window Rock before sundown. She could have stopped to see Lucas and Sloan, or her mother, or Meggie and her now only slightly wild husband, Jack, and their newest baby—but she didn't. She filled her gas tank at a convenience store, and then she fumbled for the map and kept driving. She didn't want to wait until morning to see Becenti. She wanted to get this over with, and arriving when it was nearly dark would give her a slight edge, she thought. She would be the weary traveler. He had had Katie Becenti to teach him how to behave, and he wouldn't turn her away without at least listening to what she had to say—she hoped. And, in spite of her determination not to think, her mind was busy working on precisely what she would tell Becenti when she saw him—her opening argument, as it were. Should she appeal to his better nature? To his sense of duty to his job and his family? Or should she bait him and make him angry? Lord knows, she'd had enough practice doing that.

She was so determined to find the best approach that she missed the first turnoff, a narrow dirt road that wound upward and seemed to go nowhere. But, she was reservation raised and therefore undaunted. She backed up and made the turn, and she kept going, slowly guiding her low-riding car carefully around or through the potholes, if there was no other way. The farther she went, the more impassable the road became. She stopped at one point to look at the map. "Two and a half miles" Lucas had written. He was exacting about these things, so she kept going. Eventually the land flattened and broadened, and the road became somewhat less rutted.

She drove on. She could see a cluster of trees, and experience told her that this was a likely spot for the Becenti homestead to be.

It wasn't.

She kept driving, finally stopping again to look at the map. It showed that the homestead was somewhere in the vicinity, but not precisely where, and there was nothing about this particular stretch of road. The sun was going down. There was little daylight left for her to go aimlessly looking. She should have waited until morning.

On impulse, she got out of the car and walked to a cluster of vertical standing rocks she thought she could climb to get a better view of the land around her. She made her way upward carefully and with minimal difficulty. When she reached the top, she looked in all directions, seeing nothing in the least bit helpful—another stand of trees off to her right, long shadows from the monoliths. It seemed very quiet at first, just the wind and her labored breathing from making the climb, but then she heard a different sound, the faint bleating of sheep from somewhere—from that same stand of trees.

She thought that that had to be the Becenti place, and

she scrambled down and walked back to the car, turning it around and trying to find the track that would take her in that direction. She eventually found what must be it, but her blind faith in Lucas's mapmaking had definitely been shaken. He hadn't put in the non-road to the trees.

Of course, in all fairness, he hadn't expected her to be doing this in near darkness. She switched on her headlights and drove in what she hoped was the right direction. Finally, she could see the rail fencing of a corral and beyond that, the vertical sticks of a large sheep pen. She continued until she could see a log-and-mud hogan among the trees. There was no sign of activity. No smoke coming out of the smoke hole.

She parked the car and waited, a gesture of politeness on her part to give Johnny time to prepare for company. The wind had picked up. The sun slipped behind the rock cliffs. She shivered and reached for her jacket, draping it over her arms.

She waited. The car shook in a gust of wind. She could see no flicker of light from inside the hogan. She didn't even know if she was in the right place. After a moment, she opened the car door and got out. She put on her jacket, and she stood looking toward the hogan.

Still nothing—except the continued bleating of the sheep, a bleating she instantly recognized, for all her disinterest in herding when she was growing up. Sheep in distress.

Coyotes, she thought, then immediately changed her mind. They weren't frantic enough for that; just unhappy—hungry or thirsty—and restless because of the wind.

She walked in the direction of the sheep pen. Maybe Becenti was out there. Maybe he hadn't heard her car. The bleating grew louder, and the flock crowded the fence at the sight of her, clamoring for her to take pity on them and put something over the fence. It was a decent-size flock—long-haired churros mostly, the traditional Navajo breed that had been captured centuries ago from the invading Spaniards.

She still didn't see anyone about. Someone should be out here feeding these animals. And where were the dogs? she wondered. Surely Becenti wasn't trying to keep a herd without at least one dog. It could be done, of course, but not easily, especially alone. In her experience there was always one adventurous ewe in the bunch who was forever trying to go her own way and take half the herd along with her, one whose wool was too prized or whose lambs were too healthy for her to end up in a stew pot for her mischief. God, she hated sheep.

She walked around the perimeter of the pen, still looking for Becenti. No one was outside. She walked back toward the hogan, leaving the sheep complaining after her. In spite of their noise, it was just too...eerily...quiet.

Where is he? Inside the hogan?

She didn't want to go barging in to see, and she still didn't call out to him, even though the time allotted for her to wait for his acknowledgement of her visit must be well past what Navajo decorum allowed. It was certainly past what *she* was willing to tolerate.

"Oh, the hell with it," she said aloud. "Becenti! It's Lillian Singer!"

Nothing.

She strained to hear over the bleating sheep and the wind. Still nothing.

She walked back to the car to get her flashlight, the big, six-cell nightstick variety she kept for illumination and, if necessary, protection. She was cold and she was hungry— and her mental state didn't bear scrutiny. The only positive thought she could manage was that even if Becenti wasn't here, she would have at least made her goodwill gesture on behalf of Lucas and Becenti's mother, and she could get off this family-induced guilt trip.

"Becenti!" she yelled again.

The sheep were growing more rambunctious at the fence.

She gave a heavy sigh and walked back toward the hogan. Welcome or not, wrong abode or not, she was going to have to look inside. She recognized that she could just get in the car and leave—except that Lillian Singer didn't do things by halves. She had come all this way to lecture Johnny Becenti, and that she would do—if she could find him.

The door to the hogan hung slightly askew. She stood in front of it for a moment, then pushed it open.

"Becenti?" she called, shining the flashlight beam inside.

She could see the makeshift stove in the middle of the dirt floor—half an inverted oil drum with a square cut out at the bottom for an opening and a stovepipe that went up through the smoke hole. A cooking pot sat on top of the barrel, but there was no fire burning. She could see an old military foot locker pushed against the wall, a small table, some chairs.

And a pile of blankets in the darkest corner. Someone was lying on them.

"Becenti?" she said quietly, keeping the flashlight beam elsewhere, still giving him—someone—the opportunity to invite her to come inside.

She walked closer. She couldn't tell if the person was asleep or awake. She could only hear a kind of heavy breathing—

She abruptly stopped. If she had disturbed someone's intimate tryst here, she was going straight back to Window Rock and punch her brother in the nose.

Her eyes became more adjusted to the darkness in the corner. No. This person was alone, and perhaps ill, not in the throes of passion. She stepped forward, crossing the dirt floor and kneeling down by the blankets. Johnny Becenti lay on the pile, his eyes closed, his breathing labored, painful.

Now what? she thought, trying to think of something to say to him. She wasn't supposed to be here.

But he didn't give her time to speak. He suddenly reached out for her, his hand hot against her face.

"Mae," he whispered. "Mae—!"

Chapter Three

The kerosene lamps had been lit—he could tell that much, even with his eyes closed. She had made a fire inside the oil drum, then she'd left for a time and come back again. And now...

He wasn't quite sure what she was doing now. He could hear the slight sounds of her moving around the hogan, but that was all. He thought she must be looking into the niches in the log walls to find out what he had, but he didn't open his eyes to see. It would take too much effort, far too much effort. He had to concentrate on trying to breathe. He was so cold. Everything hurt. His head, his arms and legs, and his chest.

She shouldn't be here. How can she be here?

At first he thought it was Mae who called him—her voice he heard in the wind.

Becenti! The way she always used to say it on those rare occasions when she was annoyed with him. And in his present state of mind, why wouldn't he think it was her?

He had done a great deal of late that would have caused his gentle wife annoyance.

But it was hardly less incredible to him that the voice belonged to Lillian Singer. Lillian, who never left Santa Fe if she could help it, who went to the opera and who moved in the same orbit as the artists and the musicians and the movie stars—and her longtime lover, Stuart Dennison. She was a woman who obviously needed a place like Santa Fe. She needed to be where she could live on both sides of who and what she really was. He knew that she had fled the reservation when she was still in her teens, and when and if she ever returned, it most certainly wasn't to a place like this—a one-room log-and-mud hogan with a dirt floor. No electricity. No running water. No heat save the oil-drum stove.

And yet she *was* here, and she apparently knew what she was doing. The fire was burning well. He could smell the woodsmoke, hear the oil drum pop with the heat. He wanted to ask her *how* she got here. He wanted to ask her—

He realized suddenly that she was kneeling by him, and he opened his eyes after all.

"What day...is it?" he said, clearly startling her—again.

"Friday," she answered. "Friday evening, actually." She watched him closely, he supposed, in case she decided that she needed to run. He had scared her earlier, grabbing her like that. She was still scared, no matter how hard she tried to hide it.

"Johnny, are you in your right mind or not?" she asked bluntly.

"Not," he said, sounding much weaker than he intended. To his surprise, she smiled.

"Oh, good," she said. "*That* I'm used to. Here, drink some of this."

She offered him water, the bottled kind for the relentlessly health-conscious that he had seen advertised in magazines and never had the occasion to taste or buy. He was so thirsty, and because of that, he drank deeply, in spite of the burning pain in his throat, in spite of the fact that he didn't want her here. She helped hold the bottle, because his hands shook so. His only thought was that maybe she wouldn't leave, now that she had seen his weakness.

"More?" she asked.

He took another swallow, and then another and another, thinking now of his grandfather, of a story the old man had told him once about a tiny puddle of water in the desert and two warriors. The Thirsty Warrior saw only the sunlight on the top. The Un-Thirsty Warrior saw only the mud on the bottom. There was no doubt in his mind which category *he* fell into.

"What—are you doing here?" he asked with some effort.

She completely ignored the question. "How long have you been sick like this?"

He shook his head and tried not to cough, tried not to get angry because her response was so typically Lillian. She always had her own questions, her own agenda. It was impossible for her not to be contrary. "What—are you—doing here?" he asked again.

"Feeding sheep," she said. "If I can find something to give them. Where is it?"

He shook his head again. The motion caused a sharp pain to shoot through his skull. He had to clench his teeth to keep from crying out. "I—can do—it."

"So do it," she said mildly. "But I think you should know, if they aren't fed soon, they're going to be out of the fence."

He made a feeble attempt to sit up, and then another. The third time he tried, she put both hands on his shoulders to keep him down.

"Johnny, enough already. I'll do it."

"I don't—need—your help—"

"I don't care what *you* need. I'm trying to look after the damn sheep! Never mind, I'll find it myself."

She moved away from him and grabbed up a heavy flashlight and went out the door. She was gone for a long time. When she returned, she went immediately to the stove and dropped down in front of it, holding out her hands to the warmth.

"Did you—feed them?" he asked.

"Yes, and no thanks to you."

"I want to know—why you're here."

She turned to look at him. "I'm here, Johnny, because I needed a place to hide. And I'm using you as an excuse."

"I don't know what—that means," he said, holding her gaze.

She shrugged. "I'm not exactly sure myself. But that seems to be the bottom line. You want some soup?"

He continued to stare at her.

"The question isn't that hard, Johnny," she said after a moment. "You say, 'Yes, Lillian, I do,' or 'No, Lillian, I don't.' The choice is chicken and rice *or* chicken and rice. It's the only kind you had and it's ready." She stood and lifted the lid of a small pot on the stove to verify that fact.

"I don't want you here," he said.

"I understand that," she said, stirring the soup. "Now answer the question." She went to the table and brought back two—his only two—coffee mugs. She poured the soup into one, then gave him a pointed look.

He made a gesture of impatience—and acquiescence—with one hand. She could have pretended not to understand if she'd wanted, forced him to capitulate on a grander scale, but she didn't. She brought the cup to him, but she made no attempt to help him sit. He managed to raise himself up on his elbow with difficulty. He couldn't remember the last time he'd eaten, and after a few sips, his hunger returned full force. The soup tasted exactly as he expected—essentially chickenless and canned—but it was still all he could do not to gulp it down like the starving man he was.

She left him with the cup and went to rummage in a backpack she must have brought with her. After a few seconds, she returned with a small packet of saltine crackers, or more accurately—cracker crumbs. He let her pour them into the cup.

She immediately went away again, this time to fill her own cup. She sat on the dirt floor near the stove to drink it, and much to his relief, she made no attempt to engage him in conversation.

But she kept looking at him, assessing the situation and his condition in a way that annoyed him far more than her talking would have and far more than he had the strength to be annoyed about. He didn't have the strength for anything, and he abruptly set the cup down and lay back heavily.

"When you've finished, I'll take you to see a doctor," she said.

"No."

"Johnny—"

"No! I don't want to see a doctor and I—don't want you here—"

She gave a quiet sigh. "This is the deal. If you want to get rid of me, you're going to have to let me take you somewhere to get some medical treatment."

"No."

"Then I'm staying."

"I don't need you here!"

"I told you. I'm not thinking about you. I'm thinking about the sheep. And if you die—well, then *somebody's* got to bury you."

"You'd enjoy *that,* I guess," he said with every bit of the petulance he felt at her invasion of his privacy. He was not to be bothered. Everyone on the reservation knew he was *not* to be bothered.

"Well, you have gotten on my nerves on occasion."

He swore—just loud enough to make himself feel better and not necessarily loud enough for her to hear. He *hurt* so. His chest was on fire with the effort it took to argue with her. He lay there, trying not to gasp, his hand over his eyes.

"Johnny?" she said after a moment.

"What?"

"I'm afraid you've got that hantavirus thing."

He looked at her. She was serious.

"I don't."

"How do you know?"

"Because—I'd be dead—by now—if I did."

She didn't look very reassured.

"It's something, Johnny. You need to see a doctor. You might even need to be in the hospital. If you won't do that, then I'll find Winston Tsosie. He can tell me the best person to do a chant. He'll know who can help you."

"Lillian—!" He broke off and began to cough. "I want you—to leave," he said when he was able.

She moved to the backpack, and he thought for a moment she was actually going to do it. She took out a cellular phone instead.

"What are you doing?"

"I'm going to see if I can get my sister-in-law. She can—"

"No—!"

"Sloan can tell me what to do for you."

"What you can—do—for me—is get—out of here!"

To his surprise, she did just that—but she left the backpack and took the phone with her. After a few minutes she came in again. She stuffed the phone into the backpack and came to kneel beside him.

"The transmission keeps breaking up," she said, as if this were information he had interest in or had even solicited. "I don't know if she even knew it was me. Johnny—"

"Lillian, for God's sake! Will you go away and let me be!"

"I think not," she answered without apology. "I told you. I need a place to hide—" She stopped, watching him intently. "What's wrong?" she asked abruptly.

"Nothing," he said, but he was beginning to shake. He was so *cold.* "Oh, God—"

She immediately took off her jacket and put it over him. Then she began to look around the hogan for something else to add to the pile—his heavy winter coat. But he still shook. He was ashamed to have her see him like this, but there was nothing he could do about it. Lillian was Lillian. Even if he'd been well, it was doubtful he could have made her go if she didn't want to. After a time, the chills ended, only to be replaced by profuse sweating. He threw the mound of covers off him, expecting an argument from her. But she wiped his face with a wet cloth and handed him two tablets and the bottled water.

"What is—this?"

"Aspirin," she said. "It's the only thing I've got that might help."

He hesitated, then took them, surprising himself and her. For a man who had wanted to die as badly as he had, he was now inordinately interested in anything that might make him feel better.

He must have slept afterward, but he had no idea how long. He woke up abruptly, uncertain about his surroundings but still knowing that there was something here that worried him.

Ah, yes. Lillian Singer. Where is she? he thought.

Or had he dreamed her and Mae both? He turned his head to look around the hogan. No, he hadn't imagined her being here. The fire was still burning and the bottled water was exactly where she'd left it.

He wrestled for a moment with the temptation to call out for her, but he realized almost as soon as the notion occurred to him that he couldn't do that. The idea was for her to go away, not think that he needed her. He didn't need her. As she so cleverly had pointed out, the *sheep* needed her. He could hear that they were quiet now. Fed and content—or out of the pen altogether and halfway to Albuquerque.

He lay there, listening to quiet sheep. Listening to the wind. A ghost wind.

Mae.

His wife had made her own funeral arrangements. She had lived all her life the Navajo Way, and she had remained traditional to the last. She had wanted all the taboos surrounding the dead meticulously kept. Without his leave, her family had carefully prepared her body for the long journey into nothingness. Her elderly father and her one male cousin had taken it to some remote and secret place for burial—for *his* sake, so that her *chindi,* the evil fragment of herself that remained on the earth, could never harm him. Part of him thanked her for relieving him of that terrible task. Part of him believed in the old ways enough to be at peace with what had been done.

And part of him wanted only to weep. He missed her. He'd had no idea what a great empty place her death would leave. If he had a grave to visit, if they had had children together, then he might—

He gave a quiet sigh. No. Nothing would be changed. He would still be alone—here. He would still be remembering and grieving. He didn't know what to do with it— all this sorrow. It was like a living thing that dragged him down into darkness. It was always there, whether he was asleep or awake. He couldn't bear the emptiness of the house in Window Rock that he and Mae had shared. He couldn't bear going to the law-enforcement building and doing the job he'd put before her more times than not. So he'd come all the way out here, away from everybody, not understanding until very recently that the emptiness wasn't in the house or in the job, but in himself.

And now he had another tribulation—Lillian Singer.

He lay there, still listening, and he realized suddenly how much he was anticipating her return. Surely he hadn't become that starved for human companionship—to the point that Lillian Singer would be welcome. But, even he would have to admit that her coming here hadn't been all that catastrophic—so far. She wouldn't let herself be ordered around, of course, but that was nothing new. She had done nothing but feed him, and build a fire to warm him, and look after the sheep. But the question still remained.

What the hell is she doing here?

Hiding, she'd said. From what? As abrasive as she could be, perhaps she'd gotten on the wrong side of someone during a court case, or more likely, she'd gotten a guilty client off and the victims didn't thank her for it. He certainly understood how that could happen. He'd been angry enough with her on similar occasions himself. She was a good lawyer; he would admit that. She was incredibly astute, able to uncover the smallest inconsistency or impropriety in police procedure, relentless in her questions and her arguments. Legally, she was a bane to any law-enforcement agency, and heaven help the agency if it couldn't prove the wrongdoing it claimed had been done. He had always hated to see her coming, and yet she was the very lawyer he would have wanted if he'd ever needed one.

He dozed off again, and when he woke this time, it occurred to him that Lillian's aspirin must have helped, because he didn't hurt nearly so much. She still wasn't in the hogan, but she had to have come back at some point. The fire in the oil drum was still burning and a different boiling pot sat on top of it. The lid rattled from time to time as the steam escaped. It didn't smell like more soup.

He struggled to sit up, and he realized that he had done more than doze. He could see daylight coming through the smoke hole.

So far, so good he thought as he made it to his feet. The effort sent him into another fit of coughing. He stood there, hunched over, his hands resting on his thighs in a useless attempt to stave off the pain.

"Where are you going?" Lillian said at his elbow.

"None—of your—business," he answered around the coughs.

"Do you need any help?"

"No—damn it, I don't."

"I won't look," she said.

He glanced at her and frowned.

"Well, you've been asleep a long time," she said. "All that water and soup has to go somewhere." She was smiling a bit, her chin up in that slightly defiant way she had.

"It's not—your problem—"

"Oh, I know. I'm just trying to be helpful—I *know,*" she said, holding up both hands. "You don't want my help. So sue me."

"Lillian—you could make—a man—really crazy—you know that?"

"Yes, I do. That's why I've never married—out of compassion for your gender."

"You're a damned—pain in—the—"

"Captain Becenti!" she cried in mock horror, smiling still. The smile eased a bit. "Can you make it to the privy or can't you?"

"I can—make it."

"Ah. Good. You can hold on to me until you get outside. Then you're on your own, and stop looking at me like that. I know you never planned on my finding out that even *you* have to heed the call of nature, but there you are."

She stood, holding out her hand to him.

"It's a good—thing for you—I feel this—bad," he said, letting her take his arm. He should have pushed her away, even if he did need the support, and he wasn't quite sure why he didn't.

"Yeah, well, fate loves the fearless," she said.

"What is—that?" he asked as they passed the stove.

"What is what?"

"On the stove—what is—it? You really know—how to make yourself—at home, don't you?"

"I didn't pillage your supplies. It's just hot water. Part of which I'm going to give you when you get back. You can do whatever you want with it. The rest I'm going to boil sage in—after which you will drink the subsequent sage tea. Do you have any idea how good sage tea is for respiratory illnesses?''

"Yes," he assured her. "I'm surprised—you do."

"Boil sage—drink the liquid—cure a cold," she recited for the benefit of his doubt.

"I don't have a—cold."

"No, you have pneumonia—or worse. Are you sure you can make it outside?"

"Lillian—"

"You aren't going to shock me, Johnny. I have brothers."

"And I'm not—one of them. If I don't come back—don't come—looking for me. I mean—it."

Lillian didn't go looking for him, as much as she wanted to. He was gone a long time. But, he didn't seem that much worse for wear when he returned. He was winded and still not up to looking after a flock of sheep, but he was on his feet at least and that was a vast improvement over when she'd arrived.

She had the hot water ready for him as she'd promised—threatened. And a towel, and the soap she had brought in her backpack because she couldn't find his and didn't want to go rummaging through the hogan any more than she already had. Her eyes burned from lack of sleep. She'd been afraid to sleep, because he was so sick and because of the sheep. Coyotes—both the animal and the human kind—always seemed to know when a potential victim was less than protected.

She wasn't surprised that Becenti made no effort at conversation. She wasn't welcome here, and he was barely able to stand. Neither thing was conducive to small talk, even discounting his taciturn personality.

She kept her back to him, and she could hear him pour the water from the pot she'd left for him into the wash pan, and then washing noises. Then she could hear him moving around the hogan—making a trip to the outside again, she supposed, to dump the wash pan.

"Lillian," he said when he came back, and she braced herself for Act III of "Don't Let the Door Hit You in the Butt, Ms. Singer."

"What?" she said, still not turning around.

"The sheep—"

"Are fed."

"And the horse?"

She looked around at him. He was putting on a clean shirt. "What horse?"

"The one in the corral."

"No horse, Johnny. Sorry." She supposed that when the hay and grain weren't forthcoming, it had jumped the fence, but she refrained from pointing out the obvious.

"I need that—horse," he said.

"Not yet, you don't."

"Lillian—"

"Would you mind if I fixed something to eat?" she interrupted. "It's been a long time since I had a meal." She had been making do with the fruit and nuts she'd dumped into the backpack, but now she needed something more substantial.

He looked at her. She didn't know if he was surprised that she would give him such a big opening to tell her to hit the road to the nearest restaurant or that she'd had the good manners to finally ask his permission to take over his hogan.

"In the containers over there," he said. "Coffee— flour—cornmeal—whatever. And there should be—some canned stuff—fruit and meat—milk. Eat what—you want."

The sage tea was ready, and she brought him that first. He took the cup, and for once, he didn't argue. Almost.

"Are you sure you—used sage?" he asked.

"Yes, I'm sure I used sage," she answered, insulted. She knew as much about reservation plant life as he did, or she would have if she'd paid more attention to her mother.

He almost smiled, and he held the cup closer to sniff the brew. "Smells like sage tea."

"Drink it!" she said, and this time he did smile—for a tenth of a second.

"What a wonderful—nurse you'd make, Lillian. You—missed your—calling."

"Maybe so, but I can do without your remarks. I'm not any happier about this situation than you are."

"Then why don't you—just go?"

"I told you why."

"No—you didn't."

"You're sick, Becenti."

"I'm better."

"The sheep will starve if I go."

He sighed. "Probably—so," he admitted.

"The tea *will* help, you know."

He didn't say anything to that, but he did drink some of the sage brew before he lay back down.

"Can you make—fry bread?" he asked after a time.

"I can," she assured him.

"As long as you're in—the mood to cook—if I asked you—politely—would you make some?"

"If you asked me *politely?*"

"Yeah."

"After I alert the media about this remarkable first, you mean?"

He actually almost smiled again. "Yeah."

She shrugged. "Well. If it's politely."

Actually, she had already mixed the dough and had it in the two-hour "rest" her mother had always insisted upon. It had been a long time since she'd made fry bread, but she had no trouble remembering how. She had no trouble remembering anything. Bread recipes. Details of lost court cases. Humiliations in Santa Fe restaurants. Part of her was more than ashamed of having run away from another encounter with Stuart and his fiancée. Part of her felt only relief.

And part of her still wanted to cry—when she had never been one to shed tears over anything. She always duly noted how miserable she felt, picked up whatever salvageable pieces remained of an unhappy situation, and then she moved on. She certainly didn't run to the primitive outer reaches of the reservation and force herself upon a man who was essentially a complete stranger and who had never tried to hide his dislike of her.

She gave a quiet sigh. "You must be feeling better," she said, walking closer to him.

"I don't know," he said, his hand over his eyes. "I'm just...hungry."

"I still think you need to see a doctor."

He lifted his hand. "If you're going to—stay here, don't—talk," he said.

"Don't talk? Johnny, I'm a lawyer."

"Please—don't remind—me."

On impulse, she bent down and touched the side of his face. He was still burning up with fever, and he caught her wrist too late to keep her from noting it.

"This is—none of your—business," he said yet another time, and he was still holding on to her wrist. He wasn't hurting her, but he was strong, in spite of his illness.

"Well, actually, it is. I took the retainer."

"What—retainer?"

"If I can have my hand back, I'll get you some more aspirin—"

"Answer the—question!"

"I will," she said, pulling her hand free. She moved away from him and she could feel him watching her as she searched the backpack. She found the aspirins and brought them to him. There was just enough water in the bottle for him to get them down.

"The water barrels are almost empty, Johnny. How far away is the well?" she asked.

He swore instead of answering. She understood the response to the no-water situation perfectly; it was very much like her own.

"I could drive the truck around looking for it," she said, "but it would waste *your* gasoline. And the sheep are—"

"Damn it, Lillian—!"

"Johnny, this isn't *my* fault. I didn't use up the water. I'm just the messenger. And I can't help that you're sick. You're sick and the water barrels need filling. So deal with it."

"I'm not—"

He suddenly began to cough, and there was no water to give him.

"Here," she said, offering him the sage tea again.

He was still coughing, and he made no attempt to take it.

"Becenti—"

He made a wide backward sweep with his hand, knocking the cup to the ground.

"If you think *that* is going to hurt my feelings, you're wrong," she said, bending to pick up the cup. "You can suit yourself. You're the one with the cough."

But, inexplicably, her feelings *were* hurt. Appalled that she was actually about to cry, she turned away from him just in time to keep him from seeing it. His rudeness, his rejection of her attempt to help him was not unexpected, and it was certainly nothing to cry about. She had no reason to be upset, because none of this mattered. Johnny Becenti wasn't her responsibility. She'd done far more for him than his mother's twenty dollars covered. She didn't like sheep and she didn't like him. There was no reason in the world why she couldn't just get into her car and go.

Instead, she uncovered the dough for the fry bread and tore off a piece, pressing it into a round, flat shape for frying with a good deal more force than the task required.

"You don't have to—do that," he said behind her.

She didn't stop.

"Did you—hear me!"

"Yes, I heard you. *I'm* hungry. And unless you're planning on sending *me* the way of that cup, I'm going to make the fry bread."

"Lillian, are you—crying?"

"No!" she said, her voice breaking in spite of all she could do.

"Great. You're not—crying—and I'm not—sick. Lillian, what the hell—is wrong with you?"

"Everything. Everything is wrong with me. I lost a big case I shouldn't have lost. After all those years with Stuart, I just got dumped. *Your* mother and *my* mother laid a guilt trip on me you would not *believe*. I haven't had any sleep. I'm hungry. I don't know how to get water for all those damned sheep and I'm scared *you're* going to die, okay!"

She stood there, her back to him, the piece of fry-bread dough still in her hand. After a long moment, she heard him sigh.

"Okay," he said.

Chapter Four

He watched her make the bread. She had very long fingers and delicate wrists, but her hands were sure and capable. If she was still crying, he couldn't tell it, and most certainly, he wasn't about to ask. He lay on the blankets instead—more than disconcerted. If there was anything as incredible as the fact of her being here, it was her being here and in tears.

But he was curious by nature and by former profession, and he couldn't let her revelations simply lie. He waited until the bread was made, then he waited until they had eaten—fry bread and canned Vienna sausages and canned peaches to get some kind of liquid to wash it all down. He had no complaints about the bread. He was actually grateful that she had obliged him by making it, regardless of the fact that he neglected to say so. It tasted good—like his mother always made. His mother, who had somehow gotten Lillian Singer to feel guilty.

He made no attempt at conversation while they ate, and

neither did she. She hardly looked at him except to hand him the bread or the sausages or the peaches. When the remnants of the meal had been cleared away, she left him sitting at the small table and went outside. It took a certain amount of effort on his part not to ask her where she was going. She returned eventually, with an armload of wood.

"Wait," he said when she was about to put it into the stove.

She glanced at him. "It's cold in here."

"What happened—with—you and Dennison?"

The question surprised her. It surprised him. Of all the enigmas she'd laid out for him, he would have been hard-pressed to explain why he had selected that particular one for inquiry. He thought at first that she wasn't going to answer, because she gave a quiet sigh and went back to putting wood into the stove.

"You said you—got dumped," he reminded her.

"He's getting married," she said finally, still not looking at him.

"Don't you approve—of his choice of—brides?"

"I don't know if I approve of her or not. I didn't know there *was* a potential bride until a few days ago."

"Why not?"

She finally looked at him. "Why not? Oh, I don't know, Johnny. Probably because he was taking me out to dinner with his political friends, sending me flowers, calling me every day—and it just never occurred to me to ask him if he'd suddenly found some child he wanted to marry."

He had to work hard not to ask the logical question that should follow the detail that Dennison's fiancée was "some child."

Is she white?

"So he—hurt—your pride?" he suggested instead.

She gave a short laugh. "You might say that. I could probably handle the hurt pride part—it's feeling so damned stupid that I'm having a problem with. I don't like surprises, especially when I should have seen it coming. He caught me completely off guard. And it wasn't just that he suddenly announced that he was getting married—'' She was still on her knees in front of the stove and she turned to him earnestly. "It was the *way* he did it. Stuart Dennison and I were friends. Or so I thought. Even if I wasn't the love of his life, I deserved better than—''

She abruptly got up and began brushing off her knees. It occurred to him that he'd never seen her dressed the way she was now—in jeans and a baggy sweatshirt. The narrow-legged jeans gave her a youthful, coltish look that was not unattractive. He didn't understand her at all. He had actually been witness to a breakdown of the infamous Lillian Singer's stoic demeanor, and she seemed more annoyed with herself than embarrassed. And he didn't know what to make of her candid revelation about Dennison.

"Better than what?" he asked, because he realized that, in spite of himself, *he* actively wanted her disclosures to continue.

She didn't answer him.

"Better than—what?" he asked again.

She came to sit at the table, sliding down in the chair, her arms folded over her breasts and her long legs outstretched and crossed at the ankles. He made a point of not looking. He didn't want to look. He didn't *feel* like looking. But his eyes made the trip anyway.

"He delivered his wedding announcement in the middle of a restaurant," she said. "The bride-to-be was there—well, not *there*. She excused herself from the table long enough for him to actually tell me. It was beautiful—music playing, candles burning, me thinking I'm going to get New Zealand raspberries. Believe me, a 'Dear Lillian' letter would have been a whole lot easier.''

"You're a—lawyer. You could handle it. You've had a lot of practice—at not letting—people know what you're—really feeling.''

"Yeah, well, it didn't help much that time.''

"What did you do? Throw things? Turn over a few tables?"

She smiled. "I wanted to. It's never been *my* way to brood," she said significantly.

"Meaning what?" he asked, ready to be offended.

"Meaning some of us brood. Some of us don't."

"Then what are you—doing here—if you're not brooding?"

"I'm hiding. I told you that."

"But you didn't say—why."

"Because I didn't want another encounter with Stuart and his new fiancée. Because I lost that big case and I want to feel sorry for myself. Because your mother gave me a perfect excuse to disappear for a while when she paid me to come out here and lecture you about your bad behavior."

"My mother paid—"

"Yes, she did. She actually came to Santa Fe to see me. That alone should give you some idea of the uproar you've caused. You know, I thought at first you were still grieving and that was why you didn't care if you worried the hell out of your family. But that's not it, is it?"

"Isn't—it?"

"No, I don't think so. I don't think you're all that sad, Johnny. I think you're mad."

"And who—am I mad at, counselor?"

"Mae. You're mad at Mae."

"You don't know anything—about it." He made an attempt to stand, but she reached out and caught his arm.

"I know getting dumped makes you mad as hell."

"She didn't—dump me."

"Didn't she?"

"No!" he said, pulling his arm free. "She died, damn it!"

"Right. She *died*. But you're acting like she put your saddle outside the hogan door—like she went off with somebody else, somebody younger and richer and a whole lot handsomer than you are. You remind me of my brother when he had that thing with the white woman anthropologist—"

"*I'm* not drinking," he said to get some kind of barb in.

She wasn't impressed. "You're throwing away your career—just like he did until he got some help. Now, who was it that made him get that help, I wonder?"

"I don't want to—talk about this!"

"Too bad, Becenti. I knew Mae for a long time—since we were children. You were the joy of her life. She was so proud of you—all the good you were doing for the People. She wouldn't be proud now, would she, Becenti? Poor Mae. She was always a good and loving wife. And your mother blames *her* because of the way you're acting now."

"Get out," he said, his voice deadly. He meant it. She had no right to say anything to him about Mae. He wanted her away from here!

She looked at him. He had to force himself to hold her steady gaze, because he saw only compassion there. He didn't want her compassion. He didn't want anything, least of all her opinions about what he felt and what he should be doing.

She stood and crossed the hogan, picking up the backpack on her way to the door. And she didn't hesitate. She walked out without a backward glance.

He sat there, fighting down the need to cough, his hands shaking with anger. It was a good thing she had gone. If she hadn't, sick or not, he might have—

He listened intently for the sound of her car starting. He heard voices instead—Lillian's and a man's. He didn't go to see. He didn't care who she was talking to. He just wanted to be left alone.

Even so, he strained to hear. Her voice grew louder, but he couldn't understand what she said.

Now what? he thought, but he stayed where he was. After a moment, he heard her car start and drive away, and then complete silence.

Finally. Finally!

He knew that he should go see who she'd been talking to, but he didn't. He couldn't hear anything now; there was a good chance that she'd taken whoever it was with her.

Quiet. It was good to have things so quiet.

Alone. It was good to be alone.

He expected to feel relieved, liberated now that she had gone. He didn't. He felt exhausted, sick, and completely overwhelmed at the prospect of having to look after a flock of sheep. He should have held on to his temper until *after* Lillian had figured out a way to get the water barrels filled. And, angry or not, he should have said thank-you.

He looked around the hogan. There was nothing that would indicate that she had even been here. Nothing but his own body that exuded the fragrance of the soap she'd given him to use, a soft flowery scent that belied her exasperating nature but was still entirely *her*.

"*Yah-ta-hey!*" someone called from the outside. He gave a heavy sigh—and tried not to cough. He wasn't alone after all. He stood with some effort and walked to the door of the hogan, trying to reconcile the fact that he felt both better—since he'd eaten—and worse—since Lillian Singer had made her grand exit.

Winston Tsosie stood outside, patiently waiting, and Becenti suspected he was not here by accident. Winston wouldn't come this far without a good reason. He usually worked as a volunteer at the mission men's shelter, his frail and aged appearance belying his true self. Winston was wise and tenacious—an old busybody for whom Johnny Becenti had nothing but the greatest respect. There was nothing Winston Tsosie wouldn't do for the betterment of the People—as a nineteen-year-old marine private hitting the beaches of Iwo Jima during World War II or as a keeper of drunks now. Even so, Johnny was not eager to become one of his projects.

"*Yah-ta-hey*, Winston. What are you—doing here?" he asked, bypassing Navajo decorum altogether. He had neither the patience nor the strength for it. He couldn't manage the polite period of waiting for the old man to state his business.

"Lillian," Winston answered simply.

Of course, Becenti thought. *Lillian.* She must have gotten the phone to work after all.

"She says you got trouble," Winston said. "She says the sheep need looking after. She says there's no water—"

"I don't care—what she says!" he interrupted, compounding his rudeness.

"She *says,*" Winston continued anyway, "you need somebody to look after you, too."

The sarcastic remark that came immediately to mind got lost in a sudden wave of weakness. Becenti reached out blindly for the hogan wall, and with Winston's help, he sat down heavily on a warped wooden bench by the door.

"I'm all—right," he insisted.

"Yeah, you in fine shape, Johnny—except you can't breathe and you can't stand up so good."

"I don't—" He abruptly gave up the protest, because he realized suddenly that Lillian's car was still here. "She left, didn't—she?"

"Who?" Winston asked mildly.

"You know—who! Lillian!"

"How am I going to know, Johnny? If you don't care what she says, I'm thinking you don't care where she goes, either. Not enough to ask, anyway."

"Is she still here—or not?"

"Her man took her off."

"What—man?"

"The man from Santa Fe, the one she don't marry. He didn't like her being up here with you much—and she didn't like him not liking it. He said she looked like hell. She said, thank you so much, but he really didn't have to come all this way to tell her that. If she wanted to know it, she would of looked in a mirror. And then—" Winston stopped.

Becenti had to force himself not to prod the old man into continuing.

"He came to Window Rock looking for her because nobody in Santa Fe knew where she was. He followed us when we left to come up here," Winston said finally.

"Us?" Becenti asked, still trying to keep from interrogating him about Lillian's "man."

"Me and Jack Begaye," Winston said. "Lillian, she didn't want Lucas to come along. She said he would upset your harmony even more than *she* does."

"There's nothing wrong with—my harmony," he said, not wanting to lend credence to Lillian Singer's self-proclaimed disruptiveness. And Jack Begaye was all he needed. Jack had been nothing but trouble since he was eleven years old. It was only since Jack's marriage to Lillian Singer's step-niece that Becenti had begun to have some hope that Jack Begaye would ever get himself straightened out. The very thought of having to deal with Jack *and* Winston sent him into another coughing fit.

"You ain't had your harmony for a long time, my son," Winston said. "Now you ain't got your health, either. So when Jack gets done with the sheep, he's going to look at you, see if your lungs are as bad as they sound."

"Winston—"

"Lillian said you don't want no IHS doctor—so she don't send you any. She sends you somebody from her own family. Jack was a good marine corpsman—he's still good at it. And if he says you need to go to the hospital, then you're going. It don't matter if you say no to me or not. If we got to throw you in the truck like some damn drunk that wants to sleep in the middle of the road instead of coming to the mission where he can be fed and be safe, then we'll do it. Jack Begaye and me—we can handle you."

Becenti didn't doubt it for a minute. He'd seen the two of them rescue drunks before. These two ex-marines, in spite of their extreme difference in ages and wars, made a formidable team, and he was hardly up to a physical confrontation, even with the elderly Winston.

He sat there, trying not to cough. "Do you two—do—everything Lillian Singer—tells you?" he asked when he was able.

"Lillian don't give orders to us, Johnny. She's worried, even if Katie Becenti did pay her, and she asked her family to help her."

"Yeah? When did *you* get into the Singer clan?"

The old man looked at him, and it occurred to Becenti that he had hurt Winston Tsosie's feelings.

"I been adopted a long time now," Winston said quietly. "Jack's wife, Meggie, she done it. She needed a grandfather for her and Jack's children."

"What does Lucas say—about that?"

"Lucas is the uncle-by-marriage. Uncles are important. Grandfathers are important. He knows that. Children need all the help they can get to learn which path to walk on. And even when they ain't children no more," he added significantly.

Becenti was cold sitting in the sun, and he had to work hard not to shiver. He intended to take a deeper breath, but it hurt too much and made him start coughing again—just in time for Jack Begaye to come around the hogan and hear him.

Jack didn't waste time with amenities. "You going to let me listen to that or not, Captain?" he asked.

"You mean—I've got a choice?"

"Yeah, you've got a choice," Jack assured him. "But not much of one. You know our Lillian. Hard telling who she'd send out here next."

"It's not as—bad as—it sounds."

"Oh, I'm sure," Jack said, clearly humoring him. "Unbutton your shirt."

Jack had a stethoscope in his jacket pocket. He took it out and began to listen intently to Becenti's chest and then his back.

"I can hear the congestion all over, Captain," Jack said matter-of-factly. "I think you need to go into town, especially if you've been having chills and fever. It hurts pretty bad, too, right?"

Becenti didn't answer him.

"Look, man," Jack said. "It's *your* chest. But I'm telling you I think you need medical treatment—now. Either Winston or I will take you to get it. You don't have to worry about your animals—I know where the hay and the well are."

"What—are you two—*supposed* to be doing?" Becenti asked. "What about—the men's shelter? What about—your family?"

Jack grinned. "Captain, you've known Meggie as long as I have. You know she keeps a 'worry list' and I'm sorry, but you're on it. It's a wonder she didn't come up here herself. The shelter is under control and Meggie knows where I am. So let's get this show on the road, okay? I'm going to let Winston take you in—he's dying to drive Lillian's new car, aren't you, old man?"

"Damn straight," Winston assured him.

Jack tossed him the keys. "Oh, and Lillian wanted me to tell you she found your horse, Captain," he said. "It's in the corral. She said be *sure* to mention she played hell trying to catch the damn thing."

Becenti stood with some help. He was too tired to protest anymore. Jack Begaye had been right. If he didn't cooperate, there was no telling who Lillian would send out here next. And perhaps he'd found some remnant of his good upbringing after all. These people—not to mention his own mother—had gone to enough trouble on his account, and there was no point in letting the sheep and his prodigal horse suffer. Surely he could pull himself together long enough to prevent that.

"Come on, son," Winston said, taking his arm.

"You know how to—drive a car like—that?" Becenti

asked him as they began a slow walk toward Lillian's low-slung vehicle.

"Nope," the old man said. "This is going to be an adventure."

"That's what I'm—afraid of," Becenti said. "You're not still—riding—motorcycles, are you?"

"All the time," Winston assured him.

Becenti could see the corral now, and he abruptly stopped.

"What's the matter?" Winston asked, still holding on to his arm.

In spite of his mental and physical misery, in spite of the likelihood of precipitating another series of painful coughs, Becenti laughed. Out loud.

"What's the matter?" Winston said again.

"Lillian—"

"What about her?"

"That—horse—in the corral," Becenti said. "She had to—work really hard—to get him—in there, right?"

"That's what she said."

"Too bad," he said, laughing again. "It's not—*my*—horse."

Chapter Five

He was in the hospital in Gallup for a week—long enough to reassure his mother that he would indeed recover, long enough to attend to some pressing business regarding the Navajo Tribal Police and his continued employment, long enough for Lillian Singer to come to see him.

She didn't. It both surprised and annoyed him, how much he expected her to visit. There was no reason why she *should* come, of course. She'd only been paid to get him here. No, actually she'd been paid to lecture him about his behavior—which she'd done nicely, as he recalled. Strong-arming him into the hospital had only been incidental to the task she'd been hired to do, and therefore finite when it came to her personal responsibility for a follow-up. She likely didn't visit any of her unfortunate clients who ended up in prison, either.

He wanted to see her. He wanted to annoy her about that horse she'd accidentally stolen. He wanted to tell her how much he *didn't* appreciate being here, and how easily he

recognized *her* heavy hand in the appearance of the irrepressible Mary Skeets, a longtime tribal police dispatcher,
who came to see him nearly every day—just to casually
mention the most recent and flagrant violations of Navajo
tribal law—something he couldn't help but be interested in.

But, he wasn't about to *ask* Lillian Singer to come to
Gallup, and soon, he had no excuse to ask, even if he'd
been so inclined—which, of course, he wasn't. In spite of
everything, he suddenly found himself feeling better—actually physically, and perhaps mentally, able to face a few
things, like his job and his grief and his guilt. He sent
Winston Tsosie, his other regular visitor, to bring his
mother to Gallup to see him, and as much as he wanted to,
he didn't ask the old man if he was still driving Lillian's
fast car.

Katie Becenti arrived at the hospital both rushed and
worried—clearly out of harmony. It was yet another reason
for him to feel guilty, because he'd certainly led her to
believe that she could only expect something upsetting
from him. His mother was traditional; it was vital that she
stay in tune with her surroundings. She sat down on the
chair by his bed, her weathered hands clasped in her lap.

"Stay, Winston," he said in Navajo, when the old man
was about to tactfully withdraw. "I want to tell my mother
I'm sorry. I behaved badly in front of witnesses. It's only
right that I apologize the same way."

"It was the *chindi* of the one who died—" his mother
began, careful not to say Mae's name.

He held up his hand. "No," he said. "It was not. It was
me. I held on to her and I wouldn't let go. I don't want
you to worry anymore. I'm...all right now. My lung sickness is gone. My sadness is still here," he said, touching
his heart, "but I...won't..."

He didn't go on, and his mother reached out to pat his
hand, saying nothing, because, unlike Lillian Singer, *she*
knew how to keep silent when words would only make the
situation worse.

"I want you to tell my cousin to take my sheep," he said after a moment. "If he looks after them, he can have whatever money the lambs and the shearing brings. Tell him he can put them with his flock. And tell him to watch the ewe with the torn ear. She likes to run off and take half the flock with her."

"You're coming back to Window Rock, then?" his mother dared to ask.

"Yes, my mother, I am."

"You will be the policeman again?"

"Yes."

She smiled. "It's the best thing for you. You don't have to worry, either. Your house—we took care of it. It's ready."

"Ready?"

"It won't make you sad now," she said.

The doctor came in before he could ask any more questions, and his mother left. He had given her a task, and the very nature of sheep demanded that she see to it immediately. He had to wait until Winston's next visit to find out what he wanted to know.

"What is this business about my house?" he asked the old man immediately.

"You don't want to ask," Winston said obscurely.

"I realize that—but you tell me anyway."

"You're just going to be mad at her all over again," Winston warned him.

"I'm not—" He stopped, realizing suddenly that Winston didn't mean Katie. "Who exactly are we talking about here, Winston?"

The old man sighed.

"You're not going to tell me Lillian did something to my house—"

"Okay," Winston said agreeably.

"What did she do?"

"Now, son—"

"Winston, what did she do!"

"Nothing much. Talked to your mother. Talked to the tribal council."

"She talked to the tribal council about—my house?"

"It's the *tribe's* house, Johnny. You're not going to start coughing again, are you?" Winston asked.

"Never mind about my—coughing! What did she do?"

"She just told them what you said."

"I never said anything—about my—house!"

"Maybe you don't remember—"

"Winston—!"

"She got them to fix the house up for you, that's all. New paint—stuff like that. Whole lot of people helped. Many tribal police officers came, and Lillian's half-Navajo nephew by marriage, Will—the one learning to be the *hataalii*. He's a good boy. Works hard. Going to be a good medicine man. And Mary Skeets came, because she's the one knows how you don't like clutter. And your mama was there. She said what color paint to use—what things to move. It was all done in a couple of days. It's looking good, Johnny. The People respect you. They wanted to do this for you. Maybe you won't mind being in Window Rock so much now."

"I cannot believe—!" He stopped. Of course, he could believe. Lillian Singer was in the middle of it. Lillian, who had no sense of what was intrusive and inappropriate whatsoever.

"Maybe you going to like it, Johnny."

"I'm not going to—like it."

"Maybe you ought to rest now so you don't cough."

"Maybe I ought to go find—Lillian Singer."

"No, that wouldn't do your cough no good," Winston assured him. "You rest so you can get all the way well. And then you can see the house. You need to see it—before you get all pushed out of shape and start looking for people."

But he wasn't going to like the house. Of that he was certain. How could he? He had just lost the only place he had left that was free of Lillian Singer's meddling. He hung on to his anger, nurturing it so that it was still viable when he was finally discharged. He made no attempt to go home—to his way of thinking, he didn't have one anymore. He went to the law-enforcement center instead, startling the unflappable Mary Skeets for the first time in living memory.

"Captain Becenti!" she cried loudly enough so that no one else in the building would be caught unawares. "You're here!"

"I am, Mary, yes," he said in passing.

"Good to see you out and around! You're going to your office?"

He didn't stop to answer, and the clearly unsurprised officers he encountered in the hallway had obviously heard Mary's less-than-subtle Becenti alert.

"Welcome back, Captain," they said in passing.

He didn't stop for them, either, walking rapidly now and flinging open his office door.

Lucas Singer sat behind his desk—Lillian's brother, who obviously hadn't heard Mary yelling but who didn't look all that perturbed about being caught in the inner sanctum. He'd always admired that trait in Lucas. He thought it must be something Lucas Singer had been born with, that penchant he had to never admit blame for something until it was absolutely certain that the you-know-what had hit the fan. They'd had words about it more than once over the years. Becenti would admit that Lucas was a good officer, just as he would admit that his sister, Lillian, was a good lawyer. That didn't mean that they both didn't drive the people who had to deal with them to disharmony.

"Welcome back, Captain," Lucas said, getting up. "You'll want to look at these," he said, shuffling a stack of papers and putting them back on the desk. "It's pretty quiet today. We may have an elderly couple—tourists— lost. They were supposed to be on a tour bus driving down through Lukachukai to Window Rock, but they weren't there when the driver did a head count— Or did you come in to work?'' Lucas suddenly asked.

"I'm here to work,'' Becenti said—anything to keep from going home. He sat down at the desk. In his absence, the chair had been readjusted and was now too low. "What else do I need to know?''

"Well, nothing right now. As I said, it's quiet today.''

"What about those tourists?''

"The bus driver's going to wait in Lukachukai while one of the patrol officers checks their last stop to see if he left them there. I'm thinking he did, and if they'll just stay put until somebody can pick them up, they'll be all right.''

"Okay. Close the door on your way out.'' He looked up from the stack of papers because Lucas didn't immediately leave but stood watching him instead. "Anything else?'' he asked.

"Ah, no, Captain,'' Lucas said, finally turning to go and closing the door firmly after him.

Becenti sat staring at the papers, trying to get his thoughts together, trying to get himself into the problem-solving mind-set that had always served him so well. But he really didn't feel like being here. He didn't feel sick; he just felt...tired.

He forced himself to read the top sheet of paper, and then the next one. He was halfway through the third sheet when he realized that he had no idea what any of them said.

Maybe some coffee, he thought. He was about to go get it, but someone knocked softly on the door.

"In!'' he said with a good deal more authority than he felt.

The door pushed inward and Lillian Singer stood on the threshold. She came barging right in—black power suit, white silk blouse, blue topaz lapel pin—topaz, not turquoise—high heels and all. He sighed heavily, regardless of the fact that he had just given her permission to do so.

"What are you doing back on the rez?'' he asked bluntly.

She smiled in that way she had. Chin up. A bit defiant. "Well, I had to put that horse back where I got it," she said. "Wouldn't do for an officer of the court to get arrested for horse stealing."

"As I recall, horse stealing seems to run in the Singer clan."

"That was Meggie and Jack when they were children—and neither one of them were Singers. That doesn't count."

He made a small sound that neither agreed nor disagreed.

"And..." she said pointedly to make him look up at her again.

"Lillian, what the hell do you want?"

"I want you to go ahead and get it over with."

"I don't feel like playing games. What are you talking about?"

"Well, Johnny, I thought I should come by here. You wanted to see me, didn't you?"

"No," he assured her. "Believe me. *No.*"

"I thought you did. I thought you wanted to yell at me—maybe punch me in the nose. I *know* you're upset with me. And since I had to put the horse back anyway—"

"Lillian, I'm busy."

"Well, not very, according to Mary Skeets."

"Lillian—"

"So tell me what you thought of the house."

He looked at her, incredulous that she would actually bring that up. "I haven't seen the house."

"Would you like to go see it now? And please don't look at me like that, Johnny. It's a very simple question."

"I can*not* believe—" he said more to himself than to her.

"You need to go see it, Johnny. And you ought not go by yourself. You need somebody to go with you who can explain the particulars."

"Just who did you have in mind?"

"Oh, that would be me," she assured him.

He sat staring at her for a long moment. "You know, I

am amazed that you ever reached the age you are now without somebody killing you.''

She laughed. "So are we going or not?''

He sat there—immovable.

"Do you know the way?" she asked.

"I know where I live, Lillian,'' he said testily.

She frowned. "Oh, did you think—? You *did,* didn't you! It's not *your* house, Johnny. It's another house. For heaven's sake, why would you think we'd just barge in and redo *your* house?''

"Oh, I can't imagine,'' he said sarcastically, trying to remember if his mother or Winston had actually said it was *his* house that Lillian and half of Window Rock had descended upon. They had spoken in Navajo, and unlike English, the language wasn't nearly so precise. It didn't have ten different words for everything. Sometimes there weren't any words at all.

But that in no way let Lillian Singer off the hook.

"I really think we ought to go now,'' she said. "Because if you don't, you're liable to have a hundred people pounce on you and then you'll have to go see it with a very big escort—all of them expecting you to be gracious. And we both know what a chore *that* would be. Probably half the Navajo police force and Mary Skeets and your mother and who knows who else, in a kind of—oh, I don't know— 'Welcome Home, Johnny' party. And I know how you'd hate that.''

"Is that a threat?''

"*No.* Yes. Well, actually, what it is, is the truth. If you just go quietly right now, and take a quick token look at the place, then you can come back here and tell all those *volunteers* who worked really hard on the place how much you hate it and be done with it. That way, see, they'll know you're still the same old poop you always were, and you won't have to hurt their feelings in the middle of what is *supposed* to be a really festive occasion. It's so gauche to make those kinds of announcements when people are expecting pleasant company and something special to eat. Believe me, I know. So are we going or aren't we? I'll drive.''

"No, *I'll* drive," he said, because a Welcome Home party was beyond unacceptable.

"I'll drive, too. You can follow me," Lillian said—because she was Lillian and therefore always contrary.

He sighed and followed her out the door, catching a whiff of that soap again as they walked along. Even as annoyed as he was, he wasn't beyond appreciating that the scent was very...that it was almost...

"Oh, leaving already, Captain!" Mary Skeets announced when she saw him, interrupting his pondering with an updated Becenti whereabouts report for the benefit of everyone in earshot. "You want me to say where you can be reached?" she asked, clearly hoping to find out where he was going with Lillian Singer.

"I have no idea where I can be reached," he said testily.

Mary cut her gaze to Lillian—who had the audacity to smile.

"Right, sir," Mary said. "No saying where you went."

"Did you put that horse back or not?" he asked Lillian as they walked across the parking lot.

"I told you I did. I never lie."

He laughed. "And thunder still sleeps," he said, alluding to the likelihood that she was feeling particularly free to play fast and loose with the truth, because there was no threat of being struck by lightning until after the end of May when thunder woke up again.

"Everything was under control at your homestead," she said. "Your cousin was there and thrilled to take over your operation. The sheep were fine. The horse—*your* horse, I hope—came wandering in a few days ago. The *Yei* are all in their places and everything's right with the world."

He had no comment regarding the Navajo gods being where they were supposed to be. He, regardless of his semi-traditional mind-set, knew that that could change at any minute, particularly with people like Lillian Singer doing their dead-level best to upset the natural harmony of the universe at every turn.

She hesitated when he reached his vehicle.

"You are going to follow me?" she asked pointedly. The sun was very bright and she had to shade her eyes with her hand to see him.

"Anything would be better than that Welcome Home thing you threatened me with."

"You never know, Johnny. You might like it. Really."

He made a disgruntled sound, and she laughed. He got into the Navajo Tribal Police vehicle and started the engine, watching as she ran lightly across the parking area to her own car—high heels and power suit notwithstanding. She really was an attractive woman—especially for such a meddling hardhead. As far as looks went, it rather surprised him that she had been so unceremoniously "dumped." Her disposition, of course, was something else again. He wondered if she had been her true self with Stuart Dennison the way she was with him. Surely not, or the relationship wouldn't have lasted so long. It occurred to him suddenly that Dennison had come for her that day at the homestead. Perhaps she hadn't been "dumped" after all.

He glanced toward the law-enforcement building. Lucas Singer—a very interested Lucas Singer—stood looking out the door. Obviously, the intense curiosity about what Johnny Becenti was doing with Lillian was catching. It suddenly occurred to him that Lucas must know that she had spent the night in his hogan. In fact, it must be all over the reservation by now, no doubt minus the part about Katie Becenti having paid Lillian to come to him.

So, he thought. On top of everything else, he'd likely compromised her reputation if not her maidenly virtue, regardless of his having been so ill that he hardly remembered her being there.

He watched her swing her long legs into her car. Who, precisely, was he trying to fool? He remembered, and he remembered well.

He sighed heavily and followed her out of the parking lot. As expected, she drove like a bat out of hell. It didn't seem to bother her in the least that she had a tribal police captain right behind her.

He recognized the place where she took him, but only in a vague sort of way. He had been in this area for something or other at some time in his tribal police career, but he no longer remembered the reason. The prefabricated house she parked in front of was small and rectangular. The yard had a redwood rail fence and a few Russian olive trees growing. The driveway had been newly graveled.

He pulled his vehicle in behind hers and got out. Lillian stood next to her car while she rummaged in her purse for something. The wind had died down considerably, leaving only the bright sunshine and a halfhearted promise of spring. But everything in his experience told him to expect at least one more good snow, just as it told him to be wary of this woman. Who knew what horrific thing she might have planned next?

He waited for her to find whatever she was looking for, regardless of the fact that he didn't want anything to do with this house business. On the other hand, he didn't want some kind of obligatory party held in his so-called honor. He didn't doubt for a moment that Lillian could and would carry out her threat and arrange one. He knew that he wasn't all that popular with his subordinates, but he also knew that refreshments and a little downtime could be a big draw for people who had to work almost every weekend and holiday. No, he liked her alternate plan better than her party threat; he would go see the house and then come back and tell everybody he hated it.

"Here," Lillian said, pushing a ring of keys at him. "One key opens the front and the back door—and there are two extras."

He took them and walked toward the house, surprised that she didn't follow along after him.

"Aren't you coming?" he asked.

"No," she said. "If you're going to hate it on sight, it should be because of what it is and not because you don't like me."

The remark caught him off guard, in spite of the fact that a smart woman like her would have grasped the situation a long time ago. He didn't like her, and she knew it. And that, as they say, was that.

He looked back at her once before he opened the door. She was leaning against her car, studiously picking something off the sleeve of her power suit.

The door opened easily enough. No warping, no worn lock. He was immediately assailed by the smell of fresh paint and something else—the residual scent of a Navajo ceremony. The place had been purified—by the youngest of Lillian's nephews by marriage, he guessed, the half-Navajo one, Will, who was a good boy and a hard worker, and who was studying to be a medicine man.

He stepped inside, unprepared for the pristine, unclut-tered look of the room. The walls had been painted white, and there was very little furniture. A couch and an easy chair, both of them covered with a brightly colored South-western-style blanket. There were no curtains, only the "matchstick" roll-up shades that would have come from one of the discount department stores in Gallup or Flag-staff. Three rooms, he supposed—a combination living room-kitchen area and two bedrooms. And a bath, he noted, opening one of the side doors. The place was heated by a single woodstove in the living-room area—which meant that whoever lived here would eat warm and sleep cold. He himself had grown used to sleeping cold.

He moved to open the remaining doors. The bedrooms were newly painted—white—and as sparsely furnished as the rest of the house. There was a single bed in one, a double bed in the other. Both of them had been made up by someone who had been in the military—Winston or Jack? The dark brown blankets had mitered corners and were pulled very tight.

But what would Johnny Becenti do with *two* beds? He hardly needed one.

He looked inside the closets, opened the back door to see what was outside. As much as he didn't want to admit it, the place suited him. It suited him very well—because it held no memories.

When he returned to the living room, Lillian stood just inside the front door, waiting.

"My nephew by marriage, Will, did a small ceremony to make the place ready for you," she said, confirming his earlier guess. "He's getting good at the *hataalii* thing. He says you need a really big ceremony later on—if you decide to live here."

She glanced at him, apparently expecting some kind of response.

"The front door faces east," she went on when there was none forthcoming. "You'll be able greet the sunrise."

He stared at her across the room, but he still made no comment. She presumed that such a fine point of Navajo traditional belief would matter to him. Just as she had presumed that he wanted to be well again, that he wanted to return to his job, that he wanted—needed—this house. She was right on all accounts, but he didn't thank her for it. Her penchant for intervening in matters that were none of her concern had to stop. He wasn't going to tolerate it any longer.

"You had no right to do this," he said finally.

"I know that," she said. "I'm..."

"What?" he asked when she didn't go on. "Sorry?"

She gave a quiet sigh. "No, I'm not sorry. I can't help the way I am. I see a problem and I want to fix it."

"I am *not* your problem, Lillian," he said. He walked closer to her. She didn't back away, but he had the distinct impression that she was considering it.

"I was— I thought this would make things easier for you," she said. "You said you never wanted to go back to your own house."

"No, I didn't."

"Yes, you did."

"*If* I did, if I told *you* anything that personal, then it was the fever talking. I couldn't have been in my right mind."

"It doesn't matter whether you were in your right mind or not. The only thing that matters is whether what you said is true. You told me that Mae's family had taken everything of hers away—but she was still there. You said it hurt so bad to have...nothing of her. To have only the grief and the pain of losing her. You said you wanted to believe that some day you'd see her again, but you didn't—"

"I never would have told you such a thing!"

"Well, you did. Maybe I *was* wrong to interfere. Maybe you are a truly gifted herder of sheep. I don't know. I only know you're good for the tribal police. You're strict, but you're fair and you care what happens to the People—"

"I don't need a performance evaluation from you!"

She didn't say anything. He didn't know why; she clearly had the words all ready. But she kept her opinion to herself for once, and her silence provoked him in a way that one of her notorious rebuttals never would have.

"The only thing I need from you is to be left alone. Do you understand?" he said.

She still didn't say anything.

He stepped closer. "Do you understand!"

She stared back at him, unflinching, full of challenge. Lillian Singer was not about to be intimidated.

He should have let it go then, but he didn't. It was so quiet in the house suddenly. The bright sunshine strained to get in through the matchstick shades, leaving tiny strips of light on the spotlessly clean floor. He could still smell the new paint, the burned cedar and sage.

And now he could smell her, too; that soap, that soft woman smell he'd come to associate only with Lillian Singer. He looked into her eyes. She had beautiful eyes. He was staring too long—way beyond what was acceptable

Navajo decorum. He needed to say something—or he needed to get out of here.

But he reached for her instead, his hands resting on her shoulders. She was clearly surprised, but she made no attempt to move away from him. He reached up to touch her face, to stroke her cheek. Her skin was smooth and silky soft. Warm. How long had it been since he'd touched a woman this way?

He stared at her mouth.

Beautiful, he thought. He could already taste her, and regardless of her obvious misgivings, her lips parted in anticipation of what he intended to do.

"Johnny," she said, her voice sounding strained and a little tremulous. "This isn't what you want."

He had no idea what he wanted.

Yes, he did.

He lowered his mouth to almost touch hers. He was like a man about to partake of a forbidden fruit. How dangerous was this going to be? Was he or was he not willing to suffer for it?

Yes, damn it, he thought. He was.

"Lillian—" he said, and incredibly, she leaned into him. He completely lost whatever else he'd been about to say. His mouth came down on hers. Her lips parted to give him access—she tasted so good to him! He was like a starving man—hungry—aroused. He couldn't get enough of her. His arms slid around her, pressing her against him. He wanted to feel her, touch her. He was trembling; he was aching with desire. How far could he go with this? How far would she let him go?

"Johnny ," she said, turning her face away. But, she still clung to him. His hand found her breast, and she gave a soft moan. She lifted her mouth to his again, letting him kiss her the way he wanted, the way they both wanted.

"Johnny—!" she said again, but this time she pushed hard against his chest, twisting herself out of his grasp. Her protest hardly registered. He didn't want to stop and he took a step toward her. She moved backward until she was up against the door.

She stood staring at him for a moment, breathing heavily, her look as shocked and incredulous as he felt.

Then she turned and jerked the door open, looking back at him once before she stumbled outside.

Chapter Six

Lillian headed immediately back to Santa Fe, her mind barely paying attention to the interstate exit signs and speed limits along the way. She didn't stop by to see the family. She didn't stop for anything. She just drove.

Stupid! she kept thinking.

"Stupid!"

How in this world had she *ever* let herself get into that kind of situation? She always kept her guard up; after all these years, it was second nature for her to do so. She always, *always* stayed away from men like Johnny Becenti, because she didn't want to complicate her life in Santa Fe or her career. She lived off the reservation for a reason—because she *wanted* to—and she only returned long enough to meet the absolute minimum required of her in terms of her family obligations. She was torn enough about that already. It was the price she paid to make sure that she never let herself become involved with someone who had strong ties to the kind of life she'd been so determined to escape.

She wanted nothing to do with a man who could make her feel guilty for not living Navajo.

But, for all her astuteness, she hadn't seen this coming at all. She had only wanted Becenti to look at the house without the pressure of an audience and to know that he had a place to go that wasn't inhabited by Mae's ghost. Perhaps she even wanted him to be a little appreciative of the trouble *she* had gone to. But she *never* expected that he would—that they—

"Oh," she whispered, remembering the urgent feel of his hand on her breast, and the taste of his warm mouth. She had reacted like the sex-starved and spurned old maid that she was, and she couldn't bear to think about how close to disaster she'd come. This was *not* supposed to happen to her—or to him—especially with each other. He was grieving still, and barely out of the hospital. She was supposed to be pining for Stuart Dennison. She and Johnny Becenti had nothing in common save their ethnic group. They detested each other, for God's sake! Given their history, she could only suppose that he was indulging in a little payback—deliberately trying to teach her a lesson for interrupting his self-imposed exile.

But, she assured herself, there was no point in dwelling on it. Whatever had flared so suddenly between the two of them wasn't worth all this *angst*. It was over and done with now. Nothing had happened, not really. A kiss, what was that? She wanted to believe that she had nothing to worry about. It wouldn't be like the closemouthed Captain Becenti to go telling what had happened all over the reservation even if he did want revenge. And, if the past was any indication, she could go for months and months without seeing him again. How often did he come to Santa Fe? How often did she go to Window Rock? It could well be, by the next time their paths crossed, that neither of them would even remember the incident.

"Stupid!" she said anyway. What could she possibly say to him when she saw him again?

Nothing, she immediately decided. *He* started it.

And I almost finished it, she thought in dismay. She hadn't wanted to stop. She was mortified by how much she hadn't wanted to stop. She had never encountered that dangerous and heady mixture of enmity and lust before. She'd never in all her life come so close to being completely swept away by pure, unadulterated physical need. Even now, she wanted to go to him, to lie with him in one of those austere, military-looking beds in the house with no ghosts.

Oh, God.

What if someone had seen them? she thought, her mind off on a completely different and equally distressing tangent. It would be all over the reservation by sundown—Lillian Singer and Johnny Becenti were...

No, they weren't!

Nothing happened.

But it still had to have been calculated, this sudden interest in her as a woman. He had to have deliberately wanted to show her who was in charge here, and show her in a way that would prove the most humiliating. And she had played right into his hands.

So how do you like having your harmony disrupted, Lillian?

She didn't like it. She didn't like it at all.

She nearly missed her Santa Fe exit, but by the time she reached home, she had herself under control. More or less. Self-control was a matter of understanding the situation. And it was simple, really. First, she had run to Window Rock to hide from Stuart. Now she was running to Santa Fe to hide from Johnny Becenti. She had worked hard all her life to establish a certain reputation for being capable and self-reliant and smart. The consummate levelheaded-lawyer type. And here she was behaving as if she were trapped in the lyrics of a very bad country-western song.

It didn't escape her notice that it was Becenti who was causing all this...yearning...and not Stuart. She had been upset to a certain degree when Stuart announced his marriage plans, but once the initial shock had worn off, she'd almost effortlessly moved on. It was as if some part of her had been expecting the demise of their relationship for a long time, and now that it had actually occurred, it was essentially a relief. A loose end, now neatly knotted and tied. She didn't like loose ends. She didn't like all this emotional upheaval, either. She liked a nice evenness to her life with no major ups or downs—a variation of the Navajo belief in being in harmony with all things, she supposed. There was a lot to be said for harmony, and at the moment, she was a long way from having it.

She went to bed early, slept fitfully—until it was nearly time to get up, then slept so deeply that she was late for court. Not terribly late. Just late-for-Lillian-Singer late. And it was duly noted by both her colleagues and her adversaries—not to mention the judge, a woman well-known for her penchant for punctuality.

"Are we keeping banker's hours now, Ms. Singer?" she asked, looking at Lillian over her half-rim, tortoiseshell reading glasses.

"No, Your Honor. My apologies to the court for my unavoidable delay," she said, her uncharacteristically meek reply causing as much surprise as her belated arrival had.

She had to will herself to stay focused, and the rest of the day—the rest of the week and well into the next— unfolded uneventfully enough, except that the intense concentration it took to keep from being distracted from the job at hand left her physically and mentally exhausted.

Stuart kept leaving messages for her everywhere she went. She didn't return any of his calls because she didn't want to. She hadn't liked being accused of deliberately going off to Window Rock without telling anyone just because she wanted to annoy him. She wasn't being vindictive; her feelings had been hurt. She would admit that she used Becenti as an excuse to escape another meeting with Stuart and his fiancée, but that was then. This was now, and Stuart's persistence in calling to reprove her under the guise of making sure she was "all right" was just one more aggravation to add to the ever-growing pile.

By sheer willpower alone, she lost herself in her work, refusing to dwell on the fact that all the phone calls came from Stuart and not from Window Rock. Not that she expected any—of course, she didn't. And the fact that Becenti didn't call to at least make a token apology for his uncouth behavior only served to underline the obvious. To Johnny Becenti, the clinch in the kitchen had been nothing but a well-timed joke.

On Friday, she worked late in the law library, bypassing the office and arriving home just ahead of a late-winter storm. The snow had already begun to fall as she drove the last leg of the trip up the winding drive to her front door.

Because the house was stucco instead of adobe, it was a bit of a misfit for the area—like she was. The house proper was L-shaped with a front porch that filled in the structure to make it the predictable low-roofed rectangle. In warmer weather she had all manner of chairs and rockers dragged onto the porch—wicker, wrought iron, pine—so that she or her guests could take advantage of the view of the surrounding hills. She liked having people come to visit. It was so peaceful and beautiful here, and she liked to share it—usually.

But today it was as cold and bleak as she felt. Snow was rapidly covering the ground, and the wind chimes on the porch clanged forlornly in the biting wind. She hadn't left any inside lights on, and having to enter a dark house only served to compound her dismal mood. The weekend stretched endlessly ahead of her. She was going to be snowed in. She was going to have two full days of nothing to do but think. She would have brought some legal work home with her—except that, for once in her career and thanks to her desperate need to stay busy, she was actually caught up on the research necessary for her current caseload.

She carried in a bag of groceries and her dry cleaning in one trip, nearly upending the bag in the struggle to get the door open. She stepped inside, still juggling.

"I'm home," she called softly to the empty room, needing to pour salt in an open wound, apparently—which was ridiculous. She had lived alone for most of her life. Even in her unprosperous, half-starving law-school days she had always preferred guests to roommates—people who came, had a good time, and then left again. She didn't want anyone underfoot. She didn't *need* anyone underfoot—which was why she had never actually lived with Stuart Dennison. It was truly an enigma to her as to why she felt so abandoned right now.

She saw him at the same moment she switched on the lamp by the front door, and in retrospect she would have been hard-pressed to say who, exactly, scared whom. But in any event, she retreated in a flurry of shrieks and groceries and dry cleaning, back out into the snowy evening.

"Lillian!" he yelled after her. "It's me!"

She still didn't stop until she'd reached the car and the voice finally registered. She whirled around.

"What the hell are you doing in my house!"

"Ah," he said mildly. "You don't like it when the hogan is on the other foot, I see."

"Becenti, you answer me!"

"What? Like you answered me when *I* asked that question?"

"Becenti—!"

"Come back inside, Lillian. It's cold. It's snowing. Which, if you ever paid attention, is your answer. I meant to wait outside until you got home, but it got to be too much for me. I'm still recovering, you know. And, I had the cat."

"What cat!"

"Your secretary's cat. Gracie's cat. I didn't want us both to get pneumonia—I've already had my turn. Come on," he coaxed, as if she were the one in the wrong here and it fell to him to be magnanimous.

She walked forward, but she was still angry. And unsuitably glad to see him, she noted grimly. She *hated* how glad she was to see him.

"What are you doing with Gracie's cat?" she asked, her tone of voice indicating that she was ready to accuse him of the worst kind of catnapping.

"I'm being helpful," he said, standing back so she could come inside. "Gracie's daughter went into labor. When I got to your office, she was running in circles like she had one shoe nailed to the floor and she was all worried about this cat—which, I understand, you said you'd baby-sit. So I volunteered to pick up the cat and bring it to you."

"And how did the two of you get here? *Broom?*"

He smiled. "That's good, Lillian. Sometimes I forget how witty you are."

She bent down and began picking up scattered groceries. Gracie's elderly gray tabby cat had already appropriated the half-empty bag. "Get out of there, Fred," she said. She glanced at Becenti. "I didn't see a vehicle," she said, wondering what she would have done if a Navajo Tribal Police car or some other official transportation had been sitting in the drive.

"No. No vehicle. Gracie didn't think you'd get home late, so I had young Officer Toomey drop me off. He had to testify in his first major trial today. He was scared so I came along to Santa Fe to talk him through it."

"He was probably more scared of you than he was of testifying," she said.

"He got over it," Becenti assured her. "I told him, by the way, that the absolute worst criminal-defense attorney he'd ever have to face is you."

"Oh, thank you," she said sarcastically.

"That wasn't a compliment."

She frowned. And she didn't ask him how his return to

work was going. She most certainly didn't ask him where he was living.

"So—like I said—Toomey dropped me off. He has some cousins in the area and he went to see them. I'll call him when I'm done here." He offered her her slightly askew dry cleaning. "Anything else?"

"It's cold in here," she said, because she couldn't resist his invitation to make further complaint. She took the dry cleaning out of his hand and hung it on the nearest door. "*I,* at least, made *you* a fire."

"I told you I wasn't planning on being inside when you got here."

"Oh, really?"

"Yes, really. The plan was, when I heard your car coming, I'd go back outside before you caught me."

"So much for that," she said dryly.

"Well, I fell asleep. That really is a comfortable chair," he said, of the overstuffed 1930s horsehair easy chair she'd gotten at a church rummage sale. Fred, deprived of his grocery bag, apparently recognized that fact himself, and he languished contentedly on the plush seat.

She turned to go into the kitchen, leaving Becenti standing. He didn't follow. In spite of her initial fright and her subsequent exasperation, in spite of her resolve as to the reason he'd instigated that Window Rock thing, she found that she very much wanted to continue this conversation—any conversation.

"So how did you get in here?" she asked over her shoulder.

"I picked the lock," he answered, coming along with her after all.

"You—a captain in the Navajo Tribal Police—stooped to breaking and entering?"

"Well, your nephew by marriage taught me how to do it," he said, giving her a truly feeble excuse. "I only 'entered.' I didn't exactly 'break.'"

"Meggie's Jack taught *you* to pick locks," she reiterated,

more than skeptical—not at Jack's being willing to share this useful information, but at Johnny Becenti's being willing to learn such an un-Becenti-like thing.

"He did. Your lock is the first chance I've had to practice. He's going to be so proud."

She laughed in spite of herself. *This is really...almost pleasant,* she thought—if she ignored the awkwardness and her embarrassment. But she said, "It's a good way to get yourself shot."

"In that case I'm very grateful you were only armed with a grocery bag and your dry cleaning."

"Do you want some coffee?" she asked abruptly. She tried to sound offhand, indifferent as to whether he did or not.

"Yes," he answered without hesitation.

She glanced at him. The look held.

"Day-old vegetable soup and cheese toast?" she added, still holding his gaze in a supreme effort not to seem flustered.

"Yes," he said again.

She had to turn away from him to concentrate on what exactly such a project would entail.

"Do you want some help?" he asked, his voice much closer behind her than it should have been. She didn't turn to see where he was standing. She didn't dare.

"No— Well, you could build that fire," she said, because it was clearly not a good idea to have him in the kitchen with her after all. "The stove is in—"

"I know where it is," he said.

"The wood is—"

"I know where that is, too."

He went away. She could hear him talking to Fred. He didn't seem to have that macho disdain for cats that most men had. She'd never really understood it—particularly when, to her way of thinking, cats behaved very much the same as men did. They both had their own agendas, their own intense Don't-bother-me-I'm-on-a-quest mode, and they both got around to the person who fed and took care of them when and if it suited them—at which time they could be very affectionate. No. Not much difference at all.

But, whatever the topic of conversation, Fred seemed to appreciate the effort Becenti was making. She could hear a meow from time to time in response to his considered opinions. She smiled again, wondering if Gracie had any idea that Fred apparently spoke fluent Navajo.

She opened the refrigerator, relieved that she did indeed have enough soup left for two. And bread and cheese for the toast. She would feed him, make him coffee, carry on a little conversation—and then she would find out what the hell he was doing here. She couldn't believe that he would just show up here like this. He was behaving as if nothing had happened between them. And worse, he was behaving as if they'd known each other for years—well, they *had* known each other for years, but only in a Fred-the-cat-hiss-and-spit kind of way. He must be here for a reason. He'd plainly said he was planning to call young Officer Toomey when he was "done here." Whatever that was supposed to mean.

She looked out the window. It was nearly dark now and the snow was coming down harder.

Becenti, Becenti, she thought, sighing heavily. He was indeed still recovering. He looked much better than when she'd last seen him, but not yet well. He seemed tired— tired enough so that she didn't really mind that he'd shamelessly let himself into her house. She did owe him some reciprocal hospitality, she supposed.

She smiled slightly, remembering the "hogan on the other foot" remark. He was somewhat witty himself— something she hadn't known about him and would never have guessed, just as she was unable to guess his real reason for being here.

She poured the soup into a pot and set it on a burner to heat. Then she put the cheese toast into the oven. And she listened. He wasn't talking to Fred anymore. The question now was whether or not he would talk to *her*. She had no plans to be coy. She was just going to ask him.

What are you doing here?

She couldn't get any plainer than that. And if he'd come all this way just to hurt her feelings, again, then so be it.

Becenti waited to make sure the fire had caught. He looked around the living room, marveling again at Lillian's decor. The walls were white. Everything else was desert- and sunset-toned—deep red to dark brown and every shade in between.

Assorted Native American—professionally done, he thought, looking past the huge striped sofa to a carved Zuni corn dancer and some pieces of Acoma Pueblo pottery that sat on a tall table behind it. An Ojibwa ''dream catcher'' hung on the far wall alongside a print of a Navajo man in a reservation hat who had wrapped himself in a bright red cloth that had a subtle suggestion of the American flag in the lower corner. The artist who had done it must have had an acute understanding of the conflict between a Navajo's need to be traditional and his fascination with the white world. Becenti thought it an appropriate selection for Lillian to have hanging in her house.

There were a few other more or less Navajo things around—a reasonably authentic pattern in some throw pillows, and a wedding vase on the large and low piece of furniture she used as a coffee table. Besides the vase, there were several candles in tall glass containers, a bowl of oranges and English walnuts, a blue Mason jar full of sea-shells and a few sprigs of dried desert flowers, and a decidedly non-Navajo red-and-white antique bank—a ring-master holding a large hoop for something now hidden in a barrel to pop out and jump through.

There was a large armoire with punched tin inserts in the doors, a table with a huge round-based copper lamp, an upholstered footstool with black wrought-iron legs, stacks of picture books—Rembrandt, O'Keeffe, Norman Rockwell, Tony Hillerman. She also had a number of framed snapshots of the members of the blended Singer-Baron clan. He looked at them closely. He knew everyone—all of Lillian's mixed family on display here. Some of the events—like Meggie and Jack Begaye's wedding—he himself had attended.

He took his jacket off and hung it on a nearby doorknob to keep it from becoming a cat bed. He looked down. Several sizes and colors and patterns of rugs lay this way and that, overlapping each other, on the hardwood floor. He wondered how much it had cost Lillian to be surrounded by this studied homeyness. Or perhaps she had missed her calling. Perhaps she had done it herself. In any case, this place was a long way from a dirt-floor, log-and-mud hogan.

He found the wall between the kitchen and the living room the most interesting, because there were four large, one-over-one glass windows in it. He thought that it had once been an outside wall and that the windows had been left in to keep both rooms from being too dark. They also gave him an unobstructed view of Lillian stirring the soup. He could see her, but he would have to go out a door and through a small hallway to get to her. And if she knew he was watching, she was making a point of not looking in his direction.

He checked the stove again. The fire was burning well. Not too vigorously. No smoking backdraft. He could safely go back into the kitchen now, but he didn't. He'd had a hard time explaining to Lillian what he was doing here. Not exactly a surprise, because he would have had a hard time explaining to himself what he was doing here. Both he and Toomey—and Lillian, for that matter—knew that the two of them should have been on their way back to Window Rock long before now. It was snowing, and Becenti had no apparent business being here. Even a rookie tribal police officer could see that. But here the always-in-control Johnny Becenti stood, trying to think up a way to stay even longer.

The phone rang, but Lillian wasn't in the kitchen. He couldn't see her anyplace, but after a few more rings, she returned, now wearing jeans and a T-shirt. She picked up the kitchen extension to answer, listened, then immediately held the receiver to her chest for a moment before she continued.

"Stuart, what do you want?" she said.

Because of the four windows, Becenti could hear her quite plainly—more plainly than she probably realized.

"No, I am not hiding again," she said. "No, you can't come out here. Because it's snowing, that's why. And because I have a guest. And because you and I have absolutely nothing to talk about—"

She gave a heavy sigh. "What kind of legal matter?" she said. Then, "Stuart, Santa Fe is full of lawyers—"

"Then call the office and make an appointment. Yes, I mean that. If you need legal advice and you think it has to be mine, call the office. Gracie will set you up with a convenient time— No, I'm not trying to worry you. I'm trying *not* to worry *me*. What? No. Stuart, you aren't listening. Stuart—"

She stood looking at the receiver briefly before she hung up.

She's not happy, Becenti thought, giving a loud enough sigh to draw a mild inquiry from Fred.

"Nothing, little brother," he said, reaching over to briefly stroke the cat's head. "Go back to sleep. This is nothing for you—or me—to worry about."

When he looked up, Lillian was standing in the doorway.

"It's ready," she said. "Yours, too, Fred."

But Fred preferred sleeping in the easy chair and rolled over onto his back, stretching as long as he could with both paws over his head before he curled into a furry ball again.

"It feels much better in here," Lillian said, nodding toward the stove. The stove had a glass insert in the door, and the flames were clearly visible.

She turned to go back into the kitchen, and he followed,

noting as he walked behind her that this was not the Lillian he had always known. This was the other one, the blue-jeans Lillian who had invaded his hogan and his grief—not the one in the courtroom power suit. He noted, too, that he should not be paying so much attention to those jeans—or to the T-shirt. Or to the memory of her warm, firm body under his hands. He should be thinking of her as the hotshot lawyer—not that her lawyer persona had proved to be much of a deterrent to him that afternoon in Window Rock. Still, at this particular moment, it was clear to him that he needed her to be the woman who had always annoyed him.

"Is Stuart coming?" he asked, surprising her a bit. "I could hear," he added without apology.

"No. Or I don't think so. He's been very...strange lately."

"Strange?"

She shrugged. "Like he doesn't remember he's getting married."

Becenti stood for a moment, assessing the emotion her remark caused in him. It wasn't a difficult process and it didn't take long. The emotion was easily identified, even for a person given to flagrant episodes of denial the way he was.

Jealousy.

He hadn't come here to feel jealous. He had come to try to get back his harmony, and seeing her again had seemed the only way to accomplish that. Even Winston Tsosie had noticed his uneasiness after Lillian had left, not to mention Mary Skeets. Mary must have asked him twenty times a day if he was feeling all right. But worse, Winston had immediately understood which person exactly had precipitated this disharmony.

"I think you better go to Santa Fe, son," the old man had said one afternoon, obliquely wise as always.

And so Becenti had barely made it two weeks without showing up on Lillian Singer's doorstep—and breaking into her house. All in all, though, she seemed to be taking his intrusion better than he would have thought. He just needed to make sure that she hadn't misunderstood... anything. And as soon as he knew that, everything—*he*— would be fine.

"Johnny, are you going to sit down or not?" she said, cutting into his thoughts.

"I am," he answered, pulling out a chair from the kitchen table. He was very hungry actually, and the soup smelled wonderful. He gratefully accepted the bowlful she gave him. And the coffee. And the cheese toast.

They ate in a kind of strained silence, as if both of them were waiting for an opening to speak their minds. But with such minimal conversation, there were no opportunities forthcoming.

"Did you make this?" he asked finally, well after the second bowl.

She looked up at him. "Why?" she asked pointedly, clearly expecting a resumption of their old adversarial relationship. If he had remarked upon the soup, then surely a criticism must follow.

"Because, Lillian, if you did, I was going to say that it was good."

"Good," she repeated, still suspicious.

"Okay, then, amazing," he said, deciding he couldn't resist aggravating her after all.

"Very funny, Becenti. You're pretty outspoken for a man with no transportation and a snowstorm outside," she said, getting back to her "amazing" soup.

He smiled. And he savored the sensation.

"I like to live on the edge," he assured her.

"You must—you came here."

They stared at each other across the table. He wanted to look away but he didn't. With that one small remark she had effectively removed all the pretense, however flimsy, that his arrival had been innocent. The moment of reckoning was here. No excuses. No escape. Speak the truth, suffer the consequences. The only problem was that he suddenly didn't know what the "truth" was.

The silence lengthened.

She is *beautiful,* he thought as he had that afternoon in the Window Rock house.

"Are you going to tell me why you're here or not?" she asked quietly.

He took a small breath, but he didn't oblige her.

"You're going to have to," she said. "Because I don't want to guess. Not that I can't. It's just that I don't know who's supposed to make the speech."

"Lillian—"

"Well, one of us has to, right? Isn't that why you came? You want to be reassured about what happened between us—and so do I," she continued—nervously, he thought, and very un-Lillian. "We were both...vulnerable. It took us both by surprise. It didn't mean anything." She was looking into his eyes when she said it.

"Right," he agreed too quickly. "It didn't mean anything."

At that moment, he should have been feeling a great relief to get this worrisome matter into the proper perspective, to know that she hadn't misunderstood the situation at all. But somehow the sensation escaped him.

"And neither of us should concern ourselves about it," she continued. "Our paths are going to cross from time to time—professionally—and even when I come to Window Rock to see the family, there shouldn't be any awkwardness between us because of what happened the other afternoon at the house. None. It was just—" She stopped.

"Just what?" he asked when she didn't go on—because the entire explanation sounded like a song from a Broadway musical she'd been practicing in front of the bathroom mirror—or worse, like what he'd intended to say himself. "Tell me."

She abruptly got up from her chair and began to pace the room. "You know what it was."

"No, you tell me—exactly. What was it?"

She stopped pacing and turned to face him. "All right. It was to teach me a lesson. It was putting an uppity woman in her place."

He made a slight sound and shook his head, amazed that she could think such a thing. How could she *possibly* have jumped to that conclusion?

Because she was Lillian, because she had forgotten who and what she was, that was why. The People didn't seek that kind of revenge against each other.

"You," he said, jabbing the air in her direction, "have been living away from your own kind too long! So what is it now?" he persisted. "Am I here *now* because I'm still trying to get my revenge and put you in your place?"

"Aren't you?"

"No, damn it, I'm not! I'm here because I—"

He stopped, incredulous that he'd been about to say it.

"Go on," she said. "You don't have to worry about hurting my feelings."

"Well, I am worried about it—but not in the way you think. You make me so damn *mad!*" he said. He stood too quickly, and his chair toppled over backward. He left it lying and moved around the edge of table toward her. "It's all I can do not to put you over my knee and—"

"Oh, yeah? You and who else?" she said, delivering the challenge expected of her but taking a few steps backward just in case.

"Lillian—!" he said, because at this point he was afraid he might really do it.

"What!" she said, still backing away.

"Lillian—!" he said again.

"*What!*"

"Do you have to have a house fall on you?"

"I guess so, Becenti, because I don't know what you want here!"

"I want *you,* damn it!" he yelled at the precise moment

someone knocked on the back door. They stood staring at each other, both of them transfixed by his revelation.

"You what?" she asked with some difficulty.

"You heard me."

She started to say something else but didn't, started to move in his direction but didn't do that, either. She looked toward the door, then back at him, shaking her head and making a slight gesture with one hand.

"I have to answer the door," she said, even though there was no more knocking forthcoming—not much of a surprise if the person outside had heard Becenti's bold announcement.

He gave a sharp sigh and snatched the chair upright. He expected the irrepressible Stuart Dennison to be on the doorstep. Toomey stood there instead. The young officer could see Becenti as soon as Lillian opened the door, but the expression on his face indicated that he really, *really* wished that were not the case.

"What is it, Toomey?" Becenti asked.

"Well, sir, the, uh, telephone— I called, but I couldn't get through— I guess there's a line down. So I just thought I should, uh—"

"Come in, Officer Toomey," Lillian said, taking him by the sleeve and pulling him into the room before he died there on the threshold. "Would you like some coffee?"

"Coffee?" he said, his eyes darting around the room as if he'd expected a lot more than what he was seeing. Or a lot less.

"There's some left," Lillian suggested so that he might grasp the reason why she was asking.

"Oh, yes, ma'am. Thank you. It's cold out."

"How bad are the roads?" she asked as she poured.

"Not too bad," Toomey said, gratefully accepting the cup. "If you go slow."

Becenti turned and went into the living room to get his jacket. This was not going as planned. At all.

"What? You're just going to leave now?" Lillian said behind him. He'd hadn't realized she'd come with him. He could see Toomey through those suddenly not-so-convenient windows. Toomey—nonplused, but still curious.

"Yes," Becenti said.

"Yes?" she repeated incredulously. She gave a sharp sigh, and he realized that he should be saying more—to keep her from thinking she was right about his ulterior motives in Window Rock, if nothing else.

But there was no time for talking. He picked up his jacket and headed for the small hallway that led into the kitchen, grabbing her by the hand in passing and dragging her along with him. The second they were out of Toomey's sight, he pulled her to him, his mouth coming down on hers, hard and hot and urgent.

"Don't," she whispered, but she was clinging to him, and he didn't stop. His mouth covered hers again. His hand found its way up under her T-shirt.

And Toomey stood drinking his coffee not ten feet away.

"Don't—" she said again.

He abruptly let go of her.

"Go."

"What?"

"Don't go!" she whispered, holding on to his arm.

"I have to. Toomey—" But he was reaching for her again, kissing her again. "Lillian, he'll know we—" he said between frantic kisses.

"He heard you, Johnny. It's too late—now."

Yes, Becenti thought. *Much too late.*

He thrust his jacket into her hands and stepped away from her.

"Toomey," he said, startling the rookie with his sudden appearance in the doorway. "Go spend the night with your relatives."

"Sir?"

"You heard me. Come back here tomorrow—around noon."

"Noon?" Toomey said, clearly hoping for an explanation for this sudden turn of events, preferably something other than what it looked like.

"Well, what are you waiting for!" Becenti barked.

"Nothing—nothing, sir," he said, backing toward the door. He suddenly remembered the cup he was about to take with him wasn't his, and he rushed forward to set it on the counter. "Noon—tomorrow," he said as he hurried out.

Becenti stood there in case Toomey needed more instruction, but after a moment he heard the police vehicle start up and back slowly down the driveway. This was going to put one hell of a strain on young Officer Toomey's discretion, he thought. Not telling the boys around the coffeepot that Captain Becenti had stayed the night with Lucas Singer's sister was going to require colossal self-restraint on his part. And Mary Skeets could get information out of a stone statue.

But Becenti wouldn't worry about that now. He went back into the hallway. Lillian was standing where he'd left her, still holding his coat.

"I don't want to talk this to death," he said. "I don't want to analyze it. I don't want to justify it. Whatever this is with you and me—I want to enjoy it—for as long as it lasts."

Her eyes searched his, for what truth he couldn't imagine. "All right," she said.

He took the jacket out of her hands and tossed it aside, reaching for her at the same time. She came to him willingly, holding on to him, burying her face in his shoulder. And she felt so good, smelled so good.

Lillian.

He began to kiss her in earnest, savoring the sensation and her response. She leaned into him, offering her mouth to him, returning kiss for kiss until they both were breathless.

Who would ever believe this? he thought. No one. Even if Toomey told them.

She stepped away from him and took him by the hand,

leading him through the house to the room where she slept, both of them indifferent to the meal they hadn't quite finished or to the whereabouts of the cat—to anything except each other.

The bedroom was large. The bed was large. He paid no attention to anything else. His focus was entirely upon her.

She switched on a small lamp on the nightstand and turned down the bedcovers. He tried not to think about Stuart Dennison. He wouldn't think about him. He didn't care if Dennison had been in her bed, this bed, a thousand times. He reached for her again, his hands sliding over her, trying to find bare skin. His mouth brushed over hers in what could hardly be called a kiss, but her lips parted, and he tasted her deeply now. She gave a soft moan, one he could feel, one that tripled his sense of urgency.

She kicked off her shoes. He began to unbutton his shirt, but she immediately reached to free the buttons for him herself. She looked into his eyes as she did it, playful now, and mischievous. It was no simple task getting a tribal police officer out of his uniform. Buttons and belts and a side arm.

She lay his gun belt carefully on the dresser, then took away his shirt and pulled his undershirt over his head. Then she held her arms up so that he could pull her T-shirt off. Her bra was made of lace and some kind of silky material he could barely feel. He undid it with trembling fingers and tossed it aside. And he stood staring at her. Her breasts were perfect; not large, not small. He reached out to touch them, and she stood perfectly still to let him cup her warm softness in the palms of his hands. Her breath caught when he brought her nipples to hard, tight peaks. She was so beautiful, and she knew it. She wasn't in the least embarrassed by his unabashed attention, and he found that incredibly erotic. She didn't have to be wooed so much as conquered. Everything about her said, *Here I am. Take me—if you can.*

He reached for the waist of her jeans, unbuttoning, unzipping, pulling everything down as he crowded her back toward the bed until she had to sit down on the edge. He knelt to take off her socks, the jeans, the panties, stroking her legs, her thighs as he did so. She braced herself, leaning back a bit, watching him with that half smile he always found so intriguing.

Then he stood and reached into his left pants pocket. He had a statement of his own to make—a handful of condoms he let trickle through his fingers onto the bed, the ones he'd bought in an out-of-the-way place where no one would know him. It was a bold move on his part, both the purchase and the presentation, and one that made her laugh out loud.

"You are *very* sure of yourself, Becenti," she said, making him laugh with her.

He got rid of his pants and underwear and came to her quickly, tumbling her backward on the bed and rolling her on top of him.

"You haven't seen anything yet," he promised her, kissing her hard, the laughter bubbling from her mouth into his.

The kiss ended, and they lay there, staring into each other's eyes. She was smiling still, but the smile slid away.

"Johnny," she whispered, nuzzling his cheek. "Johnny..." She pressed a kiss at the corner of his mouth, and then another.

He gave a soft moan when her tongue darted across his lower lip, and he reached up to entwine his fingers in her hair, to keep her mouth close, to accept the invitation she offered.

They were both deadly serious now and in a hurry. He wanted her. He ached with desire, trembled with it. It had been a long time since he—

No. He wouldn't think about that. Mae was gone. This was Lillian. This was now. He abruptly rolled her onto her back so he could touch her, look at her. He stroked her body, his hand finding her soft inner thighs, stroking and stroking, each time reaching higher. He bent his head so that he could kiss her breasts. She made a soft "Oh" sound and her head arched back when he suckled her, her hands clutching at him, holding him tightly against her.

His fingers touched the intimate female part of her now, gently and then more insistently when he found the place that gave her pleasure, and then gently again. She writhed under his expertise. It took everything he had to restrain himself. He wanted her. He wanted to plunge himself deep inside her now—*now*. He drew her hand downward, but the soft brush of her fingers was nearly too much for him. He couldn't wait any longer. He fumbled for one of the condoms scattered around him and tore open the pack, his hands shaking.

He knelt between her thighs, ready now, his eyes holding hers. His hands slid under her hips to lift her to him. He didn't hesitate, couldn't hesitate. He thrust into her, hard and deep, the pure pleasure of it making him give a deep, guttural sound. He tried to be still for a moment to give her time to grow accustomed to him, but then he realized that she needed no time. She was clinging to him, her body rising to meet his in a rhythm as old as time.

"Don't stop," she whispered. "Don't— Oh!"

He couldn't have even if he'd wanted to. She was so hot and tight around him. He thought he could die from this urgent need of her, but still the sensation grew. He had never felt such desire, both for gratification *and* to somehow make it last. He wanted to tell her how good it felt, how good *she* felt.

But then her body arched under him and she cried out his name.

It's so good! he thought, perhaps said. He could feel her spasms of release around him, and he thrust harder and harder until his own body exploded inside her in a rush of heat and pleasure. He lost all sense of time and place. He lost himself, and, for a brief moment, his sadness. There was only Lillian and he clung to her, giving a hoarse animal cry as he collapsed against her and finally lay spent.

Chapter Seven

Lillian awoke slowly from a deep sleep, the kind that only came from being well loved and thoroughly sated. She stretched contentedly and turned onto her back, expecting to feel Becenti there beside her.

She was alone.

She abruptly sat up, listening hard for his whereabouts. It would be just like him to suddenly remember who and what he was—who they both were—and leave—even though he didn't have any kind of transportation. She could easily picture him walking down to the road in hip-deep snow and thumbing a ride to Toomey's relatives—or all the way back to Window Rock.

She gave a quiet sigh, remembering his touch. She hadn't known it would be like that with him. Or perhaps she had. She had known him a long time, and she felt no pressure to be anything other than herself. They had seen each other at their worst; there was no need for pretense. She didn't have to worry about offending his white sensibilities with what little of her Navajo self remained. And all that freedom had translated into a passion she had heretofore only imagined. If he was somewhere now, guilt-ridden and filled with regret because they'd gone to bed together, she was going to—

She heard a sound, a door closing. She wrapped herself in the top blanket and hurried through the house into the kitchen. She found Fred oblivious to everything but a chunk of cat food on a piece of waxed paper near the back door. She stepped over him to look out the window. The snow had ended. The clouds had gone, and the sun was about to come up. But she couldn't see anyone—or any footprints in the snow. She walked back through the house to look out the front windows, and she saw Becenti immediately. He was standing on the small section of porch that was bare of snow, facing the faint glow of dawn on the horizon, already engrossed in the morning chant. And, freezing cold or not, he was completely naked.

It took a great deal of self-control on her part not to interrupt. The man hadn't been out of the hospital all that long, and standing outside with no clothes on hardly seemed a wise choice. But, she would respect his apparently pressing need to observe the Navajo Way, if not his good sense. And having decided that, she should have discreetly withdrawn, but she didn't. She stood there and brazenly admired him instead.

For as long as she had known him, he had kept his hair cropped short in a kind of military law-enforcement-officer crew cut, but during Mae's long illness and his subsequent mourning and exile, he had given up being shorn—perhaps as a move back into Navajo traditionalism for her sake— and his hair now hung down his back. He was beautiful to look at; the consummate warrior.

And lover.

Her lover.

Lillian, Lillian, what have you done? she thought. She never should have started anything with him. She was far

too comfortable and settled in her life here—and far too
old—for this kind of head-over-heels infatuation with a
man who was so unsuitable. They were completely incompatible in personality and temperament. No one who knew
them both would argue that.

But they weren't incompatible in bed.

She sighed, looking out the windows at him, still remembering last night. If she'd met him when she was twenty-one, she would never have become a lawyer. She would
have had ten or twelve of his children instead.

Fred jumped up on the table beside her to peer out the
window. She smiled and stroked his fur.

"If Toomey shows up early," she told him, holding back
the curtain so he could see, "one of us had better know
how to do CPR."

Becenti suddenly dashed back inside in a rush of cold
air and blowing snow, startling both Fred and her.

"I'm freezing!" he cried, grabbing her, blanket and all,
and lifting her off the floor.

"Captain Becenti," she said calmly, trying not to let him
see that he had rattled her with his boisterous—and nude—
enthusiasm. "I do have neighbors, you know."

"Not anymore, you don't," he insisted, covering her
face in kisses and making her laugh. If she expected any
kind of embarrassed reticence on his part this morning, that
concern was quickly put to rest.

"Captain Becenti," she said again, dodging yet another
kiss.

"Yes, Lillian, what is it?"

"Could I interest you in some coffee?"

"I'd have to put you down for that, wouldn't I?"

"Yes, I believe so."

"Then, no. There are other ways of getting warm." He
began walking toward the bedroom, still holding her off the
floor and trying not to step on the blanket.

"Oh, you think so?" she said, trying not to laugh as they
staggered along.

"I *know* so," he assured her.

* * *

She awoke with a start. Someone was knocking on the back door again, and Becenti scrambled for his clothes.

"Toomey," he said. "I forgot about Toomey—"

She looked at the clock. "Punctual to a fault," she said, stretching and reaching out to stroke his bare back. "Are you leaving?"

He looked around at her. "I think I should."

"Why?"

"Because I want to go before you want me to," he said simply.

She moved to put her arms around him and rest her head against his shoulder, her breasts pressing into his back. He reached up to stroke her hair. They stayed like that for a moment, then she sat up again.

"I don't want you to leave. I want you to stay as long as you can," she said.

He smiled. "Poor Toomey," he said, standing and zipping his pants. He didn't bother with his shirt or shoes.

She got up as well, finding a robe and putting it on in case that wasn't Toomey at the door. Whoever it was knocked again as she walked into the living room, and she could hear Becenti open the back door.

But nobody said anything.

She moved to where she could see through the windows in the wall. The door was flung wide as she expected, and Becenti was standing there in a state of undress that obviously needed some kind of explanation—only he wasn't giving one. And it was certain that Toomey wasn't about to ask.

After a moment, the young officer sighed. "I'm staying with the relatives again, right, sir?"

"Right," Becenti said. Period. And he closed the door.

She chuckled to herself when Toomey almost immediately took his life into his hands and knocked again. Becenti jerked open the door.

"Do I plan on a particular time to be back here, sir?" Toomey asked in a rush, clearly trying to get his query in before he got yelled at.

"No," Becenti said.

"Oh, well—"

But the door closed again on whatever thoughts Toomey had remaining, and Lillian laughed out loud.

Poor Toomey, indeed, she thought. Firmly entrenched in his twenties, he clearly had had no idea that people as old as she and Becenti ever indulged in this kind of behavior. And if the truth be told, she was rather surprised herself, particularly considering the consequences. All Becenti had to worry about was Toomey telling everybody in Window Rock. *She,* on the other hand, had to worry about another visit from both their mothers. Lillian was certain that when Katie Becenti had come to hire her to lure her son out of his exile, this was *not* what she'd had in mind.

"Lillian?" Becenti called, and she stepped into his arms, amazed that the consequences suddenly didn't seem to matter anymore. He had been right not to want to analyze whatever was happening between them, and there was absolutely no way to justify it. They had both lost their minds. It was as simple as that. And mindless or not, at this particular moment, she didn't care.

For as long as it lasts, Johnny, she thought.

They took a long tub bath together. It was the first time she had ever let a man wash her hair. Somehow, in all the years she'd spent with Stuart, they had never reached that level of intimacy. And it *was* intimate, and infinitely tender—a gesture she thought Becenti made simply because he wanted to.

She leaned back against him in the warm water, eyes closed, blissfully enjoying the process. When she was a little girl, she used to beg her grandmother for a yucca-root shampoo, earnestly believing that it was the suds from the yucca plant that always made her feel so much better. It was only at this moment that she realized that it wasn't the plant at all, but the caring attitude of the person doing the washing.

They ate a huge late lunch of cold cuts and bread and fruit, and then they went for a walk in the snow. The sun shone brightly, and the wind was sharp. She showed him all the places around her house that she'd found so beautiful.

"Do you ever hear the hum?" he asked.

"What hum?"

"You know—that strange sound people are always on the tabloid news saying they hear."

"No," she said, taking his hand as they walked. "No hum. What are you going to do about Toomey?"

"Do?"

"Are you going to tell him not to say anything—about us?"

"No," Becenti said, helping her through a deep patch of snow.

"Why not?"

"Because it would be wrong." He turned to look at her. "I'm not ashamed of this. I'm not going to behave as if I am."

He walked on ahead of her, leaving her standing. A hawk suddenly cried overhead, and he shaded his eyes to watch it soar higher and higher until it was little more than a speck in the bright blue sky.

Be careful, Becenti, she thought. *You are in danger of making a friend for life, here.* It was incredible to her that this heretofore exasperating man could keep doing and saying the right thing.

They walked steadily up the hillside that was visible from her front porch, and she knew all the while that she would be able to look at it again without thinking of this day. They were out of the shelter of a line of junipers now, and the sharp wind made her falter from time to time.

"Are you cold?" he asked at one point.

"Of course," she answered.

"Good," he said, smiling back at her. He waited for her to catch up, and when she did, he put his arm around her shoulders as they continued upward to the ridge.

"Do you...like living here?" he asked.

"Not a good question, Becenti," she said.

"Why not?"

"Because it's not what you really want to know."

"So what do I *really* want to know?"

"You want to know why I left the rez." She stopped, and she was looking at him as she said it. He didn't avoid her steady gaze.

"So why did you?"

"Because I wanted more."

"More what? More money?"

"Yes, more money. More prestige. More everything."

"Why?"

She frowned. "Why?"

"There must be a reason," he said. "You were brought up the same way I was, I think. Both our mothers are traditional. I didn't want to leave. Why did you?"

She shrugged. "Just one of those things, I guess."

He reached out to move a strand of hair that had blown across her face. "Now who isn't saying what she really means?" he said.

They walked on for a short distance.

"Why do you think there has to be a reason?" she asked abruptly, stopping again.

"Because I know you. You don't do things on a whim."

"I came to your hogan."

"That wasn't a whim. That was a desperate act. You were cornered."

She sighed. "You're right. I was."

"And I'm right about the other thing, too."

"No, you aren't."

"Yes, I am," he insisted. "But you don't have to tell me if you don't want to."

"Then why are we having this conversation?"

"So you'll know I understand more than you think I do."

She didn't say anything else. She was not at all sure how she felt about his assertion that he "understood." She had gone her own way for a long time now without wanting or needing anyone's acceptance or a critique of her choices.

She was out of breath when they reached the ridge. More so than he, regardless of the weakness in his lungs. They stood side by side, looking back at the snow-covered hillside they'd just climbed.

"I don't think *you* understand," he said after a moment.

She looked at him. "Then tell me."

"I don't think you understand how...strange this is for me."

"I understand," she said. "You were married to...Mae for a long time."

"I loved her."

She waited for him to go on. She'd had to force herself to say Mae's name, and she didn't know why. She hadn't believed in evil ghosts since she was a child. She had no fear of the wandering *chindi* and the harm it could do to anyone who spoke its name.

But he didn't say anything else. He moved her over and made her turn around. "Look down there—toward the road."

She looked where he told her, but she didn't see anything. "What is it?"

"Right there," he said, moving her slightly.

This time she saw it—a police vehicle parked on the side of the road, barely visible through the trees.

"I think it's Toomey," he said.

"What in the world is he doing there? Spying?"

"No, my guess is he needs to tell me something, and he's waiting for us to go back to the house."

"Tribal police business, you mean?"

"I expect so. He wouldn't be back here today if it wasn't something important—but it's not a major crisis, or he'd come on in."

"Maybe it's not him," she said, and she immediately wished she hadn't. It was entirely the wrong thing for the blasé Lillian Singer to say. It sounded too needy, and she certainly wasn't that, not by any stretch of the imagination. Johnny Becenti could go right now and it would be all the same to her. They had nothing between them but their one night together. She didn't have to be filled with regret because he was leaving. She didn't have to try to protect their nonrelationship by not saying his dead wife's name.

"No, it's him," Becenti said, and Toomey or not Toomey, he took her by the hand as they began to walk back down the hillside. He had meant what he said about not behaving as if he was doing something wrong, but that didn't mean that he wasn't all business when they finally reached the house. Toomey drove up almost immediately, eager to give Becenti his report, and Becenti was ready to officially hear it. Lillian stood back and let them talk, using the opportunity to look closely at the man who had suddenly come to mean more to her than she would ever dare admit. She couldn't admit it—not to him and not herself.

No strings, she thought. It wouldn't work any other way, because he had found himself again, and he was completely dedicated to the People and to his job.

No strings. No commitment. No complications.

For as long as it lasts.

He didn't stop to explain his abrupt departure to her. He had to go back to Window Rock and that was that. She didn't follow him inside the house to get his gun belt. She caught Fred as he made a dash for freedom instead, because the snow was deep and she had no wish to have to explain to Gracie that her beloved feline had suddenly found a place of honor in the coyote food chain.

But as much as she adored old Fred, he wasn't the only reason she didn't go in with Becenti. The real reason was because she felt awkward suddenly and didn't quite know how to tell him goodbye.

She stood on the front porch with the heavy cat in her arms, chatting with Toomey about the late snow until Becenti came back outside again.

"Start the car," he said curtly to Toomey. "I won't call you," he said to her as soon as Toomey was out of earshot. He absently reached out to scratch Fred behind the ear. "I'm not going to intrude on your life here. I guess you're going to have to say what the rules are."

She voiced her earlier thought. "No strings. No commitment. No complications. For as long as it lasts."

He stood for a moment, then nodded. He looked as if he wanted to say something else, but he didn't. He stepped off the porch and walked toward the car.

"Lillian?" he said when he was about to open the car door.

"What?" she said. "What?" she said again when he didn't immediately respond.

"Walk in beauty."

The unexpected Navajo benediction caught her off guard and, incredibly, brought tears to her eyes. He got into the car, and he gave her no backward glances as it drove away. She stood there, staring after it until it disappeared down the road.

She was barely inside the house when she heard the car coming back again. She smiled to herself and put Fred down before she stepped onto the porch. But it wasn't Becenti's car she'd heard. It was Stuart Dennison's.

Chapter Eight

"I told you I needed your help," Stuart said.

"And I told you to call Gracie and make an appointment."

"Lillian, do you think I'd come here like this if it wasn't important?" He looked over his shoulder. "That was him leaving, wasn't it? Your...guest? The one you stayed with in the hogan."

She didn't answer him, but she did stand back to let him come inside. And the only reason she did was because of the way he looked. She had never seen him so obviously exhausted.

"I need your help," he said again.

"With what?" She moved to the stove and put in some wood. There was coffee made. Becenti had done it so they would have something hot to drink when they came back from their walk. She pushed a pang of regret aside and tried to concentrate on dealing with Stuart. "Tell me," she said, standing with her arms folded.

"Can I sit down, at least?"

"Stuart—"

He held up both hands. "I know I'm trying your patience. And I know I have no right to do that." He gave a sigh and sat down heavily in the horsehair chair, his hand over his eyes.

"Are you and J.B. having some kind of trouble?" she asked.

He looked at her. "No. It's not that—exactly."

She waited in vain for him to be more forthcoming. "Look," she said. "I'm going to get us some coffee. When I come back with it, you had better be in the mood to talk."

He was sitting just the way she'd left him when she returned. He took the cup she offered him, drank very little, and then put it aside. His hands were shaking.

"You need legal advice," she prompted him, taking a seat on the couch. Fred immediately jumped up beside her and began to search for a choice sleeping spot—which she, of course, seemed to have taken.

"I need legal advice," he agreed. "And I need help."

"Stuart, will you get to the point!" she said, startling Fred into finding a quieter place.

"All right! I need legal advice now because I didn't take it before."

"I don't know what that means, Stuart."

He gave a sharp sigh. "Do you remember a year or so ago, when I was going to invest in that big land deal? You told me not to. You told me you thought the men asking me to invest couldn't be trusted."

"I remember," she said, sipping her coffee.

"Well, I didn't listen to you."

"And?" she prompted again when he didn't go on.

"And the you-know-what is about to hit the fan."

"For whom?"

"For everybody involved in it—for me."

"So how much did you invest?"

"A hundred dollars."

She looked at him. "And how much did you get back?"

"Six figures."

"*Six* figures!"

"I thought it was all on the up and up—"

"Just like Santa Claus and the Tooth Fairy?"

He ignored her sarcasm. "There's a reporter who thinks the whole deal came about because of insider information and manipulating government contracts."

"Did it?"

"I don't know."

"Can he prove it?"

"I don't know," he said again.

"Stuart—"

"Lillian, all I did was invest the money."

"No, what you did was give them the use of your name. And with that kind of profit, it doesn't matter a whole lot if it was on the up and up or not. We're not in the eighties anymore, Stuart. People are a little more touchy about unethical behavior in their elected officials. Whatever possessed you to do something so stupid!"

"I needed the money!"

"For what!"

"For…J.B."

"Ah!" Lillian said. "Well—if it's for *J.B.*"

"Don't be so damned sarcastic!"

"Oh, excuse me. You're the one who barged in here and demanded my help. Heaven forbid that *I* should be sarcastic."

"I don't know what to do."

"You get yourself a good lawyer. That's what you do."

"Will you take the case?"

"No."

"Lillian, please—"

"No, Stuart!"

"There's more," he said.

"I don't want to hear it."

"There's the reason I need you to get me off, the reason I need to keep the money."

"I heard the reason—J.B."

"No, you didn't. I need to keep the money because I...don't think I'm going to be here to take care of her."

"What do you mean, you're not going to be here?" For a brief moment, she envisioned that he might be planning to leave the country—or something much more final. But then she looked at his face. "What do you mean?" she asked again.

He tried to smile and didn't quite make it. "I'm sick, Lily."

He hadn't called her that in years—not since she was a bright-eyed and idealistic young law student. His doing so now scared her.

"Tell me," she said.

"It's some kind of leukemia," he said tonelessly. "For a long time I just thought I was tired, or I had the flu or something. I won't go into the gory details, but I'm going to have to start treatments soon. They tell me the odds aren't that good. It may all be a grand gesture at best. I don't want to go through it, but I don't have much of an option."

"Have you gotten a second opinion?"

"Of course. And a third. They all say the same thing. I'm even considering a faith healer." He managed a smile of sorts.

She looked at him, stunned and trying to absorb what he had told her. She didn't want to believe him, but she did.

"You're not going to bawl or anything, are you?"

"No," she said, but she didn't sound very convincing even to herself.

"Then say something."

"I...don't know what to say. Except that I'm so sorry."

He smiled slightly. "That's enough. You're the only person I can believe who has said that."

"Stuart, I still don't understand what you want me to do."

"I want you to be my spokesperson with the media. Keep them off my back as much as you can, without saying I'm ill. They'll find out soon enough, but I'm not going to be the one to give them any of the details. And I want you to start working on liquidating my assets. I'll make restitution if it turns out this land deal was illegal— I know, I know," he said, holding up his hands. "Santa Claus and the Tooth Fairy. And if it is illegal, I want you to defend me in court, assuming I live that long."

"Stuart—"

"I trust you, Lillian. In fact, you're the one person I'd trust to do this."

"Yes, well, the time to have trusted me was when I told you not to get mixed up in that land thing in the first place."

He smiled again, less painfully this time. "You always said white people lose every bit of sense they ever had when it comes to an inch of land."

"Did I?"

"Many times."

"You should have listened."

"Yes. I should have. There's one last thing I want you to do."

"What?"

"I want you to help me with J.B."

"Help you? How? I can tell you right now I don't want to be a bridesmaid—even if you are sick."

He laughed out loud. "Lillian, Lillian, this is just what I needed. Someone to *not* coddle me. Someone to make me laugh."

"Well, I can't help you with J.B."

"Yes, you can. I need you to let her think that you and I are...together again."

"Together," she repeated. She had to think about the

implications of that remark for a moment. "Why?" she asked pointedly.

"It will make it easier."

"Easier for whom?"

"For me. I'm not going to marry her. I don't want to give her this kind of trouble."

"You don't want to *give* her trouble or you don't think she'll *take* it."

He looked away. "The scandal of being investigated is bad enough."

"Does she know how sick you are?"

He looked back at her. "She doesn't know I'm sick at all."

"Stuart—"

"I'm not going to put her through my illness, too."

"It's *her* choice, isn't it? If she loves you, you have no right to keep it from her. She's going to know sooner or later."

"It won't matter. She'll think I'm with you."

"That lie will hurt her a lot more than trying to deal with your having leukemia."

He didn't say anything to that. He sighed heavily and sank back into the chair, the exhaustion she'd noted earlier all too apparent.

"Stuart, are you all right?"

"A weak spell. They...catch me off guard sometimes," he said, but he looked terrible.

"Are you in pain?"

"Just my legs. They hurt all the time. I understand that will get worse. Lillian, will you do this for me or not?"

"I'll be your spokesperson. I'll do what I can about shuffling your assets and making your will. But I won't lie to J.B."

He looked as if he was about to protest.

"I mean it," she said.

"There's such a thing as lawyer-client privilege," he said.

"I won't lie to her."

"You don't have to lie to her. I'll do that."

"Stuart—"

"Please, Lillian," he said. "Please! I'm not going to put her through this!"

He does love her, she thought. Enough to marry her. And enough not to.

She also thought he was about to cry, and she sighed heavily. She had loved him once—a long time ago, it now seemed. But she still cared about him enough to help him with most of what he asked.

"When...can I get your financial information?" she asked.

"Monday morning. I'll messenger it to you. My darling Lily, I can't tell you how grateful I am—"

"Don't be grateful yet, Stuart. I haven't done anything."

He stood, and she stood with him.

"Yes, you have. You don't know how much I've needed your good sense and your strength. It's such a relief knowing you're going to handle the bad stuff for me. I feel like I can concentrate now—on the other thing." He abruptly reached for her and hugged her tightly for a moment before he turned to go.

"Are you sure you can drive?"

"Yes, I'm sure. If I pace myself, I'm okay. Oh, I almost forgot," he said when he was about to open the front door. He took a folded piece of paper out of his shirt pocket and handed it to her. Her name was written on it.

"What is this?"

"A note from your guest, I think. It was propped against the ringmaster bank—there on the coffee table. I stuck it in my pocket while you were in the kitchen—in case you hadn't read it yet. I'm a selfish and desperate man. I didn't want you distracted while I was trying to present my case."

She took the piece of paper. "Stuart! Did you read this?"

"Of course not. It's not *mine.* Unscrupulous land deals are my thing—not reading other people's correspondence.

I'm a little jealous of him, though. You thought he was coming back just now. You have no idea how disappointed you looked when you realized it was only me." He gave her a quick kiss on the forehead and opened the door. "Monday," he said.

She stood and watched him go, finally closing the door just ahead of another of Fred's attempted jailbreaks. "There are coyotes out there, and snow on the ground, and you've been neutered. *Why* do you insist on going outside!"

"*Rrrah!*" he said.

"Oh, I get it. It's a guy thing."

Unfortunately, "guy things" had never been her forte. She didn't understand Stuart at all. It was wrong of him not to tell J.B. Totally, completely wrong. She had never believed in protecting people from the truth. It never turned out to be for their own good, because it never worked. The only thing that worked for the J.B.'s of the world was to be tossed into the sea of life and to have to sink or swim like everyone else.

But whether Stuart was seriously ill or not, his asking Lillian Singer for help had to be the epitome of unfathomable male logic—to come to the woman he'd just scorned and expect her to help him pick up the pieces of his bad judgment. Of course, he was right. She was going to do it. As hurt and angry as she had been about his careless treatment of her, she wouldn't have wished this illness on him. He'd done a stupid thing, but he was sick, and the latter seemed to cancel out the former. He'd been right about the other thing, as well. She had been disappointed when she'd realized that it was he and not Becenti who had returned.

She sighed again, still holding the piece of paper Stuart had given her. She wasn't quite sure if she believed his assertion that he hadn't read it. She didn't immediately open it, and she knew exactly why. She was afraid Johnny Becenti had come to his senses after all.

I won't call you, he'd said, and what he'd only hinted at in front of Toomey, he may well have written plainly here.

She was so tired suddenly, and she wasn't quite ready to absorb any more jarring news at the moment. Between Becenti's abrupt departure and Stuart's upsetting visit, she had no harmony left, whether she believed in the concept or not.

She picked up the coffee cups and carried them back into the kitchen, careful of the note as she went. Regardless of Fred's comings and goings, the house seemed so *empty,* and she knew without a doubt that it was Johnny Becenti's absence that made it so and not Stuart's. There had been more than just passion between her and Becenti, although that was certainly a significant part of it. There had been conversation and laughter as well, and a kind of teasing banter that she had never shared with anyone else, not even Stuart.

She straightened up the kitchen, put the dirty cups into the dishwasher, stared at the note she'd left lying on the counter.

When there was nothing left to do, she picked it up and took it into the living room. Then she sat down in one corner of the couch and pulled her feet up under her as she began to read.

Lillian,
I can't really say anything to you now with Toomey here. I don't want to leave, but I guess you probably know that. I want you to call me—if you want to—at home or at the law-enforcement building. If you can't reach me, ask Mary Skeets. She always knows where I am—well, almost always.

Lillian smiled at the oblique reference to that afternoon the two of them had gone to the Window Rock house—purposely not informing Mary Skeets of his whereabouts.

Take care of yourself.

Johnny

He had written both phone numbers at the bottom. She reread the note, and then read it again. It was not what she expected at all. She had expected "Thanks for the one-night stand, Lillian, but I have other things to do now." This note was in keeping with what he'd said about not intruding on her life here.

She closed her eyes for a moment, her mind filled with images of him—of him and her—together.

He was intruding, whether he intended to or not. And he didn't have to do anything at all. Just looking at his handwriting filled her with a sense of longing. Even now she wanted to get into her car and follow him to Window Rock. She wanted to stay with him tonight, make love with him, sleep with him, have breakfast with him in the morning—and she didn't even know which house he was living in. She wanted him, and she didn't care if the entire reservation found out about it.

I never should have started this, she thought. Somebody was going to get hurt, and it wasn't hard to guess who that somebody was going to be. Becenti had loved his wife. She had known that, even without his saying so.

Chapter Nine

She didn't make any calls to Window Rock—no matter how much she wanted to. For one thing, she was overwhelmed by the monumental task of getting Stuart's financial affairs in order. But even when she had a moment, she still didn't call. She had to prove something to herself. She had to know that it wasn't too late, that she could still walk away from this thing with Johnny Becenti if she really wanted to.

The only problem was that she missed him. She tried for days to attribute the empty feeling she carried around with her to something other than what it really was. She tried to convince herself that she hadn't been with Becenti long enough to feel this lonely without him and that her wanting to see him again would soon go away.

But it didn't. Not in the first week after they'd spent the night together, or the next two. Suddenly, she was well into the fourth week, and in spite of all she could do, her mind kept cataloging bits and pieces of her days under a very large heading called Things She Wanted to Tell Becenti—the funny things and the poignant things, and the exasperating lawyer/police-officer things they would likely argue about but that she knew he would understand.

During the lunch recess that Friday, she went to buy a very belated gift for Gracie's new grandchild, a little girl of singular elegance and beauty—according to her grandmother. The day was sunny and almost warm, so Lillian walked the distance to her favorite baby shop rather than driving her car and then having to find the ever-elusive Santa Fe parking space. With the recent births of Meggie's two children, she'd been in the store often enough for the salespeople to know her by name. There was no doubt that she belonged to a prolific circle of co-workers and family.

"Welcome, Ms. Singer," the middle-aged woman who owned the shop called brightly as Lillian walked in. "I'll be with you in a moment. Something for Tad and Julia today?"

"No," Lillian said, impressed that the woman actually remembered the names of Meggie's little ones. "A newborn—well, she's almost a month old. A baby girl."

"Over there next to the far wall. I've just gotten some lovely things in."

Lillian made her way through the relentlessly charming baby displays to the place the woman had indicated and began browsing. And the shop owner was right. There really were some lovely things for baby girls here. Lillian picked up a tiny white eyelet bonnet with pink satin roses and streamers, smiling as she did so. But the smile faded. She felt such a longing suddenly, when she knew that she had no reason to regret her choice not to marry and have children. She knew perfectly well that there was a lot more to motherhood than buying frilly bonnets, a lot more than she would ever have been willing to give. She was much more suited to being the aunt-by-marriage or the grandmother's boss. She reveled in it, in fact.

She realized then that someone had approached and

stood waiting. She turned around to ask about a tiny pink-and-white outfit that matched the bonnet, but it wasn't the shop owner. It was J. B. Greenleigh.

"Hello, J.B.," Lillian said immediately. She was taken by surprise, but she didn't intend to show it. And if she had been wondering if Stuart actually meant to tell his fiancée that he and Lillian Singer were back "together," she had no doubt now when she saw the expression on the younger woman's face. J.B. looked…tragic and not nearly so sophisticated as she'd been the first and only time Lillian had seen her. She seemed about to say something, but her eyes filled with tears and her mouth trembled.

"J.B—" Lillian began, but the girl abruptly turned away and rushed out of the shop, knocking over a small child mannequin and a stroller full of stuffed animals in the process.

"What in the world?" the shop owner said.

What indeed? Lillian thought. She moved to the window and looked down the street in the direction J.B. had gone, but she was nowhere in sight. Lillian had meant what she said about not lying to Stuart's apparently now ex-fiancée, but she had no time to chase the girl down.

She bought the pink and white outfit and the matching bonnet and waited for them to be gift wrapped. Then she returned to the courthouse for the afternoon session, more than a little disquieted by this arrangement with Stuart. The legal part, she could handle. The weeping child-fiancée on the streets of Santa Fe was something else again.

Thankfully, court adjourned early, and she drove home with a tension headache and a briefcase full of Stuart's financial reports. There was a Navajo Tribal Police vehicle parked in her driveway, and Johnny Becenti sat on the top step of her front porch. He stood and waited for her to get out of the car.

"This is not working," he said without prelude.

She didn't ask what he meant. She *knew* what he meant. She stood there, looking at him, appreciating everything about him. She was so glad to see him, even if he was clearly not happy to be here.

"It's not working, Lillian," he said again. "That Sunday afternoon when I left here—by the time I got back to Window Rock I was sure I'd made a mistake getting involved with you. I was sure I didn't want to see you again. And I stayed sure all that week. By the next week, I suddenly realized you weren't going to call me, regardless of the invitation I put in that note—and I thought that was exactly what I wanted—to be off the hook. So I said it was for the best. I was still saying it yesterday. I even believed it. And then today— Today I—" He stopped and gave a heavy sigh.

This was why the People believed so earnestly in Coyote, the Mischief Maker, she thought. Her weeks of agonizing over the Becenti-Lillian situation—and his—had apparently caught Coyote's undivided attention, and now the Trickster presented them both with exactly what they thought they wanted—a chance to end it once and for all.

But it was a very different matter to reject the Becenti who was standing right here, as opposed to the one out of sight and off doing his duty in Window Rock.

"Say something, damn it!" he said, his exasperation beginning to show.

"All right. How long can you stay?" she asked bluntly.

The question took him completely by surprise—and perhaps her, as well. But then he smiled. She had always liked unsettling him, and it was clear to her that she also liked making him smile. She made a mental note to do both more often.

"You mean now?" he asked when he recovered.

"No, Becenti, I mean next month sometime—of course, *now*."

"You are such a pain in the—"

"Please!" she said. "If you keep saying that, one of these days I'm going to believe it. Are you staying or not?"

"I...think I can manage to stay."

"Oh, good. There's nothing I like better than forcing a man to be where he doesn't want to be."

He reached out and took her briefcase so that there was no barrier between them. "You think I drove all this way because I don't want to be here? What have you got in this thing?" he asked abruptly, holding out the briefcase. "Dead bodies?"

"Actually, yes," she said, smiling into his eyes. She boldly rested both her arms on his shoulders. "I want to tell you something—but I'm afraid you'll think I'm trying to get us engaged."

"Maybe not," he said. "Tell me."

"I...missed you."

He frowned. "Is that the truth?"

"I never lie, Johnny," she said, her mouth just brushing his.

"Have you still got neighbors?"

"I don't know," she murmured, leaning into him. "I haven't seen them since you left."

He let the briefcase fall with a heavy thud, and he pulled her tightly against him as his mouth covered hers.

"Lillian—open the—door," he said between kisses.

"Don't you want to pick the lock?" she teased.

"Open the door, Lillian—"

But he took the key out of her hand and unlocked it himself. He didn't give her time to pick up her discarded briefcase or to put down her purse once they were inside. He all but carried her through the house into the bedroom.

"Tell me again," he said as he tumbled her backward on the bed and lay on top of her. "Tell me you missed me."

"I missed you, Johnny," she whispered against his ear.

He pulled her to a half-sitting position to get her out of her clothes, slinging each freed piece over his shoulder as he went. She tried to help, and when they were both finally, finally undressed, she held out her arms to him.

He came to her quickly, entered her quickly, thrusting

deep. She moaned, reveling in the feel of him inside her. No one had ever given her this kind of pleasure before.

No one.

She needed this. No. She needed him. And she was going to have to be very careful not to ever let him know it.

She closed her eyes, feeling, savoring.

This feels so good—

She loved everything about him. Her hands glided over the smoothness of his hard body.

Song of Solomon, she thought, remembering the love poetry that had nothing to do with her upbringing, only with her desire. *"My beloved is mine and I am his: he feedeth among the lilies...."*

Johnny.

She clung to him, awash in the passion she had for this man. She cried out his name in the final moment, wrapping herself around him until he collapsed against her and lay still.

Becenti held her close, his body sated, but his mind slowly returning to turmoil. He was like some lustful teenage boy. No matter how hard he'd tried, he couldn't rid himself of his "must have" mind-set where Lillian Singer was concerned. He had never expected to be led around like this, to think about her night and day, to remember— everything.

Everything.

But even so, he wasn't blind to the truth of their situation.

This is not working.

"I left the rez because I was ashamed," Lillian said abruptly. She had been silent for so long, he had thought she was asleep. He held her closer, but he didn't say anything. He had asked her the question weeks ago. He hadn't pressed her for the answer then, and he wouldn't now. It was her story to tell in her own way and in her own time—

if she chose to. His obligation was only to listen, and he would do that willingly.

"My father used to train horses for one of the big ranches," she continued. "There wasn't a horse alive he couldn't tame. I was so proud of him. One time, when I was a little girl, my mother let me go with him—to the ranch where he worked. I'd never seen such a place. They had a huge house, and they had water where no water should be—stone pools of it, for swimming and for no reason at all that I could see.

"It was so hot that day, and my father sent me to sit on the patio in the shade. There were all these wind chimes, made of bits of colored glass, tinkling in the breeze. And there was a pool with a fountain. The pool was filled with goldfish—I couldn't believe my eyes. Fish made of *gold*. And there was this latticework roof with vines climbing over it and pots and pots of flowers hanging everywhere— all colors and kinds I'd never seen before. One of the servants had been watering them and everything was still misty and wet—the way it is after a female rain. I thought it was the most beautiful place I'd ever seen. And I was so happy to sit there—cool from the water and dappled with sunshine and shade and smelling those wonderful flowers. I thought white people must truly have magic to know how to make a place like that out of nothing but barren ground.

"But I realized after a few minutes that I wasn't alone. There were some people talking close by, people I couldn't see. They were talking about that dumb Indian who broke the horses. "Such a find," one of them said. Completely undependable, of course—and you couldn't stand down- wind of him—but really good with horses, and ignorant enough to work for practically nothing.

"I was so angry on his behalf, Johnny. He was my father, and there wasn't a horse alive he couldn't tame. And those people were—"

She gave a quiet sigh.

"So I ran to him and I told him what they'd said—about

his being ignorant and undependable, and that he stank. He didn't say anything. I expected him to be angry, too. But he wasn't, not at them. He was angry at me, and when I wouldn't let it be, he hit me—the first and only time he'd ever done that. I didn't quite grasp the true reality of poverty then—that sometimes you have to give up your dignity just to survive. All I knew was that I didn't want to be Navajo anymore. I wanted to have the patio and the pools and the flowers—like them. I wasn't going to learn to weave or herd sheep or any of that. One way or another, I was going to school. I was going to be something big— something that would make people like them have to ask *me* for help. And believe me, *I* wouldn't work for *nothing*—''

She abruptly sat up. "I'm sorry," she said. "I didn't mean to make you listen to me whine about my childhood traumas. It isn't part of our bargain. It's just—you asked me why I left, and I've been thinking about it.''

He reached out to her, but she moved farther away. "You can talk to me, Lillian. Whenever you want.''

She smiled then and caught his hand. "No, I think it's better if we just keep it simple.''

The phone rang, and she got up from the bed and grabbed a robe.

"I'll take it in the kitchen. I need to do some work anyway. Sleep if you want to—'' she called over her shoulder as she hurried out, pulling the door closed behind her.

He lay there in her bed, thinking about the little girl Lillian, hurt and embarrassed on behalf of her father and wanting him to stand up to those people. No, she hadn't understood the reality of being poor, of being a second-class citizen then. She did now, of course, but what she didn't say was how much it still hurt. He knew about that, because he, too, had had a "moment of truth" like hers, as had all of the People, if they had any dealings with the white world. And if he remembered correctly, Lillian's father had died without ever knowing that she had become a successful lawyer and that white people came to her for help.

Keep it simple, he thought. *How am I going to do that, Lillian?*

She was a strong, smart, educated woman. Given recent events, she should know that they didn't stand a chance of maintaining the uncomplicated relationship she envisioned. Even before they had become lovers, they both worried about each other. How "simple" was that?

He sighed heavily. And even now, without knowing what she needed—without knowing *if* she needed anything—he wanted to make things better for her. He wanted to comfort her. Metaphorically speaking, Johnny Becenti wanted desperately to look after Lillian Singer's sheep. And what a joke that was—on them both. He was in a situation most men only dreamed about—great sex with no strings attached, no commitment, no complications. But it was becoming increasingly clear to him that the lack of emotional involvement was going to be difficult at best. Yes, he wanted to make love with her—all the time. But he also wanted to talk to her. He wanted to know about her childhood. He wanted to know what she was feeling and thinking. He had been married for a long time. He didn't know how to behave as if he weren't.

He must have dozed. When he opened his eyes, Lillian was dressed and seated on the side of the bed.

"Johnny, I have to go out for a little while," she said.

"Why?" he asked, whether he had the right to or not. He reached for her, and she lay across his chest for a moment.

"Oh...a problem with a client," she said, sitting up again. "It shouldn't take long. My house is your house, okay? If it's not too late when I get back, I'll take you to this little restaurant I know. They have the best chili rellenos you've ever eaten."

He caught her hand when she was about to get up. "Are you okay?" he asked because she seemed...upset.

"I'm fine," she said. And she smiled and kissed him to show him how fine she was. "Don't get into any trouble while I'm gone."

"You mean don't go outside naked?"

She laughed. "That, too. People *will* talk. They already are, aren't they? On the rez?"

"No, I don't think so. I don't think Toomey felt the need to release any news bulletins."

"Yet," she said, kissing him again. "I've got to go. Try to miss me a little."

"That'll be the day," he said to tease her, and she looked back over her shoulder to grin. He wondered if she had any idea—any idea at all—how much he *didn't* have to try.

Lillian kept looking from the road to the dashboard clock. It was nearly midnight and it was going to rain. She was in a hurry to get home. She should have told Becenti that she was going to see Stuart, that she had no choice but to go, and she hadn't. She wasn't quite sure why. She hadn't lied, exactly—it was true that she was having a problem with a client—but she hadn't been forthcoming, either. In keeping with their arrangement, she should have just *said* and left Becenti to understand or not, as he so chose. If she had, she wouldn't be feeling quite so devious and guilty now. She hated it, because it wasn't in her nature to be either, and she'd already decided that when she got home, she would tell Becenti exactly where she'd been and what she'd been doing.

The lengthy session with Stuart had left her exhausted. He was so ill from his most recent chemotherapy, and he was unreasonable and demanding. It had taken every bit of self-control she had not to walk out. For the first time, she thought that perhaps he was right not to put J.B. through this.

She abruptly rolled down the window because the aroma of the take-out order she had sitting on the front seat suddenly seemed overpowering. As she turned into the long drive to her house, she could see that the lights were still on—but the Navajo Tribal Police vehicle was gone. There was another car parked in the driveway—something small and new and black.

She had no idea who it could be—unless Gracie had had another family crisis, and someone was transporting Fred to his favorite cat motel. And she had no idea where Johnny could have gone, short of another summons via the ever-faithful Toomey.

No. He'd probably gone to get something to eat, she abruptly decided. Her cupboard and refrigerator were essentially bare, and she was late getting back. He couldn't live on the mere promise of chili rellenos forever.

But she was still puzzled about the other car, and she paused to look at it more closely on her way to the front door. She still didn't recognize it, and she didn't see anyone about. Which must mean that whoever it was was inside.

She was too tired to worry about that, but she did let herself in quietly. She didn't hear anything. She stood listening intently, the front door standing wide-open behind her in case she needed to retreat in a hurry. She made no attempt to call out the way the unsuspecting woman-in-peril always did on television and in the movies. She'd always considered that particular response the absolute height of stupidity. If there was anyone here, she intended to know their whereabouts before they knew hers.

She kept listening, and she finally heard a faint noise. It came from the kitchen and it sounded like someone... sniffing. She set her briefcase and the box of chili rellenos down and walked silently forward until she could see through the windows in the separating wall.

She abruptly stopped. J.B. Greenleigh sat at the kitchen table, dabbing her eyes with one of Lillian's yellow tissues.

Lillian moved quickly through the house to confront her. "How did you get in here?" she demanded.

J.B. jumped violently, apparently too immersed in her own misery to have heard Lillian open the front door. Her eyes were puffy and red from crying. All in all, she looked terrible.

"How did you get in here?" Lillian said again.

"I took the key Stuart had," J.B. said, her voice and her face sullen.

But Lillian was *not* the intruder here. "Stuart gave me that key back."

"I had a copy made and I didn't tell him, all right!"

"No, it's not all right! What are you doing here?"

"I'm not running from you anymore, that's for sure."

"Well, you can go do it someplace else. And while you're at it—"

"I told him," J.B. interrupted. "I *told* him."

"Told who? What are you talking about?"

"Captain Becenti didn't know about you and Stuart. He was really surprised—just like I was. Up until now, I've only heard about women like you—women who would go from one man's bed to another—in the same night."

"J.B.," Lillian said with a patience she didn't begin to feel. "Stuart Dennison is my client—"

"*Client?* Oh, please. He may be your 'client,' but it's got nothing to do with your *legal* services—"

"That's enough!" Lillian said. "What did you tell Becenti?"

"I told him the same thing Stuart told *me*. I told him the two of you were back together. I told him I saw you go into Stuart's house tonight. And I told him *he* was an even bigger fool than I was—"

"Are you out of your mind! Pay attention, J.B. Stuart is my—"

The room suddenly tilted, and Lillian reached out blindly to catch the edge of the kitchen counter. Her peripheral vision disappeared and she was dimly aware of a shriek as she pitched forward into the darkness that used to be a Spanish-tile floor.

Chapter Ten

"Who are you?"

"I'm a doctor," he said.

"You aren't paying attention," Lillian said. "The question was who, 'not what.'"

He laughed. "I think you've returned to the living, Ms. Singer. I need you to lie still for a little while longer—"

"How did I get in here?" she asked, because she was lying on the living-room couch and she didn't remember making the trip. The last thing she remembered was...

She didn't really remember a last thing, and she abruptly tried to sit up.

"Wait, wait, wait—I'm not done with your head," he said, putting his hands on her shoulders to make her lie back down again. "You hit the floor pretty hard. You've got a nice goose egg on your forehead, and a small laceration. I'm going to close that with a butterfly, okay? When was your last tetanus shot?"

"Last year—before I went on vacation to Mexico," she

said, encouraged by the fact that she could remember something, at least. "Who *are* you?" she asked again.

"Junie Blair's first cousin," he said. "She thought she was going to have to bury your body in the flower bed, so she called me."

"Junie Blair?"

"She prefers to be called J.B."

"I don't blame her— Ow!" she said, because of the pressure he used to make the "butterfly" adhesive stick.

"Sorry."

"Does Junie Blair's first cousin have a name?" she asked.

"Why? Do you want to sue me?"

"Oh, great. The first cousin does lawyer jokes."

"It helps in my line of work, believe me. Any idea why you fainted?"

"Fainted?" Lillian said.

"According to J.B., you toppled like you'd been hit on the head with an anvil."

"I can't— I don't remember fainting."

"Ever fainted before?"

"Never," she said. She did know that with certainty.

"Any chance you could be pregnant?"

"Pregnant!"

"Pregnancy can be a major cause of first-time fainting," he said. "And Junie seems to think you and Stuart Dennison—"

"Junie is gravely mistaken."

"When was your last period?"

"None of your business."

"And how do you feel now?"

"Like I'm going to throw up—but that's because of the chili rellenos."

"Try to aim for the floor and not me, okay?" he said, unimpressed.

"I don't know what's wrong with me," she murmured,

reaching up to gingerly touch the bandage he'd just put on her forehead.

"Well, these things happen," he said, "particularly in highly charged emotional situations."

"What?" Lillian said vaguely.

He didn't explain his remark. "How long since you've eaten?"

"I don't know."

"What about the chili things?"

"I didn't eat those—I was riding in the car with them. They're over there in that box," she added because of his skeptical look. "I guess the last time I ate was lunchtime. No, not lunchtime. I went to buy a baby gift during the lunch recess. Court was ready to convene when I got back."

"Well, okay, then. If you're sure it can't be pregnancy, going that long without food and having an argument with Junie Blair sounds like it could be faint-inducing to me."

"I wasn't arguing with Junie Blair. I was trying to find out—" She didn't quite remember what she'd been trying to find out.

"Whatever," he said. "The point is, you need to see your own doctor and get checked out on Monday—sooner if you have any problems—headache, changes in your vision, mental confusion, *vomiting*. As for right now, is there anyone who could stay with you tonight?"

"No," she said. *That* she remembered, too. Becenti wasn't here now—thanks to J.B. And that was what she'd been trying to find out. What J. B. Greenleigh had said to Johnny Becenti.

"Then I'm going to admit you to the hospital overnight for observation."

"No. I don't need a hospital."

"You're not the doctor here, Ms. Singer. *You* are the hotshot lawyer—which is why I'm not about to go off and leave you unattended. I've never had a malpractice suit and I don't intend to start with somebody like you."

"You think trying to admit me to a hospital against my will won't get you sued?"

"I think the obvious knot on your head, and the laceration, and the escalating mental wobbling I'm now witnessing will get me off—particularly since I have a someone here to verify it."

"Look. I don't want to go to a hospital. And I don't have anyone to stay with me. My family is in Arizona."

"No friends?"

"What? You think lawyers have *friends?*"

"I'll stay with her," J.B. said from somewhere in the room.

"No, you won't," Lillian said, trying to sit up again. A wave of dizziness made her immediately lie back down again.

"It's me or the hospital," J.B. said. "You don't have much of a choice."

"I don't want—" Lillian began.

"Please!" J.B. said. "I shouldn't have come here the way I did. It's my fault you got hurt. I want to stay. I owe you that."

"Excuse me," the doctor said to Lillian. "I'm going to take Junie into the kitchen, and we're going to talk about you. I'll be right back."

"I'd prefer to listen," Lillian said.

"I'm sure you would," he acknowledged, but he left the room with "Junie" anyway.

Lillian sighed heavily. She knew that the question about the possibility of her being pregnant was just part of a routine screening checklist for females of a certain age who abruptly lost consciousness. His asking didn't mean that he thought it likely. It was on the list and he had to ask, and that was all there was to it.

Or he was trying to find out about her and Stuart because he was J.B.'s cousin.

Oh, great, she thought. She wondered if rampant paranoia was a side effect of fainting. The man may be a Greenleigh relative, but he was also a doctor, one highly concerned about being sued.

She closed her eyes and tried to remember when her last period had been. Today was the twelfth. She'd had a period the first of the month—the *previous* month.

I couldn't be pregnant, she thought. *Not at my age—and even if I could—I used birth control. It's ridiculous. I've been under a lot of stress.*

But stress wasn't the only thing she'd been under, and her periods were hardly ever late. She knew immediately that there was only one thing of which she could be certain. If she *were* pregnant, she couldn't be pregnant by Stuart Dennison.

And where was Becenti, anyway? It wasn't like him to just leave for no reason. At least, she considered it no reason. Perhaps he thought J.B.'s mistaken announcement of Lillian's return to Stuart Dennison's bed signified the truth—in which case he should *still* be here. She and Johnny Becenti didn't have that kind of relationship. "No strings" meant no jealousy and no recriminations. They had more or less agreed that there was no place for it. He shouldn't *care* if whatever J.B. had told him was true.

But he would—because he was Johnny Becenti and he'd promised not to intrude.

She raised her head to see if there were any folded pieces of paper lying around, anything propped against the ringmaster bank.

The only thing she found was that moving around made her head hurt worse. And she still had that queasiness that had begun when she was in the car. Most of all, she felt like crying, a really self-indulgent episode, sitting at the kitchen table with a whole box of yellow tissues like J. B. Greenleigh.

What is wrong with me? she thought. It wasn't in her nature to whine, either—to anyone else or to herself. But she was remembering things better, she suddenly realized.

She remembered that J.B. had been in her kitchen when she got home; that was something, at least.

She closed her eyes, and then immediately opened them because J.B. had returned.

"Lillian," she said. She took a deep breath as if she needed it to shore up her courage. She was so *young*.

"I understand that you don't want me here," she said. "I...don't blame you. But you see, I love Stuart with all my heart, and if anything happened to you, especially if it was my fault—well, he'd never forgive me. I couldn't stand that. I'm not going to leave you by yourself. I won't stay in the house—I'll stay in the car. My cousin told me what to do and I'm going to check on you every hour or so. I mean, you can't lock me out—I've got a key." She gave a bit of a smile. "So that's how it is," she concluded, trying to sound firm.

Lillian looked at her. She was beginning to see what Stuart must have seen in this young woman—a certain intrinsic kindness and a complete lack of guile.

"Oh, for God's sake," Lillian said, giving a sharp sigh. "Stay. And you don't have to wait in the car. I'm not *that* crass. And stop looking at me like you think I'm going to bite you."

"Oh, I'm not afraid you'll bite—I'm afraid you'll faint again."

"I think that's pretty hard to do lying down," Lillian said. "You're not going to hover, are you? I really hate hovering."

"Well, I thought I'd make some tea—and some toast. How about that?"

"That would be...great," Lillian decided. She made another attempt to sit up.

"No, no," J.B. said. "I'll get it. I'm sure I can find the tea and the bread. And believe it or not, I know a toaster when I see one. I'm going to go tell Lawrence he can go now."

Lawrence came in to make a final assessment before he

left. "You can do whatever you feel like doing," he said, checking her pupils again with a small penlight. "But don't get too physical. Just take it easy, go slow. I'll check back by tomorrow—and see if I can drag J.B. away."

"Is she always this...fixated?"

"As long as I've known her, and particularly when it involves people she cares about. She really cares about Stuart."

Bump on her head or not, Lillian immediately recognized the subtle reproof. J.B. Greenleigh even cared enough about Stuart Dennison to watch over his alleged mistress.

"Stuart loves her," Lillian said, because it was a personal observation and not a lawyer-client privilege.

"Well, he doesn't act like it. So. That's it, then. It's been a pleasure to approximate your lacerated edges. Don't be in a hurry to take the butterfly off. Try not to get it wet when you wash your hair. Come and see me if you have any signs of an infection—redness, drainage, hot to the touch. Here's my card. Feel better soon—and don't get any wild notions about lawsuits or having my cousin arrested. Her heart's in the right place. Really."

"Thank you," Lillian said. "You know where to send the bill."

"Oh, this visit was a courtesy call. The next one is when I stick it to you."

Lillian waited until he'd gone before she tried sitting up again. The dizziness was much less pronounced this time. She was comfortably upright in the corner of the couch when J.B. returned with the tea and toast. She found that she was hungry in spite of the nausea, and she ate all the toast J.B. had made for her. She sipped the tea for a time before she decided she was ready to talk.

"J.B.," she began.

"Do you want more toast?" J.B. interrupted. "I can make some, if you do—"

"No, I don't want any more toast. What I want is for you to tell me what Becenti said when...he left. But before you do that, I want to tell *you* something. I don't care what Stuart said—he and I are *not* back together.''

"You aren't?''

"No.''

"I saw you go into his house.''

"Yes, you did. I'm doing some very extensive legal work for him. He insisted on talking about it tonight, and I went there to see him. Period.''

"Are you saying he lied to me?''

"I'm saying that he and I are not lovers.''

"He wouldn't tell me something like that if it wasn't true,'' she insisted. "Why would he?''

"You'll have to ask him.''

"I don't believe he lied to me.''

"You'd rather believe he was cheating on you instead?''

"No, of course not. I just—'' She sighed heavily and stared at the throw rugs. "He seems like a very nice man,'' she offered after a moment. "Captain Becenti,'' she added. "He was nice to me, anyway. When I got here, I was sort of upset.''

"Sort of?''

J.B. sighed. "Okay. I was bawling my head off. I was acting like a fool.''

"And you told him that Stuart and I were back together.''

"No,'' she said.

"No?''

"Well, not then. I used the key to get in—I don't know why I didn't think someone would be here. The police car was right in the driveway. He...was sitting at the kitchen table drinking coffee. He made me come in and sit down—and he found me a box of tissues.''

"And he said?''

She sighed again. "Nothing.''

"Nothing?''

"No. He didn't ask me anything. He just sat there and drank his coffee while I cried—but he wasn't indifferent or anything. It was more that he was just letting me do what I needed to do right then. And later he offered me a glass of water, and he asked if there was anything he could do to help me. I told him I was going to wait here for you because I wasn't running away anymore. He said it was his experience that running away never solved anything. Then…''

"What?" Lillian prompted when J.B. didn't go on.

"Lillian, you're supposed to rest and not be upset. Lawrence said—"

"I'm the best judge of what's upsetting and what isn't. I want to know this."

J.B. gave a heavy sigh. "Then…I just said it. I said Stuart wouldn't marry me because he was back with you. I said he'd called the wedding off because of it. I said you were with him right now—I saw you go into his house by the back way. And I said if he was waiting for you for a personal reason instead of a legal one, he was an even bigger fool than I was."

"What did Becenti say?"

"Nothing. Well, he said if you didn't get back tonight, I was to make sure the door was locked when I left."

"That's it? Was he upset—or angry?"

"No, he was—"

"What? He was what?" Lillian said, losing patience at having to pry the details out of this woman. One would have thought that it was J.B. who had been hit on the head.

"He was sad," J.B. said finally. "Really…sad."

They looked at each other across the room, and Lillian couldn't be kind.

"Then you have whatever revenge you wanted," she said quietly. "The only thing is—you hurt the wrong person."

Chapter Eleven

"Winston Tsosie called," Mary Skeets said.

Becenti braced himself against her intrusion into his office. It was a tremendous strain—trying to seem at one with the universe so as not to make Mary Skeets suspicious. But Mary Skeets was Mary Skeets—and had been for as long as he'd known her. At this particular moment, she was full of information, and while he knew that she was going to share it eventually—at her own discretion and in her own good time—the very fact that she had brought this particular message personally instead of putting it on a While You Were Out memo, could only bode ill for somebody. Unhappily, he thought that he knew exactly who that somebody must be.

He shuffled the papers on his desk, but he knew she was watching him closely. He also knew that she had decided at some point that there was something bothering him, something more than the loss of his wife, his health and very nearly his career. For the Navajo, the only way to happiness was to walk in beauty. The only way to beauty was to be in harmony with all things. Mary Skeets had clearly decided he was *not* in harmony—again—just as she'd apparently decided that it was her duty to find out the reason why.

"What did Winston want?" he asked, because it seemed that no subsequent information would be forthcoming.

"He didn't say."

"I don't think it would have been out of order for you to ask him, do you?" In spite of all he could do, the remark was barely civil.

"I did ask. He wouldn't say. He just said he wanted you to come to the men's mission house. Today."

"It's not some trouble with Jack Begaye, is it?"

"No, Jack's behaving. He's too busy with Meggie and the children to get into anything."

That'll be the day, Becenti thought, because Jack Begaye had in the past managed to get into all kinds of trouble simply by being Jack Begaye—and because Becenti's cynicism had blossomed of late. Regardless of the apparent success of Jack's marriage to Meggie, Becenti no longer believed in the power of a woman to bring out the best in a man—if he ever had.

"Then have you heard anybody say what it is Winston might want?"

"No. He seemed worried, though. *I* think it's got something to do with Dolly Singer."

He looked up from the papers. "Dolly Singer?"

Mary shrugged. "That's what I think."

He wanted very much to ask her why she thought that, but he didn't. It was a very short jump from Dolly Singer to her daughter Lillian, and he did *not* want to be led in that direction by any pointed questions from Mary Skeets. He strongly suspected that Toomey had told her about the weekend in Santa Fe after all, because Mary managed to work Lillian's name into too many conversations for her not to have gotten a hint of something.

He didn't say anything else, but Mary made no attempt to leave.

He looked up at her. "What?" he asked pointedly.

"Are you going to go now?"

"No," he said, looking back at the papers.

She still didn't leave. After a moment or two, she very politely cleared her throat.

"Mary, what!" he said. And he still had to hand it to her. Unlike most of his subordinates, she didn't cower because he'd raised his voice. She didn't even blink.

"Well, it's just that now would be a good time, sir. You've got to see the BIA people at two. And then after that, there's that tribal council thing. And who knows how long that will last. Winston Tsosie is old. It's not good for him to have to wait."

"Thank you, Mary. I'll keep that in mind."

"Sir—"

"Mary, I'm busy!"

"Well, not *that* busy," he thought she said on her way out—again. It was flagrant insubordination on her part, but out of the need to hide his inharmonious state, he let it go.

He gave a heavy sigh and rubbed the point between his eyes that hurt. Mary Skeets was right, of course. Now was the best time. The only problem was that he didn't want to go out looking for new aggravation when he had quite enough in his life already. He preferred the relative seclusion of his office to deliberately accosting someone who would make him think about Lillian Singer. He was determined not to think about her—and had been for weeks now. He had been right to leave her house so abruptly, and he knew that because she'd made no attempt to contact him since. He could only assume that all was well with her and Stuart Dennison. He could only assume that she was happy. He might be happy himself, or at least more in harmony, if he could stop remembering the time with her Santa Fe. But the harder he tried, the more it caught him off guard. He could go for hours without once thinking about her, and then suddenly he was with her again. He could taste her, feel her, smell that sweet woman smell of hers, so much so that he physically ached for her. Sometimes he woke up in the middle of the night, wanting her. He missed her, damn it. Exasperating, maddening creature that she was, he *missed* her. And he was so tired of pretending that he didn't.

He got up from his desk, leaving the pile of papers lying. He would go see Winston, because he couldn't do otherwise. He liked and respected the old man. And if Winston needed something done, then, in spite of his personal problems, Becenti would try to do it.

He left the law-enforcement building with Mary Skeets's obvious blessing—after he'd made a point of telling her his destination. He was ashamed of how careful he'd been of late to make sure Mary knew where he could be reached, ashamed because it had nothing to do with his official capacity and everything to do with the fading hope of a telephone call from Santa Fe.

The weather was beautiful—warm and sunny. He looked up at the sky. There was no sign of rain, but the monsoon season would begin soon, an event that always left him feeling encouraged, even during the worst times of his life. He took his time driving to the mission just to savor the day. If he didn't have much in the way of harmony, he was at least working on it. He tried not to speculate about why Winston Tsosie would be worried about Dolly Singer.

The mission was quiet when he got there; no vehicles around except the pickup truck Jack Begaye drove. All the residents seemed to be out for the day. In fact, the only person he saw was Jack—and he was in the process of leaving.

"Captain Becenti," Jack said, clearly surprised. "Something I can do for you?"

"No, I'm looking for Winston," Becenti said.

"Oh, yeah. He's at the corral—trying to decide what to

do with one of Meggie's horses. It's up that way. I think he's expecting you.''

He's expecting me, Becenti thought as he walked along the path Jack had indicated. He didn't know if he liked the sound of that or not.

The path wound through a stand of piñon pine. The air was heavy with a dusty pine scent, and the birds were singing. The walk was pleasant enough, but he didn't have to go far. He almost immediately ran into Winston standing in the shade among the trees.

"*Yah-ta-hey,* my grandfather," he began respectfully, but the old man held up his hand for silence.

"We need to stay here," Winston whispered. "We don't want to get in the way."

"In the way of what?" Becenti asked in a normal voice, an act that clearly unsettled the old man. Becenti didn't say anything else. He looked in the direction that had Winston's rapt attention.

The old man was looking at the corral. Someone—a woman wearing a man's shirt, jeans, and leather chaps— was seated on a kitchen chair in the middle of it, and a dappled mare stood slightly off to one side, its head held low. The woman was sitting with her legs folded up tailor-fashion, and her back was to them. She apparently held something in each fist. He could hear the woman talking, but not what she said. Every now and then the horse lifted its head enough to look in the woman's direction.

Becenti glanced at Winston.

"The mare lost her foal," the old man said quietly. "She is grieving too long. She ain't sick, but she won't eat nothing."

"So what's happening?" Becenti asked. "Who is that?" The chair thing was a new one on him. He couldn't tell much about the woman from their position, except that her hair was dark and she was probably Navajo—a friend of Meggie's, he supposed.

"She's telling the mare that there is some apple waiting

in her hand—but she must come for it," Winston said. "Choose the apple or choose to die—whichever she needs to do."

"How long has she been sitting there like that?"

"All morning. See how close the mare stands? When she started, that horse was down on the ground."

Becenti was duly impressed by the woman's patience, but not enough to follow her example. "Winston—"

"Now is not a good time for talking, my son. If we mess this up, she's going to come over here and bust both our butts."

Becenti frowned, but he didn't say anything else. As much as he would have liked to pretend otherwise, at the moment, he had nothing more important to do—tribal police captain or not. He stood watching with Winston. The horse gave a low rumble. The woman kept talking. The horse tossed its head and took a tentative step forward. The woman fell silent then, still holding her fist up, perfectly motionless. The horse blew and tossed its head, then stretched out its neck toward the woman's fist. The woman made no effort to move her hand closer. After a moment, the horse took another step forward, and another until it could reach the woman's fist, nudging and nibbling at it until she opened it and revealed the piece of apple in her palm.

Winston made a soft sound of approval as the horse took it. He looked at Becenti. "She has the way with horses," he said. "Like her father."

The woman unfolded her legs and leaned forward to press her cheek against the horse's soft nose. Becenti could see her profile now. He could recognize her now, and it hit him hard. It took all he had not to walk toward her, and then all he had not to walk away.

Lillian.

The sun was shining on her hair—she was so beautiful, and it occurred to him she never seemed to realize it. He should have told her when he'd had the chance. He should have told her a lot of things when he'd had the chance. He could see her smile. He could *feel* it. Nothing had changed for him. He still wanted her, and—God forbid—needed her. And he hated it.

"What is she doing here?" he asked abruptly, afraid of the intensity of his response. "And don't tell me she came all this way to look after Meggie's horse."

"She came because Dolly went and got her—brought her to stay here with Jack and Meggie and the children for a couple of days. Dolly didn't like the way she was acting up there in Santa Fe."

"What do you mean?"

"Dolly thinks Lillian has got some kind of trouble and she won't say what the trouble is—because she's Lillian and she thinks she don't want no help from nobody."

"Maybe Dolly is wrong," Becenti said, willing Lillian to look in his direction.

But he had no idea what he would do if she turned and saw him. It was better, he supposed, that she was so engrossed in hand-feeding the grieving horse.

"If there wasn't some trouble, I'm thinking Dolly couldn't get her to come here," Winston said. "Not the way she likes Santa Fe."

Becenti had nothing to say to that. He had nothing to say at all. He turned abruptly and would have walked back down the path in the direction he'd come, if Winston hadn't stood in his way.

"I'm thinking maybe you could help her even if she don't want it," the old man said. "Like she helped you."

Becenti stepped around him and kept walking. He couldn't help Lillian. Stuart Dennison was the only one who could do that.

He went back to the law-enforcement building, considerably less cheerful than when he'd left it. He had the meeting with the Bureau of Indian Affairs people—who wanted more cooperation from the tribal police but didn't grasp that the cooperation had to be reciprocal. He was late and even less cheerful when he arrived for the tribal council meeting, and halfway through the proceedings, he discovered that certain detailed statistical information was required of him, which he hadn't brought along. He immediately called Mary Skeets.

"Lucas Singer is working on that," she advised him.

"Well, get it," he said impatiently.

"He's on vacation, Captain, and he took it with him. You want me to go to his house?"

Becenti gave a sharp sigh. "No. I'm closer to him than you are. I'll go to his house." He had managed to avoid Lillian this morning, and he didn't want to talk to any of her relatives. But he had little choice. The tribal council wanted what it wanted.

There were no vehicles in the Singer driveway when he arrived, except the old decrepit truck Lucas complained was impossible to keep running. Becenti was encouraged by that—by the fact that there was no sporty little car from Santa Fe, not by the possibility that he'd made the trip for nothing. He got out and went around to the back, rapping sharply on the screen door and then inspecting some unusual wind chimes on the patio while he waited—parts from a computer hard drive, he thought. When he turned to knock again, Lillian stood on the other side of the screen door. She gave him no time to be surprised.

"Take one of these," she said, pushing open the door with her foot.

He saw immediately that "one of these" meant one of the two children she carried in her arms. He took little redheaded Julia, because she was already reaching for him. Meggie and Jack's daughter didn't seem to mind being handed over in the least, and he didn't mind holding her, not really. Neither of the children was a stranger to him.

"Lillian—" he said, but she abruptly turned and went in the opposite direction, leaving him standing. "Lillian?" he called as she disappeared down the hall and into another room with the remaining child. "Lillian!"

"What!" she yelled back. That was followed by a yelp of pain and the loud clanging of metal—and a word best not said in front of small children, even if they weren't talking much yet.

He looked at Julia. "All right," he said to her. "We're going in. *You* get to be my backup."

She grinned around the fingers she had in her mouth.

"Lillian?" he called again, carrying Julia down the hall. The house smelled of baking bread and roasting meat and some other entirely wonderful food aromas he couldn't quite identify.

Lillian was in the kitchen, holding the baby boy and trying to do something with one of the four pots that steamed and bubbled on the stove. A pot lid still wobbled upside down on the floor.

"Don't just stand there," she said. "Do something!"

"I thought I was," he said, glancing at Julia. "You need a pot holder," he suggested, because she was about to run afoul of another hot lid.

"Oh, thank you very much, Becenti. Just look at this— I don't know what to do with all these *things!*"

"Well, give me the boy," he said, not certain if little Tad Begaye was one of the "things" or not. "*Yah-ta-hey*, Tad. How are you doing, son?" he asked the little one as Lillian handed him over.

Not too well, he decided from the expression on Tad's face. The boy was only seconds away from bawling, and Becenti had no idea what to do about it. He was reasonably comfortable around children—he'd had to be in his line of work—but he wasn't a parent. He opted for trying to talk Tad out of it, soothing the boy—soothing both children in case this kind of thing was catching—in quiet Navajo. Surely, they must understand some words. Jack Begaye was their father and Winston Tsosie, their adopted grandfather.

It seemed to be working for the moment, and he turned his attention back to Lillian.

"Where's Lucas? I need to see him."

"He's not here," she said without turning around.

"Where is he?"

She gave him a look this time, and surprisingly, she answered.

"—cut his hand while he was working on that old truck. Lucas and Sloan took him to the clinic to get some stitches."

"Who cut his hand?" he asked, because she said the name into one of the pots.

"*Will* cut his hand—you know, my nephew by marriage—the budding *hataalii*—the one who lives here. I said I'd watch the kids, but I forgot Sloan was doing this—this—*food* thing. I don't know what to do with all this stuff!"

He didn't understand the problem. And of course he knew who Will was *and* that the boy was studying with Eddie Nez to become a medicine man. It was he, Becenti, who had negotiated the community-service sentence for Will Baron when he had gotten himself into trouble by agreeing to haul liquor onto the reservation to pay for his apprenticeship. Unfortunately, Eddie Nez's reputation as a healer had long ago been usurped by his reputation as a bootlegger.

"Turn off the burners," he said abruptly, because it seemed he was going to have to get involved in this cooking thing or put out a fire. And in spite of everything, he couldn't keep from smiling.

"I'd like to know what is so da—darn funny!"

"You are," he said. "You know, only a lawyer could make a big home-cooked meal sound like a major shortcoming."

"It's not a big home-cooked meal. It's one of Sloan's nostalgia dinners. She does this every so often. She gets hungry for Southern food and she cooks all these foreign dishes—I don't even know what half these things are. Sloan cooks all this—" she waved her hand over the pots "—and she scares the hell out of Lucas every time she does it."

She abruptly stopped. He stood there holding both children, still trying hard to understand.

"Your brother is afraid of Southern cooking," he said finally.

"*No*," she said in exasperation. "He's scared it means something."

"Like what?"

"Like she's had enough of living on the rez with him and she's so homesick she's going back to North Carolina."

"They've been married a long time, Lillian."

"Yes, but it doesn't keep him from getting that look."

"What look?"

"The look he had when he was a little boy and got shipped off to the BIA boarding school. The look he had when the white woman anthropologist dumped him."

The children were growing heavy, and he sat down at the table with a child on each knee. He didn't know about Lucas Singer's boarding-school look, but he did know about the white-woman-anthropologist one. Becenti had come as close to watching a man self-destruct as he ever wanted to come during that episode of Lucas Singer's life, his own recent plunge into self-pity and despair notwithstanding.

"What did you want with Lucas?" Lillian asked. "He's supposed to be on vacation."

There was just enough emphasis on the word "supposed" to annoy him even more than he already was, because he was here for a legitimate reason, one well apart from wanting to see her or holding Begaye babies.

"It's important," he said.

"I'm sure it is. You look like hell, by the way. What's the matter, Becenti, aren't you sleeping?"

"I'm sleeping fine," he said, even though it wasn't precisely the truth. Sometimes he didn't sleep "fine." Sometimes he woke before daylight, thinking about her.

They stared at each other. She was the one who looked

so tired—aside from being upset—and he realized that she didn't want him to see it, because she abruptly turned away.

"I *hate* cooking," she said, moving to take a very large pan of bread rolls out of the oven—without first making sure that she had some place cleared to set it down. It ended up more or less on top of two pots. "I don't know what's keeping everybody. *Somebody* should be back by now."

"So where are Meggie and Jack?"

"They went to get my mother and Winston Tsosie. Sloan doesn't do a nostalgia dinner halfway— You're not leaving, are you?" she asked in alarm, apparently because he stood.

"Yes," he said, surprised.

"No, don't go!"

"You've got everything under control—"

"No, I don't! I have to feed Tad and Julia. I can't feed two children at once."

"Trust me, Lillian, it's done all the time—"

"What if Julia starts crying or something? What if they *both* start crying? You have to help me! I can't— It's— I'm just not used to this, okay? I don't know anything about little children. I don't know anything about all this foreign food and ovens and bread— Stop laughing at me! Are you going to stay or not!"

"What is the matter with you? I've seen you cook fry bread on an oil drum. I've seen you tear somebody apart in the courtroom. If you can handle that, you can handle two little kids and four pots. This damsel in distress thing isn't like you."

"Well, I can't help that— And you stop laughing, too," she said abruptly to the children, coming close enough to give them both a kiss. "Poor babies. Stuck with addled old Auntie Lillian—and crabby old Becenti."

"Watch it," he said. "Crabby old Becenti is all you've got."

She laughed, a lighthearted and altogether pleasant sound he immediately realized he'd been starved to hear. But their eyes met, and her laughter ended. For a moment, he thought she was about to cry, and he'd seen her do that before, too.

"Does that mean you're going to stay?" she said, fiddling with a pot that didn't have a bread pan on it.

"Just to get the children fed. I have things I have to do—"

"Great!" she said, cutting off his self-declared importance. "What do you think they can eat?"

Not much in Tad's case, they soon realized. He was only six months old and he was breast-fed. Lillian eventually located the bottle Meggie had brought for him in the refrigerator. All in all, feeding two children *and* getting out of the tribal council meeting was more trying than he'd anticipated, but eventually it was done.

"I'm wondering who fed who?" Lillian said at one point, because he was wearing as much of the sweet-potato dish as they'd decided was suitable for Julia to consume.

"About six of one, half a dozen of the other," he said. "Actually, the sweet-potato thing was really good. Sloan's an excellent cook."

"I'll tell her you said that."

He had assumed that children, once fed, went to sleep, but that was obviously not the case. There was still the matter of washing faces and hands, changing clothes and diapering, and Lillian singing more times than he wanted to count, "Stand By Me." Or at least he thought it was "Stand By Me."

"Don't you know something *else?*" he asked at one point.

"You're just going to have to suffer," she said. "You're lucky it's me singing it and not Winston. Besides which, it's a Baron family tradition—singing the babies to sleep with old songs."

"Sort of like the Navajo, I guess," he said to keep the conversation going. Regardless of her slightly off-key singing, he preferred talking to being completely ignored.

"Exactly. Meggie says the Baron lullabies are usually

circa World War II torch songs, but "Stand By Me" works for these two."

And so it did. Both children were soon asleep, Julia on a low twin bed in the Singer spare bedroom and Tad on his cradle board. There was no sign of anyone in the family returning, but even so, he knew he was free to go now.

He helped Lillian put most of the "nostalgia" food into the refrigerator and wash the few dirty dishes that had accumulated instead. And when that was done, he still didn't leave. He sat down at the kitchen table, and after a moment's hesitation, Lillian sat down as well.

"We aren't going to talk about it, are we?" he asked quietly.

"No," she said. He could feel the effort it took for her to look at him.

"Why not?"

"If you'd wanted to talk, you wouldn't have left Santa Fe the way you did."

"No strings, no commitment, no complications. How much room does that leave for talking?"

She didn't answer him.

"So you and Stuart are doing okay now?"

She didn't answer that question, either. Once again he thought she was going to cry.

"What's wrong? Tell me," he said.

"Nothing," she said tonelessly.

"I never lie, Johnny. I wonder who said that?"

She made an attempt to get up, but he caught her arm.

"It's not your problem," she said, trying to pull free.

"But there is one."

"No," she insisted. "Let me go, Johnny."

"Look at me," he said. "Lillian—"

She gave a quiet sigh and forced her eyes to meet his. He immediately saw the plea for help in them, and the desperate wish to be left alone.

"Did you think nothing mattered to me but going to bed with you?" he asked. "Did you think I could be with you like that and not care anything about you? Or is that the way it was for you? Tell me. I'm trying to understand what it was we had.''

"We didn't have anything, Johnny. Nothing."

"That's not true and you know it."

"Johnny, please! You're the one who left."

"What choice did I have? The girl said you and Stuart Dennison were back together. You made all the rules and I told you I wouldn't intrude."

"Then what is *this* all about?"

"It's about the way you look at me. Do you think I can't tell something is wrong? Maybe I can help. If nothing else, I owe it to you to at least try. Tell me what's wrong with you. I told you before. You can talk to me."

"No."

"Lillian—!"

"No!"

"Are you in some kind of legal trouble?"

"No, I'm not."

"Then—" He abruptly stopped. "What happened to your forehead?"

She immediately reached up to touch the new scar that was clearly visible. "Nothing. I bumped my head."

"Dennison didn't do that, did he?"

Her incredulous look did a great deal to reassure him.

"Sorry," he said. "If you won't say, then I have to guess."

"What you have to do is mind your own business."

"Lillian, neither one of us is particularly good at that. Even if we hadn't been lovers."

"You're the one who hid out in a hogan for over a year," she said evenly.

"And you're the one hiding now."

He heard a car door slam, then another, and then two more. All the family must have returned.

"Lillian—" he began, trying to squeeze in one more question before they came inside. He wanted to know if he could see her again, talk to her, and he wanted it badly enough to risk asking.

But she got up and went to hold open the back screen door.

The injured Will came in first, holding a heavily bandaged hand carefully upright, and then Sloan and Lucas, and eventually Jack and Meggie. And, finally, Dolly Singer and Winston.

"What happened to the dinner?" Will wanted to know. "Hey, Lillian, you and Captain Becenti didn't eat it all, did you?"

"It's in the refrigerator, Bottomless Pit," Lillian said, glancing at Becenti. "The kids are asleep," she said to Meggie and Jack.

"You're going to stay and eat with us, aren't you?" Sloan asked Becenti. "It won't take long to reheat—"

"No," Becenti said quickly, and he didn't miss the look of relief on Lillian's face. "I just needed to get something from Lucas." He realized suddenly that everyone was looking at his uniform. "Julia fed me enough to know what I'm missing," he said. "But I have to go. Lucas?"

He got the statistical report he came for, and he tried to corner Lillian on his way out. She immediately got busy elsewhere. It was Winston who walked outside with him.

"Has Dolly got a reason to worry or not?" the old man asked without prelude.

Becenti gave a quiet sigh. "Yeah," he said.

Chapter Twelve

Lillian had no idea why she'd thought that a trip home to Window Rock would help. She had supposed it would provide her with some needed rest, if nothing else, and perhaps induce her mother to stop worrying. And maybe she herself would stop worrying, at least for a little while. She had foolishly thought, too, that if she stayed in the inner circle of her family—and no one got into any legal trouble—she wouldn't run into Becenti.

Becenti.

Of the sad eyes.

What a shock it had been for him, having her answer Lucas's door. It had been a shock for her, as well. The truth of the matter was that neither of them liked unexpected surprises—and she certainly had a surprise in store for him.

I should have told him. When he asked what was wrong, I should have told him.

Just as she should have told him that she hadn't just abandoned him and gone running back to Stuart. She should have tried to make him understand that J.B. had been telling the truth only as she knew it, and that it hadn't been the real truth at all.

But there was no point in telling him any of that now, and she couldn't tell him she was pregnant. She was hardly used to the idea herself. Even after three positive home pregnancy tests and the ultimate, definitive blood test she'd insisted upon. Even after a doctor's exam and the prescriptions for prenatal vitamins and iron and the obvious outward signs. Her days were filled now with relentless bouts of nausea and fatigue. Her breasts hurt, and she wanted to sleep all the time. And when she wasn't asleep, she wanted to cry—about everything. World hunger or the depleted ozone layer or the buzzer on the dryer going off. It didn't matter. She was an emotional and physical wreck. And she was still trying to untangle Stuart's legal affairs, still waiting for the other shoe to drop regarding his imprudent land dealings, aside from the fact that she was so worried about his illness. He had finished the first round of treatment. It had left him much sicker than he'd been at the outset—and scared. She didn't know what she could possibly say to him that would help, but it was obvious that he expected her to say it. He wouldn't even let her mention J.B. Greenleigh. The entire situation left her exhausted and short-tempered and highly negligent when it came to holding up her end of a conversation with anyone—on the phone or in person. Even so, the last thing she had expected was her mother to arrive, intent on dragging her back to Window Rock. But she went, because she'd never needed her family so much in her entire life.

I'm a coward, she thought, because she hadn't told Dolly about the baby, either. She hadn't told anyone.

I just have to get used to it—if I don't have a nervous breakdown from all this other stuff first.

Then, *then,* she would prepare the family, make announcements, tell Becenti. He had a right to know that he had a child coming. And she wanted him to be reassured that his life wouldn't be disrupted. Her plans for the baby absolutely didn't include him. She didn't want or need his money or his forced commitment. She would have the child and she would take care of it. After the initial shock, there had been no question in her mind about that. None. Even so, she had no idea how she would manage. She knew only that she would worry about the specifics later. For now, she would just have to take it one step at a time, first things first. Now, it took every bit of strength she had not to throw up in the middle of the morning court sessions; she couldn't concentrate on much else. But she *would* manage.

Somehow.

Becenti is good with children, she suddenly thought.

He'd fed Julia, diapered Tad, worn the sweet potatoes on his chest with a certain finesse that still made her smile. Who would have thought crabby old Becenti would be like that?

She would, of course, because she knew him now. Intimately. She knew that everything she'd always suspected about him was true; that for all his taciturn nature, he was a complex and intriguing man. And she knew that she cared more for him than she would ever let him know. She had promised him no complications, and she meant to keep that promise. She would not delude herself into thinking that there was anything between them except an intense physical need. She knew firsthand how much he *hadn't* wanted to give in to it. He had loved his wife, and his vulnerability after her death was the only reason he'd ever become involved with Lillian Singer. She could see that, if he couldn't.

Surprisingly, she was in a much improved frame of mind by the latter part of the week. She had a productive meeting with Stuart on Thursday morning. He seemed to be feeling better, and for once he was satisfied with her advice regarding the disposition of certain stocks. She even managed to get all the way through to the lunch hour with only one mild episode of nausea. In the afternoon, she went off con-

fidently to the municipal court building for a repeatedly
postponed case—a teenage girl who couldn't seem to keep
from speeding, sideswiping parked cars and rear-ending
other drivers. Her father was already paying a fortune in
car insurance to keep her on the road—for reasons that
totally escaped Lillian. It was her considered opinion that
it would be far better to let the girl's driver's license be
legally revoked than to let her continue to menace everybody who was even remotely in her path. But Lillian's job
was not to reason why. Her job was to present the defense,
and hopefully she was going to be able to do it this time,
because the case would finally be called and because it had
been scheduled in the afternoon instead of in the middle of
her worst spells of morning nausea.

The back wall of the courtroom was almost entirely
glass, as was the far wall of the outer corridor. It was possible for anyone facing in that direction to see straight
through the building to the out-of-doors as well as whoever
might be standing or milling around in the hallway. She
liked the openness of the design, but she'd always found it
distracting that people who weren't actually in the courtroom were still able to watch the proceedings. It took a
great deal of effort on her part to ignore it, and she almost
never looked to see how many kibitzers there were.

But she did today, just as she stood to begin a nonexis-
tent defense for this rich young girl who shouldn't be allowed even to ride a bicycle. She saw Becenti immediately.
He was in uniform and official looking, standing near the
outside windows, arms folded. She faltered when she recognized him, and it took her a moment to recover. She
eventually continued, but it was all she could do not to
keep glancing over her shoulder. It wasn't a coincidence
that he was out there. Of that she was certain. She recognized his purposeful look, and her only hope was that it
had nothing to do with her.

The case ended much as she'd expected—the girl and
her father both lectured, a heavy fine, traffic school. Lillian

had no choice now but to leave and no way out except past where Becenti was standing. She took her time gathering up papers and directing her client's father to where he would go to pay yet another fine, as if he didn't already know. But when she turned to leave, Becenti was no longer in the hallway. She didn't see him anywhere, even after she stepped outside.

She didn't waste time trying to locate him. She walked briskly down the corridor. Apparently, he hadn't come to see her after all. She was both relieved and disappointed. As she approached the elevators, she looked through the glass wall to the sidewalk below. Becenti was standing near the street, talking to someone. Lillian moved closer to get a better view. He was talking to J.B. Greenleigh—no, he was listening to her. J.B. was telling him something in that earnest way she had. Lillian stood for a moment, watching. Becenti was about to walk away, but J.B. caught his arm. And whatever she said next made him stay.

But, as much as Lillian might want to stay out of his way, she refused to hide in the courthouse. She hadn't seen or talked to J.B. since that fateful weekend J.B. had delegated herself Lillian's nurse. She felt sorry for the girl, but she had no wish to renew their acquaintance, either. It was much too exhausting. She had no doubt now that J.B. loved Stuart, and he was still insisting on "protecting" her. She wondered if Stuart had ever seen J. B. Greenleigh as strong as she was that night Lillian had tried to refuse her services as a post-head-injury baby-sitter.

Lillian walked to the elevators and waited impatiently for the doors to open, finally giving up and taking the stairs. She didn't see Becenti or J.B. as she came out of the building, but she took time to visually search the area around her before she went to the car.

No Becenti.

"Looking for me?" he asked mildly as she opened her car door.

She jumped violently, nearly dropping her briefcase.

"Where did you come from?" she said, more than a little annoyed that he'd managed to sneak up on her.

"From right over there," he answered, indicating a shady spot that would give him a perfect vantage point to see anyone who approached her parking space. "So, are you looking for me or not?"

"You, Johnny Becenti, are a very arrogant man," she said, trying to pull the door open. He put his hand on it to stop her.

"You, Lillian Singer, are evading the question."

"I'm a lawyer," she said, forcing herself to look at him. "What do you expect?"

"Not much," he said. "Lawyer or not."

"What is that supposed to mean?"

"It means I want us to talk."

"No," she said, pulling the car door open in spite of his hand.

"You have to let me say what I want to say, Lillian."

She looked at him. It was on the tip of her tongue to tell him that she didn't *have* to do anything, but she didn't. She was so tired suddenly. She didn't have the energy for this now.

"Goodbye, Johnny," she said, again moving to get into the car.

"What am I going to have to do, Lillian? Make an appointment? Or are you just going to send me something official on your letterhead? You'd have to type it yourself, though. You can't have everybody knowing you're pregnant and there's a remote possibility I just might be the father."

"What?" she said, completely taken aback.

"You heard me. Or maybe you're going to do like the white woman anthropologist did with your brother—just get rid of it and not tell me anything at all."

"I don't—" She began the denial, the I-don't-know-what-you're-talking-about, but she couldn't finish it. His remark about Lucas had wounded her to the quick. She didn't blame him for it, but it was all she could do not to cry. She took a deep breath and willed herself to stay in control. She had told him that she didn't lie, and she didn't.

"Please," was all she could manage to say. "Please, Johnny."

"We have to talk about this."

"There's nothing to talk about. You don't have to worry about any—"

"I don't have to *worry?*" he interrupted. "How the hell am I supposed to manage that?"

She didn't say anything else, because several passersby had turned to stare.

"I have to go," she said. "Take yourself back to Window Rock, Johnny. Where you belong."

She left him standing there, and she managed not to cry at all on the way home. And she might have maintained her hard-won control—if J. B. Greenleigh's little black car hadn't been parked in her driveway.

"I can't do this," she said out loud.

J.B. was already out of the car and walking toward her. It was all Lillian could do to keep from backing down the drive and making a run for it.

"Deal with it," she said under her breath. "Do what you've always done. Deal with it!"

J.B. stopped and stood waiting.

"Is it true?" she asked the minute Lillian opened the car door.

Lillian didn't bother to answer. She walked briskly toward the front door. J.B. followed right on her heels.

"Someone told me you were having morning sickness," J.B. said loudly. "Are you?"

"What have you been doing—going around interrogating the janitorial staff at the courthouse?" Lillian asked, because they were the only people who had ever seen her at her worst.

"Only if I have to," J.B. said.

"You don't have to."

"I do if I'm going to find out the truth. Have you been having morning sickness or not? Answer me!"

'Yes!" Lillian said.

"It's Stuart's baby, isn't it?" J.B. asked, her voice trembling.

"I am going to tell you this one more time," Lillian said. 'And if you ever ask me again, I'm going to slap you silly. Stuart and I are not lovers!"

"Then what are you doing pregnant!"

"That is a very good question—one I have no desire to answer. Now, please. Go away. I'm really not up to this *at all*—"

They both looked around at the sound of another car— a Navajo Tribal Police vehicle.

"Oh, no," Lillian said. She began to scrounge in her purse for her ever-elusive house key.

"It's Captain Becenti," J.B. said helpfully.

Lillian gave her a look, but she made no comment.

"Lillian?" J.B. said.

"What!"

"I wasn't— I didn't go asking around about you. This guy I know at the newspaper. He used to go elk hunting with my father. He told me that Stuart might be in some big trouble, but that's all he'd say. I thought if anybody would know the details, you would, so I went to your office—but Gracie said you had to go to municipal court again today. So I went there and I was looking up and down the halls for you, and this maid or whatever—she asked if she could help me. I said I was looking for you. She said you might be in the bathroom because you had morning sickness really bad, and sometimes it doesn't just happen in the morning. So I thought you and Stuart— Well, I guess you know what I thought."

"J.B., why in this world did you have to tell Becenti?" Lillian asked, her eyes on him as he got out of the car. He didn't look as upset now. He looked absolutely grim. And why didn't he immediately think exactly what J.B. thought—that Stuart Dennison was the baby's father?

"He asked me how I was doing," J.B. said, her voice trembling again. "And I...wasn't doing so good right then, I guess. He's a very kind man and— Oh, Lillian, I just *said* it—I didn't think. He didn't know anything about it, did he?"

"No, J.B. He didn't."

"Is he—? He's not the— Oh, Lillian! Maybe I'd better go."

"That would be good, J.B."

"You don't have to worry. He's going to be glad about it. I think he's going to be really glad."

"Does he look glad to you?" Lillian asked her as Becenti stepped up on the porch.

"I'd better go," J.B. said again instead of answering. "What about Stuart? Is he in trouble?"

"Go see him," Lillian said. "And don't take no for an answer."

"Do you really think—?"

"Go on!" Lillian said. "Now!"

She took a deep breath and waited until J.B. had scurried down the steps past Becenti to her car. Then and only then did Lillian look at him.

"I'm running on empty," she said.

The remark was as close as Lillian Singer could come to admitting any kind of weakness. He knew that, because he knew her and because he was the exact same way himself. Left to their own devices, both of them would suffer alone. The anger he felt left him. He took her purse out of her hand and began looking for her misplaced key.

"Why can't you put it on the same ring with your car keys?" he asked, as if that were the reason he'd come—to chastise her about keeping up with her keys.

"Because if somebody steals my car, they get the house as a bonus."

"And if they steal your purse?"

"Then maybe they don't get the car."

"Logic by Lillian," he said, finally locating the key. He gave her back her purse and unlocked the door.

"Don't start with me, Becenti. I mean it."

"You haven't seen anything yet," he said. He pushed open the door for her to go inside. It wouldn't have surprised him if she'd slammed it shut behind her and locked it again, but she didn't. She dropped her briefcase on the easy chair in passing and headed for the bedroom.

"I'm going to take a shower," she said tonelessly.

"Are you hungry?" he asked.

She looked at him if she'd never heard of the concept.

"Yes," she said finally. "I don't know what's in the refrigerator. Fruit and cheese, maybe."

Fruit and cheese he could handle. He went into the kitchen, and after a few moments he heard the water in the shower running. He found some oranges and seedless grapes in the refrigerator, and some kind of gourmet cheese, and he began to put together a meal of sorts for her.

Lillian, what are we going to do about this? he thought as he worked.

But the real question was, what was *she* going to do? He had to know, and he wasn't leaving until she told him. He had started out this day just wanting to see her, to talk to her, because he was worried about her. He had come to Santa Fe just for that purpose, even if it meant having her tell him again that their time together had been meaningless. He had never in his wildest dreams expected that the "nothing" relationship she'd insisted they had, might turn out to be "something" after all.

A child. Possibly *his* child. He had loved Mae with all his heart, and while she was alive, the fact that they had never had children hadn't really mattered. But now, *now*—

"Go ahead," Lillian said behind him. "Ask the question." She had put on jeans and a baggy T-shirt, and her hair was wet from her shower. He could smell the soap she'd used, and the scent of it immediately brought back a memory he'd been trying so hard to forget—the two of them bathing together in a tub of hot, soapy water. Afterward, they'd made love, long and slow and consuming. He wondered if that could have been when she'd conceived the child.

And looking at her now, he thought that she was indeed "running on empty."

"What question?" he asked. He gathered up the orange peelings and put them in the garbage.

"You know what question. 'Is it mine?'"

He looked around at her. "Is it?" He wanted to hear her say once and for all that he was the baby's father, and any doubts, any questions he had about it, he would try to put to rest later.

She waited a long time to answer. He could see her struggling to maintain her control. She had forced him to ask, and he had. But she still hated what must seem to her his total inability to believe she was a decent and honorable person.

"The baby is yours," she said finally.

He wanted to believe her. He didn't want to badger her. He *did* believe her. How could he not?

I never lie, Johnny.

If she was ever going to start, now was the time. Stuart Dennison had money, a big house in Santa Fe and a country-club membership. He, on the other hand, lived and worked on the reservation.

He handed her a plate of fruit and cheese, and some crackers. "Eat something. Then we'll talk."

"I don't want to talk. There's nothing to talk about. I'm pregnant. You're the lucky father. End of discussion."

"Don't be so damned flippant about this!"

"I'm not," she said. "It's a very serious matter. For *me*."

He ignored the sarcasm. "You weren't going to tell me, were you?"

"Of course, I was going to tell you."

"Only because J.B. upset your plans. You had plenty of chances the other night at Lucas's. Why didn't you tell me then?"

"I didn't want to."

"You didn't *want* to? Lillian—" He gave a sharp sigh. "So what do you expect me to do now?"

"Nothing."

"I'm not going to go away and pretend it's not happening. You know that, don't you?"

She sighed instead of answering. She sat down at the kitchen table, but she made no attempt to eat anything.

"What are you going to do, Lillian?"

"I'm going to stay right here. You, on the other hand, are going back to Window Rock."

"What about the baby?"

"What about it?"

"You're going to keep it?"

"Yes."

"Have you been to a doctor? Are you all right?"

"Yes. And yes," she said. "I'm twice as old as some of his other obstetrical patients, but the consensus of opinion among the members of the practice is that I'm doing fine."

"What about the morning sickness?"

"It comes and goes. Actually, my doctor says it's one symptom he's glad to see. It means there's an adequate hormone level. He says, in his experience, morning sickness is a good sign that the pregnancy will go to term— barring some other complication, of course."

"You haven't told your family," he said. It wasn't quite a question.

"No," she said.

"I didn't think so. Lucas hasn't punched me in the nose."

She almost smiled.

"Nobody knows about us except Toomey," she said. "Or do they?"

"I think Mary Skeets knows. And probably Winston Tsosie. I think you'd better tell Dolly and the rest of them before somebody else does. You don't want her to hear about it secondhand."

"Who is going to tell them? You?"

"If I have to."

She sighed again, then picked up a piece of cheese and put it down again.

"Lillian," he said to make her look at him.

"What?"

"Maybe we should get married."

"No," she said. No thinking it over. No hesitation whatsoever. Just *no*.

"Why not?"

"Because you think you have to do the right thing. You don't mean it."

"Don't tell me what I mean."

"Okay, then. Because I won't live on the rez and you won't leave it. Because we have nothing to build a marriage on. Because you and I have absolutely nothing in common."

"Except a baby. And the law. And the People—"

"We don't even like each other!" she said.

"Don't we?" he asked quietly.

"No," she said, her voice barely a whisper. She sat there, so still, her face turned away from him.

"I think we could make it work," he said, and she abruptly looked at him.

"I want you to go, Johnny."

"Lillian—"

"Please. It's not your problem—"

"It's not a problem at all, damn it! Not to me—"

"Please! I want you to go!"

They stared at each other across the table.

"You have to understand," she said, her voice quiet now.

"Oh, I understand," he said, because he suddenly got a glimpse of what it must have been like for her father—when he looked into her eyes and knew that she was ashamed of him.

Chapter Thirteen

He couldn't count the number of times he nearly turned around on the way back to Window Rock. The baby was his. He wanted it. And he wanted her. He hadn't made an offer of marriage because it was the "right thing to do." He'd made it because he—

He sighed heavily.

Because he loved her. He had no idea precisely when or how aggravation had become desire and desire had become love. It just had. He *loved* Lillian Singer. He thought that it never would have happened if Mae had lived. And if his mother hadn't sent Lillian to scold him back into the world of the living. And if he hadn't been so damned determined to take her to bed.

If.

The truth of the matter was that, unlike Lillian, *he* had no regrets. He supposed that she must be feeling greatly relieved now that he'd gone, just as he supposed she would think he had made his token gesture of marriage and then happily given up. He hadn't given up at all, but for now, it hurt too much, knowing that she could be so accepting of the child and so cast down by the man who had given it to her.

He arrived home well after sundown, letting himself into the dark and empty house that Lillian had negotiated for him.

Another house with yet another ghost, he thought as he switched on the lights. He had begun his tempestuous relationship with Lillian Singer here, and the memory was strong. He had wanted her so much that afternoon. He still did.

He considered going to the law-enforcement building under the pretense of working, but he didn't. He was too out of harmony to deal with anything else now. The incredible realization that Lillian Singer was going to have his child kept washing over him. He was going to be a father, and his male pride wouldn't let him be anything but delighted. He, who had never imagined himself having a wife again, much less a baby. Of course, if Lillian had her way, he wouldn't have either.

What she was doing was wrong. *She* was wrong—about his intentions, about their relationship, about everything. And he at least deserved a chance to try to prove it to her.

But there was nothing he could do at the moment except stare at the telephone. She wasn't going to call him; he knew that. Even so, after a few moments, he decided there was no reason why he couldn't call her.

She answered on the second ring.

"It's me," he said. "I was...angry when I left and I..." He didn't finish. It was far too presumptuous of him to tell her that he hadn't wanted her to worry about him.

She didn't say anything.

"Lillian?"

"Are you at home?" she asked finally. Her voice sounded strained and unnatural to him. He wondered if she'd been crying.

"Yes," he said.

"I—I'm glad you called."

"Are you all right?"

"I'm...fine."

"It doesn't have to be like this. You know that, don't you?"

There was a long silence.

"Good night, Johnny," she said and quietly hung up the phone.

He did try to get back into his usual work routine, but he found himself unable to manage any kind of routine at all. He slept fitfully, ate when it occurred to him or not at all—which did nothing to improve his desolate mood. He tried to do whatever he was supposed to do, to pay attention, to make the necessary decisions, but every day it became harder. The simple truth was that he didn't want to be bothered—by anyone or anything, officially or otherwise. And he didn't particularly care who knew it. He was incredibly happy about the baby and filled with worry and anxiety about Lillian, all at the same time. He wanted—needed—to go to Santa Fe, and he supposed that Lillian had been right, after all. He did think he had to do the right thing—and behaving otherwise was killing him.

He stayed at the law-enforcement building most of the time, because he found he was less disturbed there than he was at home. He might not have fewer memories of Lillian Singer at work, but at least he had less provocative ones. There was enough tribal police business to keep him occupied, if he'd been so inclined—a rash of domestic-violence cases, a family of bootleggers selling bad whiskey, rumors of some illegal "pot hunters" out to desecrate Navajo burial sites and steal the artifacts, two armed robberies. And the summer tourists, of course, who could get into more trouble doing nothing than seemed humanly possible. There was also the rumor of something called a "desert rave," a kind of sex-and-drugs-and-loud-music orgy, reminiscent of the 1960s, that hundreds of bored and aimless young people seemed hell-bent on carrying out in a "spiritual" but isolated place. This time, word of mouth suggested that the place of choice was somewhere on the Navajo reservation. Because there had been injuries and even deaths at these semisecret gatherings in the past, all the law-enforcement agencies in the area had been put on alert—even if it meant canvasing a possible party site in an area nearly the size of South Carolina.

He decided to delegate the task, and he buzzed Mary Skeets.

"Tell Lucas I want to see him when he comes in," he said when she answered. His request was met with a long silence. "Mary?" he said. "Did you hear me?"

"Oh...well...yes, sir, I did. You think you want to see Lucas."

"No, I don't *think*. I know. Send him in here," he said, frowning.

"Well, if you're...sure," Mary said.

He stared at the receiver a moment before he hung up, wondering what was the matter with Mary Skeets now.

Lucas eventually appeared in the doorway, but he was not happy about it. At all.

"Come in," Becenti said. "Do you know anything about this?" He handed him the memo regarding the "desert rave."

"How would I know anything?" Lucas asked when he'd finished reading—or pretending to.

"You've got Will living in your house. He goes all over the rez helping Eddie Nez with his ceremonies, and he's the right age to hear about things like this. I thought he might have said something about it."

"Well, you thought wrong."

"I want you to ask him about it any—"

"*You* want?" Lucas interrupted. "And what makes you think I give a rat's—"

"That's enough!" Becenti said. Unfortunately, Lucas

Singer's belligerence was all too familiar. Becenti looked at him for a long moment, searching for signs that, after all these years, Lucas had fallen off the wagon and was drinking again. But he didn't appear to be under the influence of any controlled substance. He appeared to be royally pissed.

"Close the door," Becenti said.

Lucas made no effort to do so.

"I said, close the door!"

Lucas closed it—hard enough to leave no doubt in the minds of anyone in the building that another one of the notorious Becenti-Singer "discussions" was about to commence.

"What is this about?" Becenti asked, regardless of the fact that he was certain he already knew.

"When was the last time you saw my sister?" Lucas demanded.

"Three weeks ago yesterday," Becenti said evenly.

"So what is it with you? She's only good for one thing and then to hell with her if she gets knocked up?"

"Sit down," Becenti said.

"I don't want to sit down!"

"All right, then stand! What did Lillian tell you?"

"Me? She didn't tell *me* anything. She told my mother and she told Sloan. She's pregnant. You're the father. Now I want to know what the hell you're going to do about it!"

"Nothing," Becenti said.

"Nothing? Why not?"

"You'll have to ask her that."

"I'm asking you."

"Well, I'm not answering."

"What in the hell is the matter with you two! Lillian has always been hardheaded—my mother and I thought we might have to go through this when she was sixteen, but not *now*. Both of you are old enough to know better!"

"Are you finished?"

"No, damn it! I'm not!"

"Well, wind it up and get out of here!"

"You should have left her the hell alone!"

"You're right. I should have."

"So she's just—on her own? You're not even going to try to work this out with her?"

"Lucas, it's none of your damn business!"

"She's my sister! You better believe it's my business!"

"There's no point in talking about this anymore," Becenti said. "Your sister is going to do whatever the hell she wants to do. And she's not going to consult either one of us. Now, get out. I have work to do—and so do you."

Lucas stood for a moment, then turned to go. "Don't you hurt her," he said when he reached the door. "I mean it."

Becenti sat there after Lucas had left, staring at nothing. Hurt her? It wasn't possible. A woman had to have some regard for a man before he could do that.

When he finally left for the day, Mary Skeets stopped him at the front door.

"Winston Tsosie's been waiting a couple of hours to see you," she said.

"Well, why didn't you tell me?" he asked in annoyance, regardless of his recent apathy. He was never going to be able to follow Mary Skeets's logic as to when it was acceptable for an old man to wait and when it wasn't.

"Because he wouldn't let me. He said he didn't want to talk to you while you were working. He wanted to talk to you when you were done."

"Where is he?"

"He went outside."

Becenti walked through the front doors to the parking lot, but he didn't immediately see Winston. He finally spotted him, standing patiently by one of the tribal police utility vehicles.

"*Yah-ta-hey,* my grandfather," Becenti said as he approached.

"You done working?" the old man asked.

"For now. Why?"

"I need to get someplace. I'm thinking we could take one of these." He patted the utility-vehicle door. "I like to ride up high."

"You want to tell me where you're planning on going?"

"No. But I got something you need there. You have to see it in the daylight, though. Can we go now or not?"

"Is there any chance we can call this police business?"

"Maybe this trip will give you some harmony. Maybe it will keep you out of trouble with Lucas—and help you quit yelling at everybody who works in the building there. That would be good for the law-and-order business, wouldn't it? Cost-effective, I'm thinking."

"Cost-effective?" Becenti said, wondering where Winston had picked up that particular term. But it didn't escape him that he'd just been chastised about his bad behavior by a man he truly respected. The voice had been mild, but the message strong.

He stood for a moment, then went back inside for the keys to the utility vehicle, and for once he didn't have to wrestle them away from Mary Skeets as if they belonged to her personally.

Winston was still waiting when he came out.

"Are you going to tell me where we're going?" Becenti asked as he unlocked the police-vehicle door for Winston to climb inside.

"No," he said. "I don't remember how to tell where it is so good anymore—but we can find it."

Winston had him take the road north toward Fort Defiance. They rode in silence except for the old man's occasional directions to slow down so he could look along the roadside—for what, he still wouldn't say.

But eventually he found it. "Pull in here," he said.

There was a pickup truck already parked in a small clearing. Becenti recognized it immediately. It belonged to Will Baron and was allegedly responsible for the recent injury to his hand. The boy was standing beside it—his hand no longer bandaged now, and he was waiting with his stepsister's husband, Jack Begaye. There had been a time in the not-too-distant past when Becenti had had no choice but to order both Jack and Will arrested. Either of the two would have gladly taken him on then, and Becenti would be the first to admit that perhaps they had an even better excuse now.

"Do they know about Lillian?" he asked Winston as he pulled off the road.

"Everybody knows about Lillian," Winston said. "And you."

Even so, Becenti got out of the vehicle and went around to help Winston to the ground. Both Jack and Will waited by the truck.

"Did you find it?" Winston asked them as he shuffled in their direction.

"We found it," Jack said. "So, Captain, what's new?" he added with just enough mischief to let Becenti know that Jack Begaye had found a certain humor in Becenti's situation with Lillian, if no one else did.

"Show me where it is," Winston said.

"Over that way. The junior *hataalii* here says any one of them is okay."

"Because they *are* okay," Will said, giving Jack a token punch on the arm.

Becenti followed the procession, still not knowing what was about to take place. Eventually, they arrived at a stack of cut logs several feet high—cedar, he could tell when he walked closer. He didn't understand, but he didn't ask questions. He waited for Winston to get around to explaining.

Winston inspected the logs closely. "They're in good shape still. You come and look," he said to Becenti.

"What am I looking for?" Becenti asked.

"You're looking for the right piece of wood to make a cradle board for your baby," the old man said.

Becenti looked at him. The remark caught him completely off guard.

"Ain't much a man can do to help out when he's got a baby coming. But he can do this. Jack and me—we cut these logs a while ago—cut them especially for the babies in the family that might need them, and we stacked them just right. Jack's babies got their cradle boards made from these logs here. You look for the one you think will work for yours and Lillian's."

Becenti stood there, saying nothing. There had been any number of cradle boards in his own family, but he didn't remember anything about selecting the wood for one. If he'd ever known, he'd forgotten—perhaps because he never expected to have to do it.

He looked at the logs, and then at the old man.

"You got to put your hands on the wood, my son," Winston said. "Takes more than just the eyes to know which one is good enough. Like this."

Becenti followed Winston's lead, touching piece after piece with both hands. "How—" He stopped and cleared his throat because his voice sounded husky and strange to him. This was not what he'd expected, this gesture of acceptance and perhaps understanding from the men in Lillian's family. "How many logs will it take?" he asked.

"Pick two," Jack said. "You can get the whole cradle board out of one—but it's good to have another one in case a piece splits wrong."

Becenti nodded and kept looking.

"This one right here—it's got really good vibes," Will said, regarding a particular log, and Becenti smiled at the boy's twentieth-century description of so ancient a concept.

"The color's good," Will said. "Looks like the furniture Lillian's got in her house. It might be the kind she'd like. And the spirit's good. I don't feel nothing bad in it, do you?"

"No," Becenti said. "Nothing bad. This is the one, then."

He carefully selected a second log, and he helped Jack

and Will put both of them in the back of the battered pickup truck.

"I'll just take these to the mission house, Captain," Jack said. "That way Winston can help you get started. The bowed piece that goes above the baby's head will have to be soaked for a while so it'll bend. But once you get that done and the rest of the pieces cut right, there's not much to it but a lot of planing and sanding. You can work on that at your place whenever you get a minute. When's the baby due?"

"I...don't know," he said, the admission calling home how little he had to do with Lillian's plans.

"Well—you've got plenty of time, right?"

Plenty of time, Becenti thought. Yes. But, even so, he felt incredibly rushed. The thought of trying to make a cradle board *and* trying to get Lillian to see reason was overwhelming.

He thanked Jack and Will for their efforts, and he stood and watched them drive away. He could hear the rumble of thunder in the distance, and he looked to the northwest where a bright-edged plume of gray-white cloud shot upward into the sky. He'd been hearing the thunder for days now, thunder that never brought any rain. But this afternoon would be different, he thought. He could smell the storm coming on the wind. He could sense it in the change in the air. And he should feel elated. When the rain came, everything—plants, animals, the People—all became new again. But he felt nothing. He was empty.

Alone.

I don't know what to do, he thought.

"You got to learn how to walk in beauty again," Winston said as if he'd heard him. "The one who died—ever since she left on that journey, you been acting like a white man. You keep trying to *make* things be the way you want them to be, and that don't work for us. It don't work, and some of us drink because of it. Some get in trouble. Some of us try to run away to a new place—like Lillian going off to Santa Fe. Some do like you and go and hide. First you were hiding in the hogan at the sheep camp. Now you're hiding in the policeman's office. You had relatives to teach you the Navajo Way. You know you got to get things in balance so you can do your job for the People like you're supposed to do. Some say they think you can't be a policeman no more. They think your *hozro* is too bad.''

"Maybe it is," Becenti said, looking around at him.

"Yes, but you can get your harmony back. It ain't going to be easy for you. You got to be strong. You got to let everything blow around you while you stand still. You got to be the policeman like you always was and when you ain't doing that, you go and make the cradle board for your baby. And you quit spending so much time thinking there's something you can do to change things in Santa Fe. There ain't—not right now. You got to stay here until Lillian sends for you."

"She's not going to send for me."

"She will. You're in too big a hurry. You got no patience. You're the father of this child, ain't you? If she wasn't going to send for you, she wouldn't have told you nothing about a baby coming in the first place. And she wouldn't have told the family this baby is yours. She's a good woman. She ain't going to keep you away from your son.''

"My son?''

"I saw it in a dream. The baby is a boy. You take an old man's advice. You might as well, because you ain't getting nowhere doing like you're doing now."

The wind began to pick up, swirling the dry sand around them. Becenti turned and walked back to the police vehicle. He was certain of at least one truth in what Winston had said. He wasn't getting anywhere doing what he was doing now. He would accept the old man's help, if not his advice, and he would make the cradle board. And as soon as it was ready, he would personally take it to Santa Fe.

Chapter Fourteen

I'm pretending, Lillian thought. *The way I used to when I was a little girl.*

She looked at the table. It had been set for four with her good crystal and china. She had candles ready to be lit, and a small centerpiece of daisies, eucalyptus and sweetheart roses. She had fixed pasta with garlic and tomatoes and walnuts, made a green salad, bought Italian rolls and lime sponge pudding with raspberry sauce at one of the most expensive bakeries in Santa Fe. The house was filled with the aroma of hot bread and freshly brewed coffee.

Now she was waiting for her guests—Stuart and two other people he'd hired to do damage control regarding his possible indictment for the illegal land deal. Lillian herself believed that in Stuart's case, there was only one way to manage the public scandal—straight on, while telling the truth. But that was a foreign concept to the politician in Stuart Dennison. She was reassured somewhat by the fact that he was now doing better healthwise, but she thought that having to maintain whatever persona his handlers concocted would be too much for him, especially if he had to pull it off with television cameras stuck in his face. He was having to deal with his own mortality and with having given up J.B. He was drinking too much and his emotions were far too unstable for any kind of subterfuge. She had no idea what J.B. was doing these days. Stuart never mentioned her, and it would seem that she had taken no for an answer after all.

Lillian still tired easily, because of her pregnancy and because of her constant state of worry. But she was no longer fighting the nausea, at least. She was beginning to show. She was glad that she had told the family that she was pregnant, and soon she would have to tell everyone else of any importance. Gracie. Possibly Fred.

She looked at herself now in the mirror. Black silk pants—happily with elastic instead of buttons and a zipper, a "generous" white silk blouse to hide her thickening waistline, expensive but tasteful gold jewelry. Simple but elegant.

And all a lie.

It wasn't only her clothes that didn't fit anymore. Her life didn't fit, either. Everything about this evening felt wrong—the food, the flowers, Stuart's legal woes. None of these things meant anything to her. She could pretend otherwise all she wanted, but it changed nothing. And worse, she had no idea who she really was now except in the most basic terms. An unmarried Navajo woman about to have her first child. No. An unmarried Navajo woman of "advanced maternal age"—as her doctor had so delicately put it. She was afraid. She had a whole list of things that frightened her, and the items on the list rotated in importance from minute to minute. What if she *was* too old to do this? What if she didn't have enough patience to raise a child and she completely ruined it?

What if she stayed in love with Johnny Becenti and she yearned for him the rest of her life?

She shamelessly kept tabs on him. Sloan came to Santa Fe every weekend to see her—a gesture that surprised her, because they had never really been that close, emotionally or geographically. But she'd always liked Lucas's second choice in white women. She and Sloan Baron-Singer were alike in that both of them preferred the direct approach. Sloan had announced immediately upon her first visit that she had come because she had no choice—she simply didn't know how to say no to Katie Becenti *and* Dolly Singer, or at least to come up with a no that the two matriarchs would accept. Lillian could certainly identify with that. But the thing about Sloan she appreciated the most was her concise reports regarding Becenti. Just straightforward and to the point, without making Lillian ask. Thanks to Sloan, Lillian knew that he was working long hours, and that Lucas was still angry with him for having taken advantage of his sister, and that Will and Jack and Winston minded Captain Becenti's business a lot more than he cared for.

"He also wants to ask about you," Sloan said.

"Wants to," Lillian repeated, trying to grasp the fine point she was certain lay hidden in the remark.

"Yes," Sloan assured her. "He wants to ask, but he doesn't. Just like you."

On her last visit, Sloan had brought a basket of fruit and English walnuts—a gift, she said, from Becenti, who still didn't ask anything. The gesture had brought Lillian close to tears, because he'd noticed this small thing about her and he'd cared enough to remember.

But instead of calling him and thanking him, she'd used the walnuts tonight to make the pasta dish for Stuart and his people, because she was still denying the truth, still pretending that her other life, her Navajo life, and this Navajo man meant nothing to her.

She looked around at the sound of a car.

Time for the dog-and-pony show, she thought. She quickly checked the table and the food again before she opened the front door. Johnny Becenti stood on the porch with a large newspaper-wrapped bundle under one arm.

She forgot that she allegedly didn't want or need him. She forgot that she'd told him to stay in Window Rock where he belonged. She was so glad he was here—too glad and too taken by surprise to hide it. She had to fight hard not to fling herself at him. Her heart was pounding; her knees were weak. She looked into his eyes and she waited, but he just stood there, implacable, saying absolutely nothing.

"Hello, Lillian," she finally suggested. "You're looking very well this evening. May I come in?"

He still didn't say anything, but she saw the faint workings of a smile at the corners of his mouth and in his sad eyes.

Her heart soared. If she could still make him smile even a little, then he didn't hate her entirely. She stood back and held the door open wide for him.

"You are looking well," he admitted as he stepped inside. "Beautiful," he added with a shy awkwardness she found totally endearing in so stern a man.

"Well, I wouldn't go *that* far," she said.

They stood staring at each other. His eyes traveled over her face. He looked…miserable. She couldn't stand it.

"So," she said brightly. "What have you got there?" She knew better than to ask what had brought him to Santa Fe.

He abruptly looked down at the bundle as if he'd forgotten he had it with him.

"Nothing much," he said. "It's for you."

He made no attempt to give it to her. He was still looking at her, his eyes searching hers for something she was desperately afraid she didn't have.

"Do I get to—" she gave a small shrug "—hold it or anything?" she asked.

He handed it to her finally, but he'd clearly had second

thoughts about coming here and about bringing her whatever this happened to be.

"Heavier than I thought," she said, struggling not to drop it.

"It's nothing much," he said again as she rested it on the back of the easy chair and began to tear the paper off.

"Oh," she said softly when she saw the cradle board. She ran her fingers over the finely sanded wood and the soft leather laces that would keep the baby secure. She touched the piece of turquoise that dangled on a silver chain from the bowed wood at the top of the cradle.

"You made it?" she asked, looking up at him, already knowing the answer.

"My first," he said lightly. His almost-smile faded. "But maybe it's not what you want—"

"No—no, it's fine. It's beautiful. I—"

"Lillian!" someone called loudly from the still-open front door, and she looked around. Stuart was coming in. "Right this way," he said to his entourage. "Smells good in here, Lily. What's cooking?"

She set the cradle board carefully down and turned to him. A faint rumble of thunder sounded in the distance.

"Going to rain in a little bit," Stuart said, still in his role of the cheerful and perfectly-at-home guest. She saw immediately that he'd had a glass of wine—or two or three—before he got here. "You know everybody, right?" he went on expansively. He glanced at Becenti. He was sober enough to know exactly who Johnny Becenti was, Lillian thought—and he didn't like his being here.

"This is Mary Ellen," Stuart said carefully, as if they all might have difficulty following. "This is Sam. Have you met or not?"

"Only on the telephone," Lillian said. "Come in," she said to them. "This is—"

But Becenti gave her no opportunity to make introductions. "I'm going," he interrupted. "I should have called first."

"No," she said, reaching out to stop him from leaving. "You don't have to go—"

"No, indeed," Stuart said as if he had the right to do so. "If I know our Lillian, and I do, there's plenty of food for everybody and then some. Isn't that right, Lily? I'm hoping for my favorite—perciatelli with garlic!"

She didn't answer him.

"Johnny, wait—"

"Oh, what's this?" Mary Ellen said, pouncing on the cradle board. "How perfectly *beautiful!* Did you make it?" she asked Becenti. "Is it for sale? How much is it? If you're taking orders, I'd love to buy one for my niece. She is crazy about anything Native American."

"I'm not taking orders," he said, looking at Lillian.

"Would you be willing to part with this one?" Mary Ellen persisted. "I just love the little turquoise thing."

"The 'little turquoise thing' belonged to my father," Becenti said. "He carried it in his medicine bag all through World War II. He gave it to me when I was sixteen."

"Oh, he was a doctor? How interesting," she said, misunderstanding about the "medicine bag" completely. "That would raise the price, I guess, wouldn't it? How much without the turquoise? I just love to haggle," she said to Stuart and Sam.

"It's not for sale," Becenti said. "Or is it?" he asked Lillian.

"Johnny, please—" Lillian said.

"Never mind," he said, sidestepping her to get out. "You do whatever you want with it."

The wind blew in through the open door. There was a clap of thunder as Lillian followed him outside. The wind chimes on the porch clanged loudly.

"Johnny, wait—" she said, trying to catch his arm. "The woman didn't mean anything. She just didn't know—"

He stopped walking. The rain abruptly began to fall— huge drops pelting the dusty ground. Lillian could smell it, almost taste it, because she was desert-born no matter how

much she wanted to forget that part of her life. She could
see his face plainly in a sudden flash of lightning.

"Then why didn't you tell her?" he asked.

"Tell her?"

"Yes, damn it! Tell her! You couldn't say it, could you?
You'd rather let her think I was somebody peddling stuff
door-to-door. Why couldn't you just say the cradle board
was a gift from me? What was the harm in that?"

"I don't know—it's none of her business, Johnny! These
people don't understand anything."

He gave a short, bitter laugh.

"They may not understand, but I do. Goodbye, Lillian."

"Johnny—wait—don't go!" she said, still trying to hold
on to his arm. But he pulled free, and he left her standing
without once looking back.

He sat in the dark, listening to country music on the radio
and to another thunderstorm. He'd left the windows open,
and the wind banged the matchstick shades back and forth.
He should get up and close them. He could feel the rain
blowing in, but he just...sat.

There was no hope for Lillian and him. None. She lived
in Santa Fe by choice. Period. He finally realized that tonight. He finally saw what her life there must be like. It
must be full of candlelit dinners and "perciatelli"—whatever the hell that was—and people like Stuart Dennison
and the insensitive woman who insisted on buying the cradle board. He had been such an idiot. He had a logical and
methodical mind, sharpened by years of police work, and
he hadn't even considered that Lillian would actually *want*
to be around people like that. He kept misjudging her, kept
thinking that if he waited long enough, she would turn into
someone traditional and sensible like Mae—a complete ex-
ercise in futility, when he knew that it was Lillian's unpre-
dictable and untamable nature that had made him love her
in the first place.

He loved her, and as far as he could tell, there was no cure for it.

The telephone rang, and he fumbled in the darkness to pick up the receiver.

"Becenti," he said.

"Open the door," a woman's voice said.

"Open the—?"

He dropped the receiver and went to the front door, throwing it wide and stepping outside onto the stoop. It was raining hard now, but he saw her immediately, running toward him from her parked car.

She stopped before she got to him and stood there in the yard, looking up at him, wet and shivering in the downpour.

"Lillian, what are you doing—?" he started to ask, but she stepped forward, closing the distance between them, reaching for him and wrapping her arms around him. He could feel her trembling.

"I'm sorry," she whispered, clinging to him. "Johnny, I'm *sorry!*"

Her mouth found his, and his response was overwhelming. He couldn't kiss her hard enough, hold her close enough. He lifted her up and half carried her into the house, incredulous that she had actually followed him back here.

"I don't want to talk," she said, her body straining against his. "I mean it."

He tried to hold her away from him so he could see her face. "Lillian—"

"Don't talk," she whispered urgently, leaning into him again, her hands clutching the front of his shirt. "Kiss me, Johnny. Don't talk—don't think. Take me to bed—"

She grabbed him by the hand, and he followed her blindly into the bedroom.

Old enough to know better.

Who had said that? Lucas?

Becenti did know better. He knew perfectly well that whatever they did in the dark now would in no way cancel out the pain of her leaving in the morning. And she would leave. She would leave and go back to Santa Fe as if tonight had never happened.

He didn't care. He loved this woman. She belonged to him—for now. He began to strip away her wet clothes, his hands trembling in his urgency to have her again. When she was naked, standing before him, he abruptly turned her around. He buried his face into her neck and shoulder, his hands sliding to caress her rounding belly. He could feel it. His child growing inside her.

She turned in his arms, her mouth finding his again. She pulled him down on the bed with her.

"Is it—all right for us to do—this?" he asked, struggling to get out of his clothes.

"Yes," she said, still shivering. "I'm so cold." She rolled against him when he stretched out beside her, and he held her close, pulling the sheet around her, trying to stop her shaking.

How many times had he dreamed of lying with her like this again, skin to skin, feeling her warm body and her breasts pressed against him, breathing her sweet breath, feeling her strong hands on his back? He never expected to make love with her again, never expected to feel her rise under his touch, never expected to have her want him, need him.

"Lillian…"

He moaned when she reached down to caress him. He couldn't wait any longer. He moved over her, thrusting himself into her.

Old enough to know better, he thought, feeling her body hot and tight around him and already giving him the oblivion they both so desperately needed.

My woman. Mine…

He opened his eyes, wondering what had awakened him. Lillian still slept, curled up in his arms. He lifted his head slightly, careful not to disturb her.

Cigarette smoke.

It was coming from the outside. He got up quietly and looked out the window. The rain had stopped. Someone— he thought it was Toomey—stood on the front steps, smoking a cigarette.

What the hell is he doing? Becenti thought, and then he realized that the boy must be trying to get up enough courage to knock. Toomey would know exactly who owned the small car parked in the drive. And he could guess what he might be interrupting.

Becenti put on his pants and walked to the front door, intercepting Toomey just when he was about to pound on the door.

"What?" Becenti said, making the boy jump.

"Oh, uh, your phone's off the hook, sir—" Toomey began. "That's why I..." He didn't finish the sentence.

"Is it?" Becenti said, realizing only then that he hadn't taken the time to hang up the receiver.

Open the door.

Lillian—

He took a deep breath to banish the rush of desire the memory caused in him.

"We found that 'desert rave' thing, Captain. It was about over, I guess, but some of those kids hung around and got caught in a wash after it rained. It's—a mess."

"Any fatalities?"

"Yeah. Three so far. The night sergeant thought you'd want to handle things. He sent me to get you." He looked over his shoulder. "I've got the last utility vehicle. You can't get up there in a car."

"Wait for me," Becenti said. "I'll be out in a minute."

He dressed quickly, not waking Lillian until he was ready to leave. He switched on a small lamp and sat down on the side of the bed, stroking her back until she opened her eyes.

"I've got to go," he said when she was awake.

"What's wrong?" she murmured.

He sighed. "Some kids got caught in a flash flood. I've

got to go see how bad it is. Will you be here when I get back?''

She turned over and sat up, sliding her arms around him and resting her head on his shoulder. "I want to be," she answered.

"Not good enough," he said.

She leaned back to see his face. "What do you mean?"

"I mean—" He broke off because Toomey was knocking on the screen door. He gave another sigh and got up to go see what Toomey wanted now.

"What is it?" Becenti asked without opening the door.

"It's the, uh, car phone, sir—in Ms. Singer's car. I thought it might be important—this time of night and everything. The car wasn't locked," he finished awkwardly, holding up the trilling device so Becenti could see it. "It was ringing when I got here, too, so I thought—"

Becenti opened the screen door and took the phone, carrying it back through the house and depositing it on Lillian's knees. It was still ringing. She looked up at him, and she had a slight frown when she answered it.

He didn't want to stand there and eavesdrop, but he didn't have time to wait. Toomey was right to think that a call at this time of night—or morning—might be important, but at the moment, he earnestly wished that the young officer wasn't quite so conscientious.

"What's wrong?" Lillian said into the receiver, and she was listening intently to whatever the caller was telling her.

"Lillian—" he said anyway.

"Hold on," she said into the telephone—or to him. He wasn't quite sure which. She pressed a button on the phone.

"If you're here when I get back, we'll talk," he said.

"I have to go back to Santa Fe. Now."

He looked at her, but he didn't say anything. And he had no doubt who was on the phone. The same person who had called her away the last time they would have spent the night together.

"I have to, Johnny," she said again.

"Why? Didn't Stuart get his perciatelli?"

He had said the wrong thing, and he knew it. He knew Lillian well enough to recognize that it was all she could do to keep from telling him what she thought of his crass remark.

"Thank you for the cradle board," she said with some effort instead.

But he couldn't let it go.

"Don't worry about it," he said. "You more than paid for it."

She looked at him, in that defiant, challenging way she had. But her eyes filled with tears and her mouth trembled slightly.

"Nice shot, Johnny," she said. "I didn't even see it coming."

"You don't understand at all, do you?"

"Understand? What is there to understand? What do you want from me!"

"I don't want *this.* I don't want you to come here and make me think what we have matters to you—and then you go running back to Dennison! Do you have any idea how that makes me feel?"

"You knew the rules—"

"To hell with your *rules,* Lillian. I care about you. I want you and the baby and I'm not going to pretend whatever it is you're doing now is okay with me, because it's not! You're going to have to choose. The situation we're in is hard, but it's not impossible."

"Maybe not for you," she said, wiping furtively at her eyes.

"We can try to work something out or we can just let it go. If it's not worth it to you to even try, then leave me alone. Stay in Santa Fe with those people who matter so much to you."

He stood in the doorway, waiting for her to say something. She didn't. He turned to go.

"You were right, you know," he said, all his anger spent

now. "I did ask you to marry me because I thought I had to do the right thing. We don't have anything to base a marriage on. Maybe you were even right about the other thing, too. Maybe we don't like each other, either. I don't want you to come here again," he said. "I'm too damn old for all this. Stay in Santa Fe. I mean it."

Chapter Fifteen

Don't cry, she kept thinking. *Just drive.* She would give Becenti what he said he wanted. He hadn't asked any more of her than she had of him.

Stay where you belong.

She had heard of people who would walk a mile to get their feelings hurt. None of them could compare to what she was willing to do.

Nice shot, Johnny.

Don't think about it and don't cry!

She tried to concentrate on the radio. Stuart had assured her that the other shoe was about to drop. He had been forewarned that the story of his lucrative land project would be in today's newspaper and on all the television stations. She expected to hear something about it on the radio newscasts, but she didn't. She also expected that she would have to wade through a herd of reporters as soon as she arrived in Santa Fe, and she earnestly hoped that she could get home and change clothes beforehand. At the moment, she looked exactly like what she was—a walking morning-after-the-one-night-stand. It was bound to affect her credibility.

She stopped paying attention to the radio. She'd been preparing ways to justify this fiasco of Stuart's to the media for months, and if she wasn't ready by now, she never would be. Whether she wanted to think about it or not, she had other, more important things to consider. Like her baby. Like the rest of her life.

Like Johnny Becenti.

She and Becenti were very good at hurting each other. In her case, she didn't want to, didn't mean to, but the result was the same as if she'd meticulously planned it. He, on the other hand, had deliberately made his remark about the cradle board. And if she wasn't careful, she was still going to cry about it.

"I don't need this," she said aloud. She'd done more crying in the last few months than she had in her entire life.

He just didn't—or wouldn't—understand that she hadn't *wanted* to go back to Santa Fe. But then she hadn't wanted to explain herself, either. She wanted the same courtesy he would expect from her. She wanted him to accept that, when it came to her profession, she did whatever she did with good reason—whether it seemed so at the time or not—even when it involved Stuart Dennison. She shouldn't have to explain that her business with Stuart was just that, business.

She made good time driving, but she was feeling the lack of sleep by the time she reached home. The kitchen hadn't been cleaned up. All the physical and emotional debris from the night before was very much in evidence. The cradle board still sat propped up in the easy chair.

She showered and changed clothes, but she also needed a big breakfast and a long nap. She didn't take time for either. She went directly to Stuart's house. She tried calling him on the cellular phone several times on the way to tell him she was coming, but she kept getting a busy signal.

He wasn't at home when she arrived, and there were no reporters encamped in his driveway. His housekeeper said he had left for his office around seven. Lillian went there, expecting to find him and his handlers in an early-morning strategy session. The door was locked.

Puzzled, she had no choice but to go back home. She bought a newspaper first. There was absolutely no mention of Stuart Dennison. She took a nap after all, ignoring the dirty dishes and the wilted sweetheart roses. She slept deeply, in spite of her agitation, finally waking when someone rang the front doorbell. She hurried to answer it, ashamed of how much she was hoping that Becenti had changed his mind and come to Santa Fe. But Stuart stood waiting on the porch.

"Where have you been?" she asked without prelude, and she made no attempt to hide her annoyance. "I thought the story about the land deal was breaking."

He stepped inside, and he didn't answer her. It took what little self-control she had left, but she was determined to stay civil—for the baby if nothing else. She'd had enough emotional upset of late.

"I made a mistake," he said. "No story."

"You made a mistake," she repeated.

"Right," he said, and he didn't quite meet her eyes.

"I don't believe you," she said.

"*C'est la vie,*" he said, grinning.

"You called me in the middle of the night to tell me I had to get back here and it was a mistake?"

"That's about the size of it. But you'll thank me later. So," he said lightly. "Did you finish whatever you were doing with Becenti?"

"None of your business," she said. "And suppose you tell me what that means—I'll thank you later."

"It means that you've let your judgment become completely clouded."

"About what?"

"About Becenti, Lillian. A clearer head had to prevail."

"Yours, you mean."

"Of course, mine. Who knows you better than I do? If I've learned one thing from being ill, it's that you can't waste time standing on the sidelines. You have to get in there and *do*. All you need is a little breathing space so you can come to your senses, and I arranged for you to have it. You had no business trying to deal with Becenti when you were in the emotional state you were in last night. He was playing you like a violin—it really wasn't a pretty sight, Lily. And, as I said, you'll thank me for getting you out of that situation—"

"Stuart! Who do you think you are!"

"I think I'm the man who's taken care of you all these years."

"Taken care of me? I'm not a child. I'm not J. B. Greenleigh. I have my own law practice. Since when have *you* taken care of *me*?"

"Who taught you all those fine points about the law, Lillian? I did. And who do you think sends all those upscale clients your way? *I* do. What is it with you and Becenti, anyway? It would be different if there was any real attachment there—but it's obvious that the two of you don't get along."

"What do you mean you send clients my way!" she cried, but he wasn't listening to her.

"The man is rude and overbearing, Lillian. He's obviously not your equal, and he does nothing but upset you. I don't see why you put up with him."

"Because, Stuart, he's the father of my baby!"

There was a stunned silence. She had his attention now. Becenti would certainly appreciate the irony of her timing. She couldn't tell people that Johnny Becenti had made her a cradle board, but she had no problem saying he'd made her a child.

"He's what?" Stuart said, completely astounded.

"You heard me."

"You're *pregnant?*"

"Yes. I am."

"Lillian, have you lost your mind?"

"Probably."

"Well, when is it due, for God's sake?" he said, staring at her belly. "You said you never wanted children."

"December—and I didn't."

"But now all of a sudden you've changed your mind?"

"Believe me, Stuart. A theoretical pregnancy is a whole lot different from an actual one."

He kept looking at her.

"Does Becenti know? Yes, of course, he knows. That's what the cradle-board thing was about. Well, *that* certainly didn't go well, did it?" he said with more satisfaction than she cared for. "You're not planning to marry him, I hope."

"No, I'm not. But what if I was? What's wrong with that?"

"What's *wrong* with it? You mean besides the things I've already named? You know perfectly well he's not a suitable choice for a husband. Marrying him would cancel out everything you stand for."

"I don't *stand* for anything, Stuart."

"Well, of course you do. You didn't leave the reservation just because you wanted a better life. You left because you had to prove something."

"When did I ever say that? Like what?"

"You wanted to show everybody back in Window Rock and everybody here that you could be successful in the white world and that you didn't have to stay where the government put you. If you let yourself get tangled up with Becenti, you'll end up back on the rez with a bunch of kids to raise and it's all for nothing. For God's sake, Lillian. Look how well you've done."

"Yes," she said tonelessly. "Look how well—all my clients are people obligated to *you*. How could you do that? You could have told me you were sending people my way.

But no. You let me think I—'' She took a deep breath to keep from crying. "Get out, Stuart."

He actually smiled. "I know you're upset now. But you'll get over it, Lily, and you'll realize I'm right. But," he said, his smile disappearing, "this pregnancy of yours changes everything. I need your undivided attention to get through this land-deal business, and the farther along you get, the more distracted you're going to be—"

"Get out!" she said. And if he hadn't gone, she thought she would have pushed him bodily from the house. She shut the door behind him—hard—and she locked it. She stood there, head pressed against the wood, trying to stop shaking.

"Who do you think sends all those clients your way? I do—"

The tears slid down her face. No matter how much she wanted to call Stuart a liar and rant and rage and throw things, she believed him. He actually thought her involvement with Johnny Becenti would make her life and work in Santa Fe "all for nothing." He was wrong. It was her involvement with *him.* He had no right to prop up her practice, no right to let her think she was succeeding because of her own reputation and hard work.

She shook her head and pushed herself away from the door.

"Take strength from this story," her grandmother would say when she was about to tell some sad tale of long ago. As a little girl, she had loved her grandmother's stories, sad or not, but she hadn't learned from any of them.

"Take strength from this story, Lillian. Once, a long, long time ago there was a little Navajo girl who thought she could fly. She climbed the highest cliff in the canyon and leaped over the edge. The Wind People were very strong that day, and they lifted her up and up until she was as high as the eagles. 'Look at me!' she cried. 'I really can fly!'

"But the Wind People only laughed and took themselves far away to another canyon.

"'*Fly now*,' they said...."

"Don't cry, damn it!" Lillian said aloud. "Take strength
from the story." She had to find the strength somewhere.
In the last twenty-four hours she'd both jumped *and* been
pushed off that proverbial cliff, and the Wind People hadn't
been on hand for either occasion.

She went into the kitchen and stood looking around at
the shambles of the night before. After a moment, she began to clear away the dishes and clutter. She carefully
washed and dried each piece of china and each crystal gob-
let and put them away in the antique mahogany china cab-
inet she'd saved for months to buy.

What good are these? she thought. They were nothing
but the trappings of the lie she'd been living.

When she was done and everything in the kitchen was
in order again, she stood there in the middle of the room,
wondering what to do with herself now. She could see the
cradle board through the inside windows, and she abruptly
walked into the living room.

She stood staring at the board. It had been lovingly made.
She knew that. She reached out blindly for it. Her hands
stroked the smooth wood. She sat down with it in her lap,
clutching it to her, trying not to cry. She wanted to talk to
him—to Johnny. She wanted to sit in his lap and tell him
what had happened with Stuart, just as she'd told him about
that long-ago afternoon on the rich man's patio. In spite of
their ups and downs, she knew he would understand, and
she needed someone who understood. She needed him.

But he was too far away. She could reach him physically,
perhaps, but she couldn't reach his heart.

"*Sha'awéé',*" she whispered, still clutching the cradle
board.

My baby.

It was nearly sundown when Becenti returned to his
small house in Window Rock. He didn't expect Lillian to

still be there, and she wasn't. Still, hope sprang eternal, and
he unrealistically looked around the house for a note she
might have left him—a fact he would have vehemently
denied if anyone had accused him of it.

He shouldn't have said what he had about the cradle
board. He shouldn't have said any of it. He would never
forget the way she'd looked at him. How could he want
her so badly and yet deliberately say the things he knew
would drive her away?

There was no note, no sign of her at all, except for the
fact that the house was so much more empty than when
he'd left it. No one would ever have guessed she'd ever
been here.

But he knew. He could tell by the great loneliness that
had come to take her place. He was tired and depressed,
and restless all at the same time, his harmony completely
gone. He opened a can of pork and beans he didn't want
and dumped it into a pot to heat. Then he turned on the
television and sat down on the couch to stare at nothing.
And he tried to think about something besides Lillian. The
only thing left in his mind was the three drowned young
people—two girls and a boy—who had been too drunk or
too drugged, or too ignorant to know the dangers of roam-
ing a wash in the rainy season. He had seen death before—
young and old and every age in between. Many times. But
it was different now, because *he* was different. He had a
child of his own coming, and for the first time in his long
career, his thoughts focused on the parents of these dead
ones instead of on the job at hand—that they must be somewhere waiting and worrying, and how sad they would be
when they were told that their son or daughter wouldn't be
coming home again.

He gave a sharp sigh, annoyed with himself for being so
uncharacteristically sentimental. There were plenty of parents who couldn't care less where their children were or

what happened to them. He knew that firsthand, too, just as he knew that he had no intention of being one of them.

Lillian.

It was clear to him that all thoughts led right back to her. He closed his eyes, remembering. She had never said that she cared about him, much less that she loved him, but she had made him feel it. Last night, when they'd made love, he had felt it—intensely—or thought he had. But now it seemed that he had been totally wrong.

He didn't understand the bond between her and Dennison, no matter how hard he tried. His mind searched for some reason that would make her drop everything and go whenever he called—a reason other than the obvious one. He refused to accept that it was some kind of jealous delusion on his part that made him think she always deferred to the man. He had seen it—that first time at the hogan, and twice since.

And yet Lillian had told the woman Dennison was going to marry that there was nothing between them now. J. B. Greenleigh didn't believe her. Incredibly, *he* did. He knew Lillian to be an honorable and honest person. She wouldn't have been going to bed with Dennison and him both, and she wouldn't have lied to Dennison's ex-fiancée.

But he didn't understand the situation, and he couldn't ask, because he couldn't get Lillian to stay in one place long enough to answer any questions.

He looked around at the sound of a vehicle pulling into the yard. Not Lillian's. The motor was too loud and uneven to be her expensive car. Someone Navajo, he thought, someone who gave the occupant of the house time to get ready for visitors instead of coming immediately to the door. He got up to stir the beans and set them off the burner before he stepped outside.

Winston Tsosie sat in his truck, waiting patiently for Becenti to invite him in. As much as he didn't want visitors, Becenti did so, holding the door open for the old man to come inside, offering him a chair and his choice of television channels, or a glass of water, or anything else he wanted. Then he waited politely for Winston to state his business, a wait that grew and grew until it became completely unwieldly. It suddenly occurred to him that Winston had played a pivotal role in keeping Jack Begaye out of trouble until he could marry Meggie, and that perhaps the old man was now extending his services to Johnny Becenti, regardless of the fact that there was no question of a Becenti-Singer marriage whatsoever.

"You made a fine cradle board," the old man finally said.

Becenti made no comment, because none was required. Given the level of his carpentry skills, he supposed that it was adequate, if not precisely "fine."

"But you took it to Santa Fe too soon," Winston added.

"Yes," Becenti said.

Much too soon.

"What are you going to do now?"

"I don't know," he said.

Winston looked at him. They sat in silence.

"Joe Bill Toomey's youngest boy—he goes to Santa Fe to see his relatives a lot," Winston said. "When he's not being the policeman. You know the one I mean?"

Becenti knew exactly the one Winston meant.

"I'm thinking you could trust him."

"For what?" Becenti asked.

"If a man wants to marry a woman, he ought to be giving her gifts," Winston said. He paused significantly.

Becenti had no idea where this conversation was going. He had sent Lillian a small gift with Sloan the last time she went to see her—but he wasn't about to own up to it. His feeble efforts at courting a woman who didn't care were not something Winston needed to know about.

"You ain't got no business going to Santa Fe right now," Winston said. "Your harmony is still bad, and you got death on you from those drowned ones. The way you are now, you couldn't help but make things worse between you and Lillian. But it might be you could keep Lillian thinking about you if you was to send her something now and then—let Toomey's boy take it for you."

"I never said I wanted to marry her."

"No, but she's got your baby coming, and you're too damn miserable not to be wanting to," Winston said. "Lucas suffered like this when he was trying to marry Sloan. And Jack, too, when he wanted to get married to Meggie. First thing *he* could think of to do was go dancing with another woman—right where Meggie could see him, too. He made Meggie cry, when he would of rather died than do that. And Lucas and both her brothers were ready to kill him. A man can't think straight when he wants a woman he thinks don't want him back. That's the truth and you know it."

Becenti gave a quiet sigh. Yes. He did know it.

"We got to get you ready," Winston said. "You come out to the mission house to the sweat lodge. Maybe you'll need Will and Eddie Nez to do a ceremony for you, too—a long one—if you got enough money. But we got to do first things first. You understand what I'm telling you? You got any questions?"

Becenti smiled slightly. He had to think about that. Did he have any questions?

"You ever say things you don't mean?" Becenti finally asked the old man.

"Used to," Winston said. "Don't now."

"Why not?"

"Ain't got no woman now, that's why not," the old man said matter-of-factly.

They looked at each other in mutual understanding, and Becenti smiled again, regardless of how little he felt like it.

But the smile quickly faded.

This is crazy, he thought. *He* was crazy to even think there could be a possible solution to his problem. The situation with Lillian was hopeless. He knew that because he'd done his best to make it that way.

"You got to be patient," the old man said. "If you are, I think you can find out what you want."

But Becenti already knew what he wanted. He wanted Lillian Singer. And in lieu of that, he wanted his child beyond the influence of people like Stuart Dennison. He wanted his child raised Navajo.

Chapter Sixteen

If Lillian had been the younger, more contentious version of herself, her pride would have gotten the best of her. She would have had to go out of her way to show Becenti that he meant absolutely nothing to her. She would have had to show Stuart what she thought of his "taking care of her" all these years. And she would have had to show them both in a way that left no doubt in their minds about how little she valued either of them. She would have had to close her office and go someplace else and start over, even if she went bankrupt or starved in the process. She would have had to prove once and for all that Lillian Singer didn't have to depend on anyone.

But she wasn't younger, and vindicating herself no longer mattered to her. She was alone and pregnant. She couldn't afford to give in to her hurt feelings or try to maintain any high-minded principles. The only thing that really mattered to her was her baby.

And her baby's father.

She had no idea what to do—because there was nothing to be done, as long as she and Becenti were at such an impasse. And it was one thing for *her* to want him to stay away, and something altogether different when he returned the favor.

She took several days off to get herself together, and she did a piecemeal job of it at best. She wasn't sleeping. She had to keep busy, or worry herself sick. If she couldn't shut down her practice, then the other alternative was to earn the loyalty of the clients Stuart had deigned to send her. She began working to that end immediately. She expected him to call any day to tell her he'd found himself another lawyer. She knew now that he held little regard for her legal skills, and she suspected that he or Mary Ellen or Sam must have thought that having a Native American woman defend him in a crooked land deal would put a more positive spin on the situation. She knew, too, that, in spite of his illness, she wasn't going to make it easy for him and ask to be replaced. He had a choice. Let him worry about her pregnancy-induced lack of concentration or let him fire her.

She kept her doctor's appointments, tried to eat what she was supposed to eat and not forget to take her prenatal vitamins. And she tried not to think about Becenti. But some days she still entertained the idea that he might come to Santa Fe to see her, regardless of what he'd said. The rest of the time she knew better.

She still saw Sloan every weekend, but Sloan had very little to report regarding Becenti's comings and goings. He was as strict as ever and he was underfoot a lot more than Mary Skeets and the rest of the officers would have liked. And he'd had another argument with Lucas. Lucas had blatantly remarked that the worst mistake he'd ever made was sending his sister to talk Becenti out of that hogan. Becenti hadn't realized that Lucas had had a hand in that, and he did *not* appreciate it.

Lillian could understand Becenti's need to stay busy, if not the rest of the male posturing. Work had always been her salvation; perhaps it was his, as well. She won most of her court cases. She even acquired a few new clients, ones she knew didn't come from Stuart. The days slipped into a kind of predictable sameness, broken only by the visits from Sloan and by two weekends of cat-sitting Fred so Gracie could go see her newest grandchild. Lillian had to put the cradle board into a closet to keep Fred from using it as a combination scratching post and cat perch. But she forgave him for presuming; he was much too good a listener for her not to. Fred, the cat, knew more about her true feelings for Johnny Becenti than any other creature on this earth.

As her pregnancy became more and more obvious, she finally announced her condition to Gracie. And once Gracie's amazement subsided and she quit saying, "But you're so *old*," Lillian's longtime right hand was ecstatic. Genuinely so, it seemed. Gracie's enthusiasm did wonders for Lillian's unhappy mood. Sometimes Gracie insisted that the two of them go baby shopping during their lunch hour. She had had five children of her own and had made a good start on the grandchildren. She was a wealth of information as to what babies required. With Gracie's help, Lillian began to see this event as something considerably less than the end of the world.

Even so, Lillian realized one Saturday afternoon in mid-September that the summer was nearly gone—and she'd missed it. She'd paid no attention whatsoever to anything associated with the change of seasons. Nothing about it had caught her attention. She had been marking time by her gestation and nothing more. She had three more months of her pregnancy to go, and then her life would be changed forever. She'd had a sonogram—several sonograms, as they tried to pinpoint an elusive delivery date—but she wouldn't let them tell her the baby's sex. As modern as she pretended to be, there were some things better left to the old ways.

On a beautiful Friday afternoon in mid-October, as she walked—waddled—back from the courthouse, she thought she saw Becenti in a passing vehicle. The car was white like the ones used by the Navajo Tribal Police, but she couldn't see the emblem on the door. She didn't take the time to see it, actually. Her only concern was the man who looked like Johnny Becenti, the one who drove right by her, oblivious to her presence.

She stared after him. If it was Becenti, he could be here for any number of legitimate reasons, none of which had anything to do with her. But she still waited on the corner to give him time to circle the block—in case it was him. In case she wasn't too pregnant for him to recognize. In case he did want to see her.

The vehicle didn't come back again.

By the time she got home that evening, she had convinced herself that she had no reason to think Becenti even wanted to see her. He had clearly abandoned her. And yet she still hoped to find his car parked in the drive when she got there, hoped to find him on the porch later, hoped that before she went to sleep he would at least call.

But there was nothing. And, if he could come to Santa Fe and make no attempt to see her or talk to her, then she had no hope at all.

She went to bed finally, but she slept very little, because she was too pregnant now to ever really rest. Her life seemed to consist entirely of sitting with her feet propped up or looking for a bathroom. She lay in the dark, restlessly turning this way and that, willing herself not to look and see what time it was, willing herself not to think about Johnny Becenti.

But she missed him so much. She wanted to see him— just see him. That's all. She didn't have to talk to him.

She fell asleep shortly before dawn, just in time to be wakened by the telephone. She fumbled to answer it, putting the receiver to her ear, too sleepy to say hello.

"Lillian?" the male voice said.

She opened her eyes.

"Lillian, I need you."

But it wasn't Becenti, and disappointment washed over her. It was Stuart, disclosed at last.

Chapter Seventeen

Stuart held his press conference early, when his own energy level was at its peak.

"They're going to ask you why you've got a lawyer with you," Lillian whispered as they were about to be led to the slaughter. "Do *not* say I'm just here for moral support or I'm just a friend. You say that in public and the lawyer-client privilege is out the window."

"I know that, Lillian," he said tiredly.

"Are you up to this?" she asked.

"Are you?" he countered.

They stared at each other.

"Thank you for coming. I...really didn't think you'd be here for me," he said.

She didn't want to be here, and they both knew it. The time when she would put her hand in the fire for him was long gone.

"You've paid my retainer," she said. "I can behave professionally—regardless of what you may think. Our personal differences aren't part of the equation. If you'd rather get somebody else—''

"No," he said. "Let's do it."

She stepped back and let him walk up to the battery of microphones. He stood for a moment, calling up his hail-fellow-well-met politician's persona. He was good, easily remembering the different reporters' names, fielding their questions with all the skill he'd learned from so many years in public office.

The questions and answers dragged on. She began to notice an uncomfortable twinge in her right side, one that slowly spread to her middle and met an equally uncomfortable twinge that had originated from the left. She shifted her position. It didn't help.

She took a deep breath and tried to discreetly press her hand to her belly where it hurt the worst. And it did hurt now. The sensation was well past "uncomfortable."

She couldn't stand still, and she realized suddenly that Stuart had said something to her or at her. She had no idea if she was expected to make a comment or not. She smiled, and tried to stifle the pain.

"See?" Stuart said, precipitating a round of laughter and getting back the questions.

She could feel the perspiration beading on her forehead. She abruptly turned to leave, but she was hemmed in by the crush of reporters who had been freed up for the event by a slow news day.

The pain was increasing steadily. She had to get out of here.

"Lillian," someone said, pulling at her arm.

She looked around. J. B. Greenleigh stood behind her.

"Telephone, Lillian," she said pointedly—apparently for the benefit of the people around them. "It's important."

"Telephone?" Lillian said, still not understanding.

"This way," J.B. said, taking her by the arm and leading her through the crowd. She didn't stop until they reached the outside hall. Then she led her briskly into Stuart's office.

"Sit down," she said, pulling around a chair. "Before you fall down. I could see you from the back of the room. What's the matter?"

Lillian sat. The pain shot through her midsection like a knife. "I—don't know," she whispered.

"Where does it hurt?"

"Everywhere," Lillian said, bending lower.

"You're not bleeding or anything?"

"No. It just— Oh! It really *hurts.*"

J.B. put her hand on Lillian's forehead. "You feel like you've got a fever. What's your doctor's name?"

Lillian told her, and J.B. was immediately on the telephone, giving someone in his office the particulars.

"They want you to come to the office right now," she said when she hung up. "Is this your purse? I'll drive you."

J.B. took Lillian by the arm again, and she hurt too much to object. Stuart's press conference had apparently ended. He met them in the hallway just as they were coming out.

"What's wrong?" he asked. "Where are you going?"

"I'm taking Lillian to the doctor," J.B. said. "She's in pain."

"Damn it, I knew this would happen when I needed you—"

"Stuart! This is not about *you* and that stupid mess you've gotten yourself into. This is about Lillian's baby. Now get out of the way!"

"You—certainly—handled that," Lillian told her as they made their way outside.

"I get so mad at him," J.B. said. "It's crazy. The way you can love a man to death and get so *mad* at him."

Tell me about it, Lillian thought.

She let J.B. help her into the car—and she earnestly wanted to tell her to stop talking and pay attention to her driving, but she sat huddled against the door instead and tried to endure.

"I heard about the indictment on the morning news and I came straight down here," J.B. said. "I thought I should be around in case Stuart needed me—then I was all hurt because there *you* were—right where *I* ought to be. It's a good thing I didn't get all huffy and leave, huh? I was about to, and then I realized something was wrong with you." She sighed. "I wish I didn't like you, Lillian. It certainly does complicate things."

"I wish—I didn't—like you—too," Lillian managed. It was the truth. She had been mistaken about J. B. Greenleigh. The woman had seen that Lillian needed help and she'd taken it upon herself to do something about it. She was clear-thinking and levelheaded. She just wasn't a very good driver.

"Stuart underestimated you," Lillian said.

"What do you mean?"

"Just that. He needs a good—talking to— Oh!" Lillian said, but it was more their near sideswiping of a parked car than the pain.

"Easy," J.B. soothed her. "We're almost there."

Lillian was whisked right in, and then sent to the obstetrical floor at the nearby hospital for observation.

"They'll monitor you this afternoon, and if nothing develops, you can go home," her doctor said. "I'm pretty sure a urinary-tract infection is all we're dealing with here—your cervix is still closed—but I want to make sure. We have to be careful because you're—"

"I know, I know," Lillian said, holding up her hand. "I'm *old*."

"Old-*er*, Lillian. I was going to say old-'*er*.'"

"Yeah, right," she said. "I don't know how you expect us mature pregnant women to come out of this joint with a shred of vanity left. This has been a very humbling experience."

He laughed. "Somehow, I think you're going to be all right. Gorgeous woman like you?"

"Too late with the—'gorgeous,' Doctor," she assured him around another wave of pain.

The obstetrical floor was quiet. Not a single person in labor, one of the nurses told her. Lillian lay in an airy, pastel pink-and-blue room, hooked up to a fetal monitor, listening to the sound of her baby's heartbeat—essentially abandoned, except for J.B.

She came in shortly after lunchtime with the latest newspapers and an announcement that she had called Window Rock.

"J.B., I didn't want you to do that!" Lillian said.

"Well, tough," she countered. "You're having a problem with the pregnancy. Becenti should know—"

"Becenti—not *Becenti*," Lillian said in exasperation.

"He wasn't there, so I asked the receptionist—Mary Something—where I could get in touch with him. She didn't know. She said he was making a lot of stops—but he could be in at any time. And she asked what it was about. I said I needed to talk to him about Lillian Singer. She said your brother was there. So I talked to him. And he was *very* glad I called."

"Only because he wants an excuse to punch Becenti in the nose," Lillian said.

"Oh," J.B said. "Well, he didn't sound like he was going to punch anybody. Really, he didn't."

Lillian was not reassured.

"Are you feeling better?" J.B. asked.

"I still hurt," she said.

"Can I do anything for you?"

"No," Lillian said. "I believe you've done quite enough."

"Oh, you're mad at me," J.B. said. "I *always* make you mad."

"I'm not mad. I'm just…I don't know what I am."

"As long as I've already upset you, I think I've got something you should know."

"What?" Lillian asked.

"I don't know how bad you need whatever money Stuart is paying you—"

"The point," Lillian said. "Get to it."

"He's been advised to seek other legal counsel."

"Good," Lillian said. "He has my blessing. I hope he does it promptly."

For some reason this pleased J.B. immensely. She sat there for a while, not talking.

"I just love that," she said finally. "Listening to the baby's heartbeat. Isn't it just the greatest thing?"

"Yes," Lillian said. "It is."

"So how come you didn't want me to tell Becenti?"

"Becenti and I are not—together."

"But you and Becenti are still having a baby. That's pretty together, if you ask me. I...think maybe you love him. You look like you do. You look like *I* do—whenever anybody mentions Stuart. Do you love him? If you do, I wish you'd tell me."

"Why?"

"So I won't feel so jealous all the time. I *hate* that. It's awful. Do you?"

Lillian found herself looking into J. B. Greenleigh's completely guileless eyes. She sighed.

"Okay," she said.

"Okay what?"

"Okay...I... Yes," Lillian said.

"Could you be a little more specific? This is kind of hard to follow."

"No, I couldn't! I don't talk about Becenti to anybody— except Fred, the cat. *He* doesn't care if I'm specific or not."

J.B. laughed, a lilting sound that must have swept Stuart Dennison completely off his feet.

"Did you do what I told you?" Lillian asked. "Did you talk to Stuart and not take no for an answer?"

J.B. sighed. "No. I...chickened out, I guess."

"Well, do it. Now's a good time. He's out of the frying

pan and in the fire. He can be a jerk, but the only time I know for certain he rose above it was for you.''

"For me?"

"Go pin him down," Lillian said. "Don't let him *not* tell you.''

"Tell me what?"

"If he loves you. And don't accept any answer you don't like. Understand?"

"No," J.B. said. "But I'll do it. I think I'll do it right now. Barge in, throw that Sam person *and* Mary Ellen out—and get some things settled. Unless...you need me to do something for you. I can take you home if they discharge you.''

"No. Gracie will do that. Go on. You won't have a better opportunity than today.''

J.B. smiled her dazzling smile. "Okay," she said. "And thanks, little mama.''

Becenti was late getting back to the law-enforcement building. He was tired and more than a little aggravated. There was nothing like a meeting with a government agency—in this case, three of them—to make him wish he was back being a patrolman on some reservation side-road instead of having to deal with all the bureaucratic nonsense that came with his current position.

But he realized as soon as he walked into the building that he might soon wish there had been a longer meeting. Both Lucas Singer and Mary Skeets followed in behind him from the front door to his office, and both of them were far too agitated for his comfort level.

He waited until he was behind his desk before he allowed them the opportunity to ruin what was left of a really bad day.

"Okay, what is it?" he asked.

"Lillian—'' they said in unison, then looked at each other as if they were both surprised to find themselves in the same chorus, much less singing the same tune.

"Lillian what?" he asked when neither one of them continued.

"—is in the hospital," Lucas said.

"—is on television," Mary Skeets said.

"Well, which is it?" Becenti said, close to becoming alarmed.

The instant replay wasn't much better.

"Mary, you go first," he said. His suggestion caused Lucas to fidget.

"I just saw Lillian on television," Mary said. "On the six o'clock news."

"She's in the hospital," Lucas argued. "She can't be on television."

"Well, she was. Stuart Dennison is being indicted for something, and Lillian was standing right there with him. I saw her."

"I talked to somebody from Santa Fe. She called around noon—" Lucas said, still arguing.

"Who?" Becenti interrupted.

"She said her name was J. B. Greenleigh. She said Lillian had to go into the hospital and she—this person with the initials—wanted to let her family know. She didn't say what was wrong—"

"Actually, she wanted to let Captain Becenti know," Mary put in. "She asked for him when she called. You were out of the office, sir."

Lucas ignored her. "I came in to tell you I need to take some vacation time. I'm going to Santa Fe—"

"No, you're not," Becenti said. "That's all, Mary," he added to clear the room.

"Why not?" Lucas demanded.

"Because I'm going. The message was for me. I need you to look after things here. That's all, Mary!"

"Well, all *right*," she said, but she wasn't happy.

"Lillian doesn't want to see you," Lucas said.

"Then she can tell me that when I get there. I'm going to Santa Fe. You're staying here. Period."

* * *

But he couldn't find Lillian. None of the hospitals had a
Lillian Singer listed as a patient. He remembered Meggie
Begaye and her troubled pregnancy. She'd had to be sent
to a hospital in Albuquerque. He finally decided to go talk
to the woman who worked for Lillian, and he drove to her
house. A boy about ten years old answered the door.

"Is Gracie at home?" Becenti asked.

"Yeah, but she's busy—she's got her hands in bread
dough."

"Who is it?" Gracie called from somewhere inside the
house.

"Tell her it's the tribal cop," Becenti said.

"The tribal cop!" the boy yelled.

"Who?" Gracie yelled back.

"Johnny Becenti."

"Johnny Becenti!" the boy yelled.

"*Who?*" Gracie yelled again.

"Fred's friend," Becenti said as a last resort.

"Fred's friend!"

"Oh!" Gracie yelled. "Tell him to come in."

"Grandma says to come in," the boy advised him.

Becenti stepped inside, wondering how many people in
this world had ever been vouched for by a cat. "Which
way?" he asked the boy, who had plopped himself in front
of the television—upon which the unwittingly helpful Fred
slept soundly.

The boy pointed over his left shoulder.

Becenti found Gracie in the kitchen, and she did indeed
have her hands in dough. She was clearly a vigorous bread-
maker. There was flour everywhere.

"I'm looking for Lillian," he said immediately.

"She's at home," Gracie said, still kneading the ball of
dough. "Didn't you try there?"

"I thought she was in the hospital," he said, unable to
hide his relief. "Or on television," he added, and Gracie

laughed. "Well, she was. But she's at home now. I took her there a little while ago."

"She's...all right?"

"Well, she's felt better, Mr. Becenti."

"She didn't sign herself out of the hospital or anything, did she?"

"Of course not! Why would you think that?"

"Because she was on the six o'clock news with Stuart Dennison," he said. But he didn't say that whenever Dennison called, Lillian went no matter what. It wasn't much of a stretch for him to think she would leave her hospital bed to go do something he needed. He realized that Gracie was watching him intently, and he grew uncomfortable under her steady gaze.

"Stuart's press conference was about ten this morning," Gracie said patiently. "She went to the hospital after that. And they discharged her late this afternoon. Okay?"

He nodded. "Thanks."

"Are you going to go see her?" Gracie asked as he turned to go.

"Yeah," he said. "Unless there's some reason—"

"No, no," Gracie assured him. "I just wanted you to take her a casserole." She went to the freezer, then decided she had too much dough on her hands still. "Would you?" she asked him.

He opened the door for her.

"That one right there," she said, pointing with her little finger.

When he turned around, Gracie was smiling.

"You're the one responsible for this," she said.

"Pardon?"

"For Lillian's baby. You're the father, aren't you?"

He didn't answer, and she didn't press.

"Take her the casserole. The instructions are written on the foil. Tell her to call me if she needs anything. Oh, and take these keys," she said, pointing to a set on the counter with her elbow. "They're Lillian's. I had them so I could get in—so she wouldn't have to get up and come to the door if she's resting."

He didn't take the keys.

"Or would you rather pick the lock?" she asked, and he couldn't help but smile.

"I guess she told you about that," he said, not precisely embarrassed, but not comfortable, either.

"She doesn't say much about you—but she did tell me that. And Mr. Becenti," she said when he was about to leave, "I'm *so* glad it's you and not Stuart Dennison."

The small candlestick lamp had been left on, but Lillian woke up for other reasons. Because she never slept for very long anyway. Because she was on the couch and she had been covered with a blanket she didn't have when she lay down.

And because someone very close by was snoring.

She rose up on her elbow. Becenti was sprawled in the easy chair, sound asleep.

"How did—?" she started to say out loud, but she saw her keys lying on the coffee table. She quietly sat up so she could see him better. He had moved the easy chair closer to the couch, she supposed, to be handy if she wanted anything, but he was too dead to the world to be of much help at the moment.

She smiled, her eyes traveling over him. He looked younger asleep. And vulnerable. She could have reached out and touched his hand if she'd wanted, but she didn't. She was glad suddenly that J.B. had made the telephone call to Window Rock. And she was glad that Becenti was sleeping. She would have a little time, at least, just to look at him—before he woke up and they had to knock the chip off each other's shoulders.

I love you, she thought. And it was as startling as if she'd said it out loud. She had worked so hard not to dwell on that aspect of their situation. But it was true, and his self-imposed absence had only served to point it out to her.

She kept looking at him. There were scrapes and scratches on his hands and knuckles. She wondered what he'd been doing—not fighting with Lucas, she hoped. He'd had a haircut recently—she actually liked his unhip, pseudomilitary look. There was so much about him that pleased her. She loved that his reserved personality was actually rife with mischief and laughter. She loved that she could see a smile coming in his eyes a long, long time before it ever reached the rest of his face. She loved the way he looked at her—with desire *and* with respect. The thing that had been so hard to bear was seeing how much she hurt him.

I don't know how to be the person you want.

And she didn't know if she could change—or even if she wanted to. She wasn't in the least like Mae. Mae had been gentle and kind and quintessentially Navajo. Lillian didn't bother with the Navajo Way, and she was a royal pain in the butt and always had been. Becenti himself had said so.

I can't give you what you need. I can only make you miserable.

That was the final truth, if she could just accept it. She gave a quiet sigh and looked down, her hands gently caressing her belly. The baby immediately stirred under her touch.

She looked up to find Becenti awake and watching. Her eyes filled with tears.

"Johnny," she whispered. "Where have you been?"

Chapter Eighteen

It wasn't what he'd expected her to say at all. She stared into his eyes. He wanted to touch her, but he made no attempt to do so. He had missed her so much, needed her so much.

"I've been waiting for you," he said in answer to her question.

"Waiting for—? You told me to stay away."

"Since when do you ever do what I say?"

Great, he thought. They were going to pick up the argument exactly where it left off.

But, surprisingly, she smiled.

"So why did you come?" she asked after a moment.

"I owe it to you. You drove me crazy when I was sick. I figured I should return the favor."

She laughed softly. It pleased him to be able to make her laugh. He had so much he wanted to say to her, so many things he wanted to know, but he was afraid nothing had changed, and he wasn't ready to hear that yet.

"How are you feeling?" he asked.

"I've been better," she said, echoing Gracie's report.

"Can I do anything for you?"

"No, I have everything I need—Gracie went to the grocery store for me."

"Are you hungry or anything?" He was happy to sit with her like this, precarious as the situation might be. But if she needed something, anything, he wanted to take care of it for her.

"No, I'm just—" She stopped and took a deep breath. "I just don't want to talk about...anything."

Their eyes met; hers looked away. He remembered only too well the last time she hadn't wanted to talk.

She shifted her position on the couch and leaned back, and an expression he couldn't quite identify passed over her face.

"Are you okay?" he asked. He reached out as if to touch her, but didn't.

She took another deep breath. "I—"

She abruptly leaned forward.

"Lillian?" he said, still not touching her.

She looked at him. "I'm...okay," she said, but her answer did nothing to reassure him.

"I'll be right back," she said abruptly, standing.

He stood with her. "Are you sure you're—?"

"I'll be right back," she said again.

"Okay," he said, worried now.

She was gone a long time. He finally went looking for her. She was in the bedroom, sitting on the foot of the bed. She gave him a funny little half smile when he went in.

"I think I know how you felt," she said.

"About what?"

"About my coming to the hogan that time—when you were sick."

He didn't say anything, because he didn't understand the direction the conversation had taken. At all.

"You wanted me to go away and leave you alone," she said.

"Yes," he agreed.

"And I think you wanted me to stay, too."

"Yes," he said again. He could admit that—now. He sat down on the bed beside her. She reached out to take his hand.

"You know what really scares me?" she asked.

"What?"

She licked her lower lip and gave a wavering sigh. "You do," she said.

He laughed. "Lillian—"

"I am so afraid of needing you," she said in that earnest way she had sometimes. He'd first seen that side of her when she'd come to see him at the hogan, when she'd told him Stuart Dennison was marrying someone else.

"Would that be so bad?" he asked.

"Of course it would, Johnny. Don't you understand?"

"No," he said, truthfully. He had seen many sides of her complex personality, but he had no idea which Lillian this might be. "You're tired. Maybe you should lie down."

"I'm trying to tell you something," she said.

"Then tell me."

"I need to be strong, Johnny. I *have* to be. It's the way I cope with things. And most of the time I *am* strong—but tonight I—" She stopped. "Maybe it's just the pregnancy—or it's the other thing."

"What other thing?"

"I'm not making any sense, am I?"

"Not much, no."

"I've never been any good at being coy—you've probably noticed," she said, squeezing his hand slightly and letting it go.

"A time or two," he said.

"So I'm just going to say it. I…want you to stay for a little while. It doesn't mean anything. I'm just a friend, asking for a favor. And that's all," she said, and he had the distinct impression she was trying to convince herself as much as him. "I feel so bad and I want to go to sleep— with you here. And don't ask me why, because I don't know why. I just—" She lifted her hands slightly and let them fall back into her lap.

"Okay," he said. "You lie down and go to sleep, and I'll be here."

"I mean *here* here," she said, waving her hand over the bed. "So I'll know..."

"No problem," he assured her, wondering whether there would ever be a time in his life when he could consider her "just a friend."

She was looking at him so intently, as if she were trying to see if he meant it.

"Okay," she said, apparently deciding that he did. She reached to pull down the covers. He helped her get situated, then took off his gun belt and emptied his shirt pockets and lay down beside her. She turned so that she was facing him.

"You know it's the antibiotic talking—not me," she said, still trying to lower any great expectations he might be harboring.

"Oh, I'm sure of it," he said. He reached out to tuck a strand of her hair behind her ear.

"Or maybe it's the fever. You know what fever can do to you— What happened to your hands?" she asked abruptly, taking one of his and looking at it closely. "They're all beat-up."

"Oh—Lucas and I—"

"Don't tell me you had a fight."

"No, nothing like that. We had to take a rifle away from a man who'd had too much to drink. He wasn't happy about parting with it."

"Lucas or the man?" she asked, and he laughed softly. It was a reasonable question, given her brother's disapproval of him.

"You and Lucas are supposed to supervise," she said.

"Don't you have some nice Toomey types to do things like that for you?"

"The Toomey types were all on vacation or elsewhere. Lucas and I had to take the call. I thought you wanted to sleep," he said, because she was still looking at him so intently.

"I do. I'm just waiting for the baby to settle down." She placed the hand she was holding firmly on her belly. "See?"

He was unprepared for the insistent scrambling he felt, or for his emotional response to it.

"Strong," he said, his voice sounding husky and strange to him.

"You should feel it from this side," she said.

He reached for her then, moving her closer to him so that her head rested on his shoulder. "Don't worry," he said to reassure her that he wasn't taking more than she'd intended to give. "It doesn't mean anything."

He held her close for a moment, and he had to brace himself against the rush of feeling her nearness caused him. He loved her. And he couldn't say it without risking what little ground he'd gained. She was sick and she was scared and she didn't want to be by herself. He was handy. And he had to be satisfied with that.

She went to sleep easily, and so did he. But it was he who woke up alone. He sat up. There was a hint of daylight at the windows. He listened intently, but he couldn't hear her moving around anywhere.

He began to look through the house for her, finally finding her outside, sitting on the front-porch steps. It was a cold morning, and she sat huddled with her head resting on her knees.

"Lillian?"

She looked up at him, her face tearstained and anxious. "I think I'm in labor," she said.

He didn't remember much of the trip to the hospital— except that he held her hand. Her fingers were cold and clinging in his. He kept looking at her as he drove. She was in intense pain; he could see it on her face. And there was nothing he could do about it—except drive.

He took her in through the emergency entrance, where a woman wearing a blue scrub dress immediately whisked her away. He didn't know if she remembered Lillian from yesterday or if "I think I'm in labor" was the magic phrase to get a patient seen in a hurry. He wanted to go with Lillian, but he wasn't give the option. He stood there, staring at the door she'd gone through, completely at a loss as to what he should do. He'd been in a hospital since Mae died—as a patient—but he'd forgotten—hadn't realized—how much he hated them, how much the smell and the sounds of the place could bring all that pain and sadness back again. He had been down this road before: *Wait here. Stay out of the way.*

The sense of helplessness was nearly more than he could bear.

He forced himself to sit down in the waiting area with the rest of the extraneous people. He wasn't even sure anyone would come to tell him how Lillian was. He wasn't her husband. He wasn't even her "significant other." When everything was said and done, he was merely the donor of the sperm.

The place was busy; he could understand what that might entail, but it didn't help the waiting. Finally, Lillian's obstetrician—a young man with thick glasses who looked like a college student—called his name.

"She's in labor," the doctor said bluntly, because he was too young and too white to do anything else. "She's almost thirty-five weeks—five weeks from her due date. We like for a baby to be as mature as it can be before it's delivered, but in this case, we can't wait any longer."

"Why not?" Becenti asked, already fearing the answer.

"The tests we're doing show some problem with the fetal circulation."

"I don't know what that means," Becenti said loudly enough to cause everyone nearby to look at him.

"It means something is interfering with the baby's blood supply. Every time Lillian has a contraction the baby's heart rate goes way down. She's going to have to have a C-section. We're going to have to take the baby—right now."

"Is she going to be all right? Is the baby going to be all right?"

"I think Lillian will do fine. I'm...hopeful about the baby. I've got to go. You can wait in the waiting area on the obstetrical floor—somebody will tell you how to find it. I'll look for you there—after."

Becenti stood there, stunned.

Hopeful? What the hell did that mean? Hopeful?

Coincidence had played a big part in his being here with Lillian, now. He remembered what his mother always said to remind herself to stay alert for the Navajo's metaphysical trickster and bringer-of-disaster.

Coincidence is always Coyote.

He had to think, and he was completely numb. Everything was moving too fast—he didn't even get to speak to Lillian beforehand. He didn't get to tell her—

But he wouldn't have told her anything, because she was afraid of *needing*. Just like he was.

He asked for directions to the obstetrical-floor waiting area, and the pay phones, and some place where he could get change. As soon as he had a handful of quarters, he made the call to Window Rock, to Lucas Singer's house. Lucas had gone already, a sleepy Will told him. And Sloan wasn't there, either. She was in Albuquerque attending a nurses' workshop "or something." He looked at his watch and tried the law-enforcement building. It was too early for Mary Skeets, and the night dispatcher told him that Lucas hadn't come in yet.

He didn't leave a message. This wasn't the kind of thing

he wanted Lillian's family to learn from a While You Were Out memo. He did the only thing left to do. He waited.

And waited.

There was no one else in the waiting area, and he was grateful for that small blessing. He didn't want to talk to anyone. He didn't want to see anyone. Except Lillian. And their baby.

He eventually called Window Rock again. This time he got Lucas easily—which was not necessarily a good thing.

"You took your own good time calling back," Lucas said, and Becenti had to hold the receiver away from his ear for a moment to keep from responding to the remark. He knew that it was the worry talking as much as the disdain for the man Lucas thought had used and then abandoned his sister. He had little to tell Lucas, Lillian was still in surgery. The only other thing he knew was that he had no energy left to be interrogated.

"What did Lillian say?" Lucas wanted to know.

"I didn't get a chance to talk to her."

"Why not?"

"Because they took her to surgery and then they told me about it."

"Yeah, well, whose fault is that?" Lucas wanted to know. Becenti understood the question perfectly. If he'd been her husband instead of a fly-by-night son of a bitch, he might have been better informed.

"I have to go," Becenti said. "If you've got anybody going out my mother's way, I'd appreciate it if you'd tell her about Lillian."

Lucas didn't say yes or no, and Becenti let the noncommittal silence go. He hung up the phone and went back to waiting.

He must have dozed off, because he realized suddenly that Lillian's doctor was there.

He got up immediately. He wanted to be standing when he heard the news. He wanted to meet it head-on and face-to-face.

"Lillian's okay," the doctor said. "The baby is stable. He's—"

"He?"

"It's a boy," he said. "He's having some breathing problems. We're going to have to keep him in the 'baby box,' give him oxygen, make sure he stays warm—help him breathe if it comes to that. And when all that straightens out, he's still going to have to gain some weight before he gets to leave here—but he's got all his parts and everything. Lillian's still in the recovery room. She'll be there for a while yet. We have to make sure she's stabilized before we bring her back to this floor. You can go see your boy in the meantime, down that way. Tell them who you are and they'll try to roll him close enough for you to get a look at him."

The doctor turned to leave.

"Wait," Becenti said. "You didn't say if the baby will be all right."

"I'm still hopeful. He's in the right place with all the best and latest equipment. Right now we make it as easy as we can for him."

Becenti stood in the hallway. He heard every word—but he still didn't know what he wanted to know. Breathing problems, he heard. Make it as easy as we can for him, he heard.

He turned abruptly and went in the direction the doctor had indicated. The nursery had a number of "baby boxes," all of them occupied, and he couldn't begin to guess which baby was his.

"What name?" one of the nurses said through the glass. He could barely hear her.

"Singer," he said.

"Singer-hyphen-Becenti?"

He stood there. He loved Lillian Singer. He wanted to marry her. This was *his* baby, and Lillian had done the only thing she could—or would—do to acknowledge that. But he was not happy being relegated to the other side of a hyphen. He intended to be more of a father than that.

"Yeah," he said. "Singer-hyphen-Becenti."

She motioned for him to move to another window farther down the hall. He made the trip more quickly than she, and he stood waiting. There was only one incubator in this room. It had a tiny baby inside, one that lay surrounded by equipment and wore a pink-and-blue knit cap.

"Here he is—young Mr. Singer-Becenti," she said to him, her voice still muffled and surreal sounding. She moved the unit closer to the window and then checked the baby's status—he supposed. He pecked on the window to get her attention. "Why is he in here by himself?" he asked.

"No more room over there," she answered. "This is better. One baby—one nurse."

He didn't know if he was reassured by that or not. What if the ratio was an indicator of how sick or weak the baby was?

This is not working, he thought. His son was too far away. He wanted to see him up close. He wanted to be able to tell Lillian what he looked like.

He pecked on the glass again. "Can I come in?" he asked.

She hesitated.

"Please. Can I come in?"

"No, I'm sorry. Not yet. Soon, though," she promised him.

But he had no faith whatsoever in hospital promises. He wanted to stand close to his son. He could feel his eyes filling with tears. He swallowed hard, then again. He wanted to touch his little boy, but he had to make do with touching the glass window instead.

The baby lay with his eyes closed. Becenti could see a few strands of dark hair sticking out from the knit cap and the rapid but uneven rise and fall of his tiny chest.

Please, he thought. *Please.*

What would he do if anything happened to this little boy? He had lost Mae. He had never had Lillian. He couldn't go through it again.

"He's sleeping," the nurse said. "This getting-born business is kind of rough—especially if you weren't planning on making the trip. He's little, for right now. But they do have a way of getting six feet tall and asking for the car keys."

He looked at her, trying to see if she thought *this* baby would do that.

"In a few days, if everything goes okay, you can hold him."

"Hold him?" he asked, not sure he'd heard right.

"Yes," she said, smiling slightly. "He needs to be held by his mom and dad as soon as he's able."

He stood there for a long time, watching for some sign of his son's strength and willingness to hang on. Finally, the tiny hands opened and closed.

He turned abruptly and walked away.

"Where is he?" Lillian asked. She had been trying not to, but she couldn't stand it any longer. She'd been trying not to cry, too, but the tears slid from the corners of her eyes in spite of everything she could do. It wasn't just the pain of the surgery or worry about the baby that made her cry. It was Becenti. He should be here. She couldn't be with their son—he had to do it.

"I don't know," Sloan said. "He was here. He saw the baby. That's all I could find out."

"He wouldn't just *leave*, would he?" Lillian asked, when apparently that was exactly what he had done.

"Lillian, I don't know."

"I need him," she said, still trying not to cry. "Damn it!"

She turned her face away; Sloan handed her a tissue. Lillian had no idea why Becenti would just *go*. Somebody had to look for him. Somebody had to find him and tell him to come back here.

She gave a wavering sigh. "I don't know what's wrong with me," she said. She kept *crying*, and she was talking too much—when she didn't feel like talking at all. She was so tired, and so—everything.

"You just had a baby. And major surgery," Sloan said. "And you're worried about your son."

"You've seen him?" Lillian asked. She didn't know if she was repeating herself or not.

"Yes, I've seen him. He's beautiful."

"Who does he look like? And do *not* say Winston—Churchill."

"No, he doesn't look like Winston Churchill," Sloan assured her. "He looks like...a sweet baby boy you can't wait to get your hands on."

"And his breathing is...better?"

"Yes."

"And you'll wheel me down there to see him?"

"As soon as the doctor says it's okay and you can make the trip."

"He didn't have to go back to Window Rock for some kind of police thing, did he?" Lillian asked, abruptly switching the topic of conversation.

"Lillian—" Sloan said in obvious exasperation.

"What?" Lillian said. "I suppose you want to—run off, too."

"Actually, I want to take a stick to you," Sloan said.

"What is that supposed to mean?"

"It means— Never mind what it means. I've given up on you. You just don't get it."

"Get what?"

"The man loves you!"

"Then why isn't he here?"

"Because he can't take any more grief from you, that's why!"

"Did he say that?" Lillian asked, and she couldn't keep her mouth from trembling.

"No, he didn't say that. It's just what I think."

"What he *said* was that he wanted—to marry me."

"But you took care of that right quick, I'll bet," Sloan said.

"Yes, I took care of it! I'm not coming back to the reservation. I need a little sympathy here!"

"Well, you're not going to get it," Sloan assured her. "Not from me."

"You don't understand."

"I don't *understand?* Who do you think you're talking to, here? I left everything I knew, everything I owned, to come live on the rez with Lucas, only I had three children that *weren't* his instead of one that *was*."

"It isn't the same at all."

"Of course, it is—except my situation was worse. I had my brother's children *and* the cultural differences. And then there was Lucas's history with alcohol—and that anthropologist person flitting in and out of his life whenever she felt like it. But I *still* took the chance, because I loved him and because there was no other way. I had a career, but I didn't *have* to work in North Carolina any more than you have to work here in Santa Fe. There are plenty of lawyers on the rez, and you already do legal work there whenever your mother or Lucas asks you to. I really don't see the difference."

"Maybe I don't like to get paid in sheep."

"There are worse things," Sloan said, clearly ignoring the sarcasm. "Lucas and Becenti both belong to the People. You and I don't. What do you think life is about, Lillian? You can't have what you want without some kind of strings attached. You have to make choices *and* sacrifices. You think it's been easy for me here? This is beautiful country and I love it—but it's not my *home*. And I have to struggle every day not to do something culturally wrong that will embarrass Lucas or Will or Dolly—or cause a meeting of the tribal council. It's hard. Sometimes I get so homesick I could die.''

"I know. I'm sorry."

"You know?"

"Those nostalgia dinners you have to have every so often—the grits and the fried green tomatoes and all that other stuff, right?"

Sloan gave a small sigh. "Right."

"If it gets so bad, then why do you stay here?"

"I said I get homesick enough to die, not *leave*. And I told you. I love Lucas, and I couldn't have him any other way. If I have to be homesick sometimes so we can have a life together, well—it's the price I'm willing to pay. And have paid for quite a few years now. Lucas didn't give up on us. He came all the way to North Carolina to get me. He found a way for us to be together, but only if I could do most of the compromising. He knew what he was asking—how hard it would be for me. But I made the choice—for us."

"So Lucas is worth it?"

"Of course, he's worth it. How often do you think you can find a man to love and respect, who loves and respects you, too? It's close to a miracle, Lillian. If I have any regrets, it's that he and I never had a child of our own."

"But you're telling me that to be happy you have to be miserable," Lillian said in exasperation.

"On some level, yes. Intermittently, yes. And if you love Santa Fe more than you love Becenti— Well, then, you're an idiot."

"Gosh, Sloan, why don't you say what you *really* think?"

Sloan smiled. "Because you just had a baby—and major surgery."

"And I'm worried."

"That, too."

"Becenti still loves—Mae," Lillian suggested.

"Some part of Lucas still loves the anthropologist. So we're both second choices. So what?"

"So—" she started to say, but she had no answer to that question. She only knew Becenti wasn't here, and she wanted him.

"Lillian," Sloan said. "What I really think is that whatever you ran to Santa Fe to get away from—you took with you. And I think you should deal with Becenti and whatever feelings you have for him with that in mind. Because if you don't, you'll regret it for the rest of your life. You've got that little boy to think of."

Lillian had no more to say. She was so *tired* and everything seemed to hurt. She closed her eyes. She wanted to see her baby, and she simply didn't have the strength to get there.

"Will you go see him again?" she abruptly asked Sloan. "I want to know how he's doing."

Sloan didn't point out that she'd just come back from the nursery, and Lillian appreciated that. She lay there after Sloan had left the room, thinking about the things her sister-in-law had said. The logic was flawless—even if Lillian's career success had been her own and not something Stuart had machinated. It did all come down to choices and sacrifices. How much was she willing to give up for a chance to be with Becenti and their child? Contrary to what she'd always believed, living on the reservation wasn't the real problem. She understood the *real* problem perfectly now. She was afraid, and perhaps with good reason, because Johnny Becenti had apparently gone.

Where is he? she kept thinking. *Where is he!*

In spite of everything, she fell into a deep sleep. She was alone when she wakened, and the sun was coming up. She was able to turn over on her side with considerable discomfort to her belly and to the hand receiving the intravenous fluids, but she made it, finally. A nurse came in almost immediately.

"I want to see my baby," Lillian said, trying to rise up

on her elbow. It was entirely the wrong thing to do. The pain that shot through her midsection made her eyes water.

"Easy," the nurse said. "First things first, here. You get your plumbing to work, eat a little something, sit on the side of the bed for a while—in whatever order pleases you—and *then* we'll talk."

"I haven't even seen him yet!" Lillian protested.

"I know. And we're going to fix that. So which is it? Tinkle, bath or what?"

"You people are all alike," Lillian complained. "My sister-in-law is a nurse and she's just as hardheaded as you are."

The nurse grinned. "What can I say?"

Lillian impatiently suffered the indignities of being an invalid—primarily because she couldn't do otherwise. She didn't have the strength to do anything but complain.

Sloan appeared when Lillian had just finished her bath and was attempting to sit on the side of the bed for a while to meet phase two of the proposed trip-to-the-nursery criteria. She was doing all right—so far—as long as she kept her forearms propped on the over-bed table for stability.

But she was not happy.

"Where the hell have you been!" she said without really meaning to.

"Oh, *I* see," Sloan said. "It's going to be *that* kind of a morning, is it?"

"Sloan, I'm sorry. I—" She stopped, because if she didn't, she was going to ask her if she'd seen Becenti, and she didn't want to do that anymore. He hadn't stayed around, and that was that.

"I've been looking at your boy. He's stirring some. Vital signs are stable. They haven't had to put him on a ventilator. He's tinkled *and* had a bowel movement. Oh, and I don't think I told you, he's wearing a nice hat."

"A...hat?"

"A pink-and-blue one. To keep him warm. You're going to love it. Looks like a little lumberjack."

"A lumberjack?" Lillian said, and she was going to cry again. "What is *wrong* with me?" she said, wiping at her eyes. "And don't say it's because I've just had a baby and major surgery."

"Oh, I wasn't. I was going to say it's because you're so *old.*"

Lillian laughed in spite of herself. She was still smiling when Sloan suddenly nodded toward the door.

Lillian looked around. Dolly Singer and Katie Becenti stood there, their faces impassive. Sloan greeted them both—her Navajo really wasn't half bad—then she took herself elsewhere. Lillian was left to face the two matriarchs alone. She reached for Dolly's hand, and then she waited, albeit impatiently, for one of them to begin the conversation. She couldn't help but think of their last visit to Santa Fe all those months ago. But, as tired and upset as she was, she made a concentrated effort to behave well now.

"My grandson is beautiful," Dolly said, hugging her tightly, and Lillian had to fight hard again not to cry.

"I haven't seen him yet," she said, her voice sounding small and strange to her. She hadn't seen the baby's father yet, either, but she didn't say so.

"What do they tell you about him?" Katie asked, and Lillian gave her Sloan's most recent report.

Katie listened silently. "What do they tell you about my son?" she asked when she was certain Lillian had finished.

"Nothing," Lillian said, surprised by the question. "No one has seen him."

Katie looked at Dolly.

"My son goes off to be by himself when he's troubled," Katie said unnecessarily. "Like when he stayed at the sheep camp all that winter. You know that." The tone was kind. And Lillian felt the incredible urge to cry again.

"Do you think he's...gone there now?" she asked.

"No. His baby isn't there. Or you."

They sat in silence again.

"My son asks for a marriage," Katie said after what seemed a long time.

"He what?" Lillian said—and got a warning look from Dolly.

"My son asks for a marriage," Katie said again. "He has no uncle to speak for him. You have no uncle to hear the offer. Your mother and his mother—*we* will do the talking for you and him. What do you say to marrying my son?"

"I say no," Lillian said, because she had been caught completely off guard.

"Why does she say no without asking to hear what he offers?" Katie asked Dolly.

"Because I—" Lillian tried to say.

"She doesn't mean it," Dolly said, looking at Lillian hard. Again. "And she doesn't say no. She's listening. Tell her what your son will give."

Katie looked doubtful—as did Lillian—but after a moment, Katie continued. "All his property," she said. "Everything he owns now or will own. He says to tell you he understands that you have to be away from the People. He says he understands it is something you need for your harmony. He says he won't try to make you live somewhere you don't want to be. He says he will come here. He says he can find a job with the county sheriff's office or something like that. But he asks if you will let his son come back to the People every summer. He says he wants his son taught the Navajo Way, so that when he is a man, he'll know who he is, even if he chooses to live away from the People, like his mother. He wants your relatives to help teach the boy how to walk in beauty. These men, he names. Your brother, Lucas Singer, and your nephew by marriage, Will Baron, and Winston Tsosie, who was adopted into your family, and Jack Begaye, who is your other nephew by marriage. He says all of them are wise in their own way and will teach the boy well. He wants all of this for his son—and for any other children he has with you."

Other children? Lillian almost said.

"*When* did he say all this?" Lillian asked, whether it was her turn or not.

"The day he brought the cradle board to show me was the first time," Katie said. "And every time I've seen him since then. And this morning," Katie added.

"This morning?"

"Yes. Last night, he sent Joe Bill Toomey's boy to get me and bring me here. And your mother. Toomey's boy drove the car fast so we could get here quick. This morning I talked to Johnny again so I would remember all he said and I wouldn't get it wrong."

Lillian didn't say anything. She looked at her mother—who smiled.

"What do I tell my son about a marriage?" Katie asked.

"She'll need time to think about all this," Dolly said.

"No. No, I don't need time to think. Tell Johnny I need to see his face when I answer."

Becenti sat in the waiting area, staring at nothing, hearing nothing. He was exhausted; his mind numb. And it didn't help, knowing that his mother and Dolly Singer were still talking to Lillian. He imagined all kinds of protests on her part. He fully expected that she wasn't going to want him, regardless of the concessions he was willing to make. Winston had been entirely right. A man trying to marry a woman he thought didn't want him suffered for it.

He looked up because someone stood close by—Lucas's wife.

"What's going on?" Sloan asked. "What are the big guns up to?"

He didn't try to pretend that his mother and Dolly had only come to see the baby. He knew exactly what Sloan meant. "I'm trying to get engaged," he said, deciding that there was no reason not to tell her. He didn't know whether she approved of his marrying Lillian or not—given her husband's position—but if she did, he wanted all the help he could get.

She sat down on the closest chair, but she didn't say anything.

"They've been talking a long time," he said after a moment.

"Well, you never know. That might be a good sign. I've just come back from visiting your son. You brought the turquoise for him, didn't you?"

"Yeah. It's still there, then."

"One of the nurses taped the chain to the side of the incubator," she said. She abruptly smiled. "Where he can see it."

They sat for a time in silence.

"This waiting is killing me," he said abruptly. He stood. "I have to go see her."

"Good luck, Johnny," Sloan said, using his given name for the first time in all the years he'd known her.

The door to Lillian's room was closed still. He didn't hear any raised voices. He stood outside for a moment, then pushed the door slightly ajar. Lillian lay sleeping—probably from the sheer exhaustion of their mothers' visit. He felt a pang of guilt at having subjected her to this. Surgery, the birth of a baby, *and* the matriarchs would be too much for a strong person, even Lillian. He went in and quietly moved a chair close to the bed and sat down. Someone had sent her a huge bouquet of exotic-looking flowers. He didn't look at the card. He didn't have to. The arrangement had Stuart Dennison's heavy hand all over it.

He watched Lillian sleep, thinking how beautiful she was, marveling at the number of years he hadn't even noticed.

Well, perhaps he had. But it had been different then— for him and for her. Now, nothing about her escaped him. He loved her. He even loved her stubbornness.

He wanted to touch her; he didn't want to wake her. But she opened her eyes suddenly, and she reached for him. He leaned forward, taking her hands, because he was afraid of hurting her.

"Hold me," she said, her mouth trembling. "Johnny—"

He put his arms around her then, burying his face in her neck, savoring the warmth and the feel of her. He didn't say anything, and neither did she. They clung to each other, until she finally moved to see his face.

"Sloan says he's beautiful," she whispered. "Is he?"

"Very beautiful. And loud. Little-but-Loud, is what they call him down in the nursery."

She smiled. "I want to see him so bad," she said.

But her smile faded.

"What are you trying to do, Johnny?" she asked sadly.

"I'm trying to marry you."

"You're trying to ruin your life, your career. Everything—"

"No, I'm not—"

"Your mother never should have sent me up there to that hogan."

He could argue with her about that. Her arrival had been unwelcome at best, and he would be the first to admit it. But it had changed both their lives—and made a new one.

"Lillian—"

"Your mother asked me that day she came to my office— 'What is he if he's not a policeman?' I understood exactly what she meant. Being a tribal cop isn't what you *do*. It's what you *are*. Even *I* know that."

"It's my choice, Lillian, if I leave the tribal police. And it's what I'm willing to do so we can be together—"

She gave a sharp sigh. "Have you been talking to Sloan?"

"About this? No. Don't cry," he said, because she was very close to it.

"You just don't understand," she said.

"Then help me. I'm listening."

"Giving up everything and coming to Santa Fe—for

me—and *my* so-called career is—'' She put her hand over her eyes for a moment. "I can't let you do that, Johnny."

"It's my decision," he said.

"Then I can't be the reason for it."

"Lillian, I want us to be together. You and me and our boy." She was right. He didn't understand.

She wiped at her eyes. "My career isn't worth that kind of sacrifice," she said, and she told him about Stuart Dennison's claim that he was responsible for her success. Becenti listened without comment, amazed that Dennison could have been so stupid and so callous as to tell her such a thing. He had to have known about her sense of pride, and he had to have not cared. And Becenti could see plainly that Dennison's "looking after her" had been minimal. He hadn't prepared her cases for her, hadn't gone to court with her. He'd only directed people to her door. *She* had done the rest. She had done the part that mattered.

"I was living a lie," she said.

"No, you weren't," he said. "What's a referral? Nothing. You did all the work. And I know what they say in the tribal police."

"About what?"

"About you, counselor."

"What...do they say?"

"They say they *hate* to see you coming—but if they ever kill somebody, you're the lawyer they want. And I can promise you, Stuart Dennison didn't have a thing to do with it."

She smiled, a bit tremulously, but it was a smile nonetheless.

"Did you hate to see me coming?"

"I can't begin to tell you how much," he said—and this time she managed a small laugh.

He was looking into her eyes. "I love you. I want to be your husband. I want the three of us to be a family. It's as simple as that."

"Johnny—"

"It's as simple as that," he repeated. "Now tell me. What are you going to say to my mother?"

She would have turned away; he made her look at him.

"You know what people are going to think," she said.

"What people?"

"All those people who are going to pass out from the shock of hearing about a Singer-Becenti marriage."

"I think they did that already—when they heard about the Singer-Becenti baby. Hearing about a marriage isn't going to do it for them."

"Johnny—"

"Do you love me or not?"

"I—yes. But—"

"But what?"

"Maybe we'll get on each other's nerves," she said.

"Maybe," he agreed.

"All the time."

"That's possible—but we managed to stand each other long enough to get a baby boy, so who knows?"

"Maybe I can't live on the reservation again and you can't live in Santa Fe. Maybe it just won't work."

"I already know what it's like living in Window Rock without you. I hated it."

"Maybe I—"

"Lillian—"

"I'm scared, Johnny!"

He reached for her again, and he held her tightly. He was scared himself, but not that they didn't love each other.

After a moment, he moved so that he could see her face.

"Are you too scared to even try?" he asked, his eyes searching hers.

She didn't answer him.

"Are you?"

She gave a wavering sigh. She couldn't quite say it—but he was encouraged by the fact that she was trying.

"No," she said finally, her voice barely a whisper, and she smiled at him then, that mischievous smile he'd been waiting for, the one that was totally, completely Lillian. "You're probably going to regret this," she said.

"I don't doubt it," he assured her. "And I don't care."

"You don't?"

"No, Lillian, I don't."

"Well, then…Captain Becenti…" The smile broadened. "I guess somebody should tell your mother. You're… getting married."

Epilogue

Lillian stood on the patio watching the sun go down. She could hear all the noise from inside Lucas's house, the conversation and the laughter, the squeals of delight from the children. They were having another one of Sloan's nostalgia dinners—only this one wasn't an attempt to stave off homesickness. This one had come about by popular demand, because somewhere along the way the Singer-Baron-Begaye-Becenti-Tsosie-and-sometimes-Nez family had discovered that it really did like grits and fried green tomatoes—and all the love that came with them.

She looked around at the sound of the screen door opening. Becenti crossed the patio to her. He was carrying a folded newspaper in his hand. He tossed the paper onto the picnic table next to her.

"Where's our boy?" she asked.

"On Winston's lap," he said. "But I'm not sure who rocked who to sleep."

She laughed and leaned against him, giving a quiet sigh when he put his arms around her.

"Are you okay?" he asked.

She knew why he'd asked the question. Because of the small mention of Stuart Dennison on the evening news. Because after she heard it, she'd left the house and abruptly come out here.

"I was just…surprised, that's all. I didn't know Stuart was sick again. The last time I heard anything from J.B. he was still in remission."

"It's in the paper, too," he said. "I think you should read it."

She didn't want to read it. Stuart Dennison was dead, and she felt—

She didn't know quite how she felt. Sad, yes. For him and for J.B., whom he'd finally gotten around to marrying and who had apparently not taken no for an answer, after all. And for herself, she supposed, because, in spite of everything, he had once been an important part of her life.

She'd made no attempt to keep in touch with him after she and Becenti had married. Stuart had managed to get out of the land-deal scandal, without her help and with minimal damage to his career, but Lillian had been too busy with the baby and with teaching a law course to the Navajo Tribal Police part-time to really concern herself about what happened to him after that. She'd gotten a card from J.B. at Christmas, but that had been it. In fact, Stuart had almost never crossed her mind. Until tonight. Until she'd seen that brief report that he'd died.

She turned in Becenti's arms and put her head on his shoulder. She loved Johnny Becenti with all her heart and she hadn't regretted marrying him for an instant. She hugged him tightly. He wasn't a jealous man, but she still didn't want him to be distressed by her behavior.

He kissed her cheek, and then her mouth, and then he let her go.

"I'd better get back inside. The men are doing the dishes."

"What men?" she said incredulously, and he laughed.

He picked up the newspaper. "You need to read this," he said again.

She took it, and after a moment, she moved where the light from the kitchen window made it bright enough for her to see.

She began to read. The article contained all the usual obituary facts—most of which she already knew and some of which she herself had been on hand to experience.

She stopped reading, wondering why Becenti had been so insistent.

"An' Wee-wee-ann!" Tad called through the screen door.

"What, baby?" she said, turning around to see him. But he squealed suddenly and ran away, with Julia in hot pursuit.

She smiled and looked down at the paper again. And she finally saw it at the bottom of the page. The very last sentence.

"Dennison is survived by his wife, Junie Blair—J. B.—Greenleigh Dennison, and his infant daughter...Lillian...."

* * * * *

More stories in Cheryl Reavis's compelling
FAMILY BLESSINGS *series are coming your way soon.
Don't miss* TENDERLY, *Benjamin Toomey's romance,
in the winter of 1997!*